THE LIE SHE TOLD

CATHERINE YAFFE

Cover design: Books Covers Art

For Mum and Dad, with love and gratitude

1

L eeds Magistrates Court 1998

"This isn't over, BITCH! I want my son," shouted Darren as he was led away. He struggled against the restraints around his wrists and tried to pull away from the guards leading him from the courtroom but they were too strong for him, despite Darren's huge frame. Spittle flew from his mouth as he continued his threats: face burning with rage.

K ate stared at her ex-husband as he was led from the dock, before grabbing her bag and fleeing from the oppressive courtroom.

. . .

"Kate, wait," called DI Ziggy Thornes but Kate wasn't stopping for anyone. Her desire to escape was all-encompassing, and drove her forward. Racing down the courthouse steps, she faltered for a second as she saw Ryan leaning against a plinth, cigarette hanging from the corner of his mouth. He casually waved but she ignored him.

"Kate!" Ziggy was still chasing after her, urging her to stop or at least slow down but Kate continued on her way, ignoring the shouts. She hurried to the main road and jumped into the car that was waiting.

Once inside she let out a deep breath. She turned to her son strapped into his booster seat. "You OK sunshine?" she asked, leaning through the gap and rubbing his leg. Joe nodded his head as he sucked furiously on the lollipop that was rammed firmly in his mouth.

"Are *you* OK?" asked Fiona. Kate didn't answer her sister immediately, not really sure what to say as Fiona pulled away from the kerb.

Kate loosened the scrunchy that was holding back her unruly red hair and tried with little success to neaten it up. "I'm fine, I just need to get home." Kate slumped down in her seat, breathing deeply in an attempt to calm her racing heartbeat and stop her hands from shaking.

"So, what did he get?"

"Four years."

"Shit, did you know?"

Kate was instantly alert. "What do you mean 'did I know'?"

"That he would get that long?"

Kate exhaled. "Oh right, yeah his solicitor said it might be longer though."

Fiona turned onto the ring road, heading towards North Leeds where Kate and Joe currently lived. "So, what happens now?"

"I'm not sure. I need to get home. Ziggy is meeting me there."

With little traffic around, Fiona made the journey in no time and pulled up outside the two-bedroomed terrace that until recently had been home to Kate, Joe, and Darren. Fiona was shocked with how quickly events had progressed, but she fully understood Kate's reasons for needing to leave.

The three of them exited the car and made their way to the front door. Kate hesitated and turned to Fiona. "I think it's best if we say goodbye now."

Fiona was taken aback. "Really? Don't you want a hand?" She was reluctant to leave until she knew her younger sister and nephew were safe.

"Yeah, honestly Fi. You've been brilliant and I can't thank you enough but it's for the best." Kate was fiddling with the front door key, torn between wanting to enter the house and prolonging the goodbye to her sister. "Joe, give Aunty Fi a kiss, she has to go now."

Joe had been standing in the front yard, hopping from foot to foot. He was desperate for a wee, willing his mum to open the door. He stepped forward and threw his arms around his Aunt. Fiona leant down and kissed the top of his head whilst returning his cuddle.

"Be a good boy for mummy OK?" She squeezed him a little tighter and Joe feared he would wee right there and then.

"OK, I will." He released himself from the bear hug and looked up at his mum. "I really need to pee."

Kate looked down at her son, smiled and opened the front door. Joe pushed past her and headed straight for the downstairs loo. She turned back to her sister. "Don't cry Fi, if I start I'll never stop."

Fiona shook her head and wiped her face with her coat sleeve. "Well I guess I'll see you soon then?"

"I'll let you know when we're settled." Kate took a step forward and held onto her sister tightly not knowing when or if she would see her again. "Come on, go. You know we both hate goodbyes." She playfully pushed Fiona away.

"Please take care of yourself," she whispered as she returned Kate's hug then turned away.

Kate pushed the front door open and stepped inside, closing it slowly behind her. The glass pendant light in the hallway flickered into life, illuminating the narrow corridor which housed myriad shoes and discarded coats. The house felt empty, lifeless. She walked down the hallway and trailed her hand along the flowered wallpaper. The smooth journey of her fingers along the wall was interrupted with the fist-sized hole that had torn the paper and dinted the plasterboard. She studied it, as though it was the first time she'd seen it, which of course it wasn't. It had been there for the last seven months. A lifetime ago, she thought.

"Mum, I've finished," came a little voice from the end of the hallway.

Before Kate had a chance to respond there was a loud banging on the front door. "Just a second sunshine."

"Kate? Kate, are you there?"

Kate recognised the brusque voice and the slight Liverpudlian accent and threw the front door open. "Of course I'm here, where the hell else would I be?" Tension and stress spilled over into her voice. She took a step back, allowing the imposing figure to enter.

"Mum, I've finished!" demanded Joe again. At the sound of her son's voice she softened.

"OK sunshine, wash your hands then." She turned back to the visitor and gestured for him to enter, closing the front door behind him. Kate led the way into the kitchen.

"We don't have much time I'm afraid," said Ziggy.

"Yeah, I figured," replied a resigned Kate as she leaned her back against the cool granite worktop. She hadn't realised how clammy her hands were. The cool surface felt good, providing an anchor to reality. Having removed her coat and hung it on the back of a chair she tugged at either side of her woollen grey cardigan and wrapped it around herself, hoping to find a sense of comfort and security.

"How long do we have?" she asked.

"30 minutes."

"Oh wow, you're kidding me right?" Her Yorkshire accent coming out stronger for some reason. She wanted to slam the brakes on this rollercoaster ride she had unwittingly boarded with her son. Everything she thought she knew, everything she had believed in had been tipped on its axis and if she wasn't careful even the tiniest piece of control would escape her grasp.

"Fraid not," said Ziggy. "You'll just have to grab the basics and replace the rest but it's imperative that we get a move on. There's a car waiting outside for you."

Joe, having wandered into the kitchen, looked up at his mummy. "Where are we going?" he asked.

"Good question sunshine," said Kate as she pulled him to her and held him tightly.

2

Gairloch, Spring 2000

Kate waited at the community school gates for Joe to finish his day. She said hello to some of the other mums and looked for her son's face which was always beaming at her as he ran across the playground. He'd started at the school a few months after the relocation and he had taken to it instantly, making new friends and had even starting to speak with a soft Scottish burr. His comfort in his new surroundings had gone a long way to helping Kate feel settled.

"Look mum!" shouted Joe before he had even reached the gate. He was waving a piece of paper over his head and grinning like a Cheshire Cat. "Can I go, can I go?"

"Whoa there, hang on a second." She braced herself as he threw himself at her legs and thrust the paper into her hands. "Let me see it first." She knew exactly what it was, it had been the talk of the school gate for about a week and she had also overheard conversations from the regulars in the cafe. The annual school day out to Applecross was due over the Easter holidays, and it was the highlight of the school year.

"It's a trip to Applecross. Can I go?" asked Joe excitedly.

"Well, we'll have to see won't we?" Kate took hold of her son's hand, knowing full well she would let him go but she couldn't resist the urge to tease him.

"Aww mum, see about what?" he said, dragging out the vowels. He pulled his hand away sulkily. "That means I can't go," he huffed.

"Well, let's see. Can you keep your bedroom tidy?"

"Yes."

"What about helping out with the washing up?"

"Yes." His voice was rising an octave with every answer.

"And what about helping Jack tidy the café?"

"Oh yes, yes, yes. Please mum, please. I'll never ask for anything ever..." He was practically begging her. She glanced down at the boy who was now walking backwards in front of her so he could see her face.

"Hmm I'm not sure..." But she couldn't keep it up and started laughing whilst she ruffled his hair. "Of course you can go, but you still have to do all those things I mentioned."

He almost tripped them both up as he crashed into her.

"Steady on, you'll have us both over." She pulled him from her and took hold of his hand once more but he wriggled free.

"Can I tell Jack?" he asked, already starting to break into a run.

"Yes, but go carefully," she called after him. As Joe shot

off, Kate followed at a slower pace. She was more concerned about him tripping over his own feet than busy roads or stranger danger; everyone knew everyone else in the small coastal village. Smiling to herself, she took the short walk back to the café knowing that Jack would be waiting for his wee pal.

Jack Bruce was the owner of the only café in Gairloch, a Lochside village in the Scottish Highlands. He had taken over the run-down building after the previous owners retired and although he wasn't getting any younger, he hadn't wanted to miss the opportunity of making a few pence for his own retirement fund. A couple of weeks after arriving in the village, Kate had spent an entire day knocking on doors at the few souvenir shops, the local pub and various tourist attractions in the area, hoping for a part-time position that would top up her savings. When she was exhausted and just about to give up, she sat on the bench overlooking the Loch, gazing out across the vast expanse. Jack had joined her on the bench and after a wee chat he had offered her a position in the café. It wasn't much, he had said, but to Kate it meant everything. A few months later he had offered her the little flat above and she had snapped his hand off. It was small and needed updating but anything was better than their previous accommodation above The Old Inn pub.

Now, with Jack's health not being what it was, he had offered her the chance to take over the café full-time, on a profit-share basis. She had been beside herself and, much to Jack's embarrassment, had kissed and hugged him every day for a week. He had sensed that Kate was looking for security and, having no children of his own, he had taken both her and Joe under his wing. With his guiding hand he had helped them settle into the rhythm of Highland life and now they were an integral part of the small community. Breathtakingly beautiful, the Lochside resort nestled on the banks of Loch Gairloch with natural sandy beaches and crystal blue waters. Kate had now lived there through every season. When they had first arrived it had been the depths of winter, infinitely bleak with persistent rain, snow and howling winds. Before spring had poked its head through the clouds Kate had been ready to quit. She had chosen Gairloch as she had fond memories of family caravan holidays spent there when she was younger. She figured it was far enough away to not attract any attention to herself but when she'd visited before it had been summer and she wasn't quite prepared for the isolation of winter. As the surrounding mountains had woken from their winter sleep, Kate felt her spirits shifting with the weather. The gorse bushes bloomed with their spiky yellow flowers and as the purple heather sprang forward, ready to start its new life, Kate had a sense of synchronicity and decided to stick it out. Moving Joe again would be too much for him she had thought, and now she had the job and flat she could build on the foundations and create the secure, happy home that she had always yearned for.

She caught up with Joe just as he was charging through the café door, nearly knocking one of the regulars off their feet.

"Hey, hey, hey steady on there young man, where's the fire?"

"Sorry Mr Wheeler," called Joe as he headed into the kitchen.

Kate apologised, but Mr Wheeler brushed it off. "It's nae bother hen, no harm done."

Kate shook her head and held the door open to let Mr Wheeler and his wife through. She followed Joe into the kitchen at the back of the café where Gill, the part-time chef, server and all-round life saver, was piling Joe's plate full of sausage and chips.

"There you go wean, go find yourself a seat." Gill was used to Joe taking over the café after school and she always had a plate of food ready for him.

"Thanks Gill, what would I do without you?" said Kate, shrugging out of her coat and back into her work apron. "Has it been busy?"

"Steady away, Jack's been busy with his measuring tape and doing a lot of tutting and sighing. What's that all about?"

Kate laughed. "I've given him a list of jobs that need doing. I don't think he's too happy about it."

"Ach, yes that will explain it. Giving the place a do over then?"

"Just a minor one before it gets busy in the summer. A new coat of paint and repairs to the floor and kitchen units, nothing too drastic."

"This place hasn't changed in years. You're a breath of fresh air Kate."

Kate had built a good working relationship with Gill who was as much a part of the furniture as Jack. Gill had worked at the café on and off since Jack had taken over the place years before, and Kate appreciated her hard work. She could turn her hand to anything, and the regulars loved her. Plus, her homemade cakes were a sight and taste to behold.

Kate walked out into the front of the café and sat opposite Joe whilst he tucked into his tea.

The little chime above the entrance tinkled and Kate looked up to see Jack. She smiled affectionately as he ambled into the café, wrapped up in his heavy waxed coat, cap in place and feet firmly encased in all-weather boots. He was rarely seen in anything else, even in the summer. He removed his cap and unfastened his coat.

"Now then," he greeted Kate in his usual brusque way, and tickled Joe on the back of his neck. Joe didn't look up from his plate of food. He sat in the chair next to Kate and nodded his head towards Joe. "Hungry as ever then? That boy's got a fair appetite."

Kate smiled affectionately. "I know, I have no idea where he puts it all."

Jack, not being one for mixing his words got straight to the point with Kate. "I've been doing a bit of measuring and weighing things up."

"OK," said Kate, bracing herself in case Jack had had a change of heart.

"There's more to this DIY than meets the eye," he explained. "If we're going to do this then it needs to be done right." He hesitated briefly whilst he rummaged in his pocket. He pulled out a scrap of paper that was covered with measurements and numbers. "So, I've had a word with Adam." Adam was the local odd job man that Jack knew. "I've given him the list and he's agreed to do the work."

Kate was taken aback. "Oh, OK, but won't that cost money?" Though Jack wasn't tight-fisted she didn't want to see him out of pocket.

Jack rubbed his hand across his wiry beard, once a fiery red but now heavily flecked with grey. Kate knew he always did this when he was thinking. "Aye, it will cost but will save you money in the long run and you'll turn a profit quicker."

"But Jack, I can't afford to pay for the work. I had planned on doing much of it myself, with your help of course."

"Nah, it's too much lassie. I've agreed a deal with Adam and he's starting on Monday." Jack was very matter of fact and Kate knew better than to argue. When Jack made a decision he very rarely went back on it.

"Oh right, that's good then?"

"Aye. Now that's sorted can I throw this to-do list away?" He crumpled it in his hand.

Kate laughed. "Yes of course, unless you want me to write you another one?"

"Away with ya hen, I've enough to do without your lists." He pushed back from the table. "Mighty Joe and I have things to do, isn't that right wee man?"

Joe took the last bite of his tea and nodded his head. "Aye." *'That Scottish accent,' thought Kate.*

Joe left the table and followed Jack over to the huge windows at the front of the café that looked out onto the expanse of the Loch. He climbed onto the chair that Jack had pulled up for him and the two of them looked out with binoculars firmly in front of their eyes. Bird spotting had become a habit that the two of them enjoyed, and Jack encouraged Joe to keep a notebook full of the birds that they saw. Kate knew that they would be there until the light faded, so she left her seat and started to clear the tables.

. . .

A lovely warm glow of muted orange light filled the café as the sun began to sink behind the mountains across the way. Kate looked through the windows and thought she would never tire of the view, or the feeling of contentment that settled around her. She felt a rush of love for her son, and for the old fisherman who had done much to bring peace to their lives.

3

From his position on the bench outside the local shop he had a clear view of the school gates. If they followed their usual routine, then Joe would come rushing out of the school gates and Kate would be there waiting. He knew he needed to time his approach carefully. Too soon and all his plans would be for nothing.

He couldn't believe his luck at first. Having abruptly left Leeds to return home a couple of weeks ago, it was only by chance that he'd overheard barmaid Janice gossiping with the locals. He'd quizzed her afterwards and was convinced they were talking about Kate and Joe. A few days of snooping and he was 100% certain that it was, in fact, them. He hadn't given either of them much thought since the court case. He knew she'd moved away, and he had no idea where, but he also had no feelings either way. Their affair had been brief, and a massive mistake, but it had all worked in his favour in the end.

What were the chances of them turning up in his home village? He knew Kate had holidayed there as a kid; she'd told him one day when they talked about their past. They'd laughed at the coincidence, Kate believing it was a sign, one that he quickly dismissed.

Right now, the biggest question he had was what to do with this piece of good fortune. That he would profit from it there was no doubt. He had enough over Kate to ruin her new life, and he wouldn't hesitate to use what he knew to his advantage. But Kate was smart, so he knew that he had to think carefully.

He watched closely as Joe came running across the playground, waving a piece of paper above his head. He saw Kate take his hand and turn to leave the school grounds. His eyes followed them as they headed back towards the harbour and into the café. Flicking his cigarette into a nearby puddle, he left the bench, mind working overtime, convinced there was a way to manipulate the situation he found himself in.

B ack at The Kingfisher, his family home until he'd left at 15, Ryan let himself into the rear entrance and had hoped to sneak upstairs without attracting his dad's attention. Too late, Len was stood there waiting for him.

"Where the hell have you been?" he demanded.

"Out," said Ryan, offhandedly. He was sick of his father already. He'd always been a bully, and despite his age and ill health he still thought he was the big man. When Ryan had phoned up out of the blue and asked if he could stay for a while, it had worked out well for Len. He was due in hospital for a knee operation and had been fretting over what to do with the pub whilst he was out of the game.

"You were supposed to help with the beer delivery," snapped Len, following his son as he headed upstairs to the flat above the pub.

"Yeah? You should have said."

"I did say, you useless piece of shit. I knew it was a mistake letting you back here."

"Whatever." He paused. "I'll sort it out in a bit."

"Do it now. The barrels are off."

'Oh for fuck's sake,' he thought. All he wanted to do was figure out how to approach Kate but he knew his dad wouldn't let up so he turned and pushed him out of the way, heading for the cellar.

Len limped along behind him. Years of bar work and standing on his feet all day had taken its toll on his knee and he would be glad when he'd had the op. Ordinarily, Ryan would be the last resort he would ever turn to for help. Their relationship had always been strained. Ryan's mum had died when he was 13 and his behaviour, which had never been perfect, went from bad to worse. His older sister Molly had been a breeze to raise and though losing their mum had been hard on all of them, Molly had stepped up and taken on much of the work that she used to do. When Molly met Steve at 18 she'd moved out and now lived over in Inverness, only visiting occasionally and speaking to Len maybe once a month. Len had no worries about Molly. She was a sensible girl, a loving mother and though he thought her husband was a bit of a prick she seemed happy enough. He'd told her about the knee operation, but she was yet to learn that Ryan would be running the place. Len knew she'd disagree, but he really had no choice. He made his way to the top of the cellar steps and watched as Ryan rotated the barrels and moved the new stock.

"Keep the new stuff separate, and make sure you've connected the barrels properly," he shouted down.

Ryan closed his eyes and muttered under his breath. He'd been doing cellar work since he was old enough to lug a barrel, he didn't need constant supervision. And he was 27, not 15.

"Hurry up and get into hospital or I'll put you there myself, " he seethed under his breath. Once he'd finished, he headed behind the bar to grab a wee snifter out of Len's view.

"Don't be drinking the profits." It was Janice, and Ryan inwardly flinched. He couldn't stand the woman and had no idea why his dad still employed her. He had wondered if there was more between them than Len let on. He shuddered at the thought and totally ignored her.

"You'll no be doing that when your pa's out of the way." Her thick Scottish accent, and whiny voice went right through him, setting his teeth on edge.

He turned and looked at her. 'She would need bringing down a peg or two,' he thought. As if she could read his mind, she backed away and made a show of cleaning the glasses.

Reaching for his jacket, he headed back outside for a smoke and some time to think.

H is chance came a few nights later. After another blazing row with his dad, Ryan had set off walking to the local shop for some cigarettes. As he walked along the uneven grass verge, the weather had taken a turn for the worse, and with only a thin denim jacket on he had quickly been soaked through. He could hear an approaching car, and in the vain hope it was a local not some hapless tourist, he stuck out his thumb.

L ady Luck was definitely smiling on him.

4

The Highland weather never failed to amaze Kate. When she'd set off to drop Joe at Cubs it had been dark and overcast. Less than thirty minutes later it was like the end of the world was on its way. Dark, stormy clouds had advanced and descended quickly. She was grateful she knew these roads or she would have become disoriented and lost. Despite using her headlights on the Ford Fiesta she'd recently purchased, she could barely make out the road ahead. She switched to full beam and leaned forward to peer through the windscreen.

"What the hell," she muttered. Some poor sod had been caught in the storm and was walking along the grass verge. She flashed her lights, slowed down, and pulled over. She beeped her horn, the sound somewhat lost in the melee but it was enough to attract the attention of the figure which stopped and turned, heading towards her.

Kate leaned over to open the passenger door. The wind was howling, it was raining sideways and although she could barely make out whether it was a male or female at the side of the road, she knew it would be someone local. It was a common enough occurrence for her not to worry about it being a stranger.

The grateful figure stepped forward and practically threw themselves into the car. "Good of you to stop. I thought I was stranded there for a minute."

"It's no bother. The storm came in pretty quickly. It's like the end of days." Kate indicated to pull away from the verge.

The stranger laughed. "Do you often pick strangers up from the side of the road?"

"Haha, no but I figured you might be a local. Are you from round here? Your accent doesn't seem local?" Kate was seriously regretting her decision to stop.

"Erm, kind of..."

The passenger had brought in the rain and chill of the night with him and Kate shivered. She felt a sense of recognition but couldn't quite put her finger on it. "Where are you from?" she asked.

Ryan couldn't believe that she didn't recognise him but he played along. "I'm from here originally but I've been living in Leeds."

"I thought I detected a bit of Yorkshire. Wait..." She glanced sideways. "Ryan?"

"Haha, I wondered when it would dawn on you."

"What the hell... how..." Kate was speechless. She'd last seen Ryan on the final day of the court hearing, hanging around the court steps. As memories slowly clicked into place, her hands started to shake. Heart pounding, she moved from recognition to anger in a split second. She swerved violently and pulled haphazardly onto the side of the road. "What the actual fuck? What are you doing here?" She removed her seatbelt and despite the lashing rain, she opened the car door and got out. "Get the fuck out of my car now!" she yelled above the cacophony of noise that swirled around the hills.

Ryan leaned over into the driver's seat and shouted something but Kate couldn't hear for the pounding in her ears. Rage, shock, and fear took over.

"I want you out of my car now!" she screamed again, shaking with anger. Reluctantly Ryan did as she demanded and stepped into the monsoon.

"Come on Kate, don't be like that." He headed around the front of the car towards her but she backed away.

"Oh no you don't Ryan, stay away from me."

Ryan carried on forward, relentless. "Kate, what's wrong with you?"

"Seriously? You seriously don't know?" Kate fumed. "Tell me why you're here? How did you find me? Why did you..."

Ryan moved closer to Kate and reached forward, pinning her arms to her side. She struggled furiously and lashed out, but Ryan was much bigger and stronger than Kate and he soon had her gripped to him. "You were always a bit of wild cat. Will you calm down and listen to me?" Ryan risked losing his grip and held her by the forearms. "And for God's sake let's get back in the car, we're getting soaked."

Reluctantly Kate shrugged free of Ryan's grasp and sat back in the driver's seat, slamming the door to vent her anger.

"Jeez," said Ryan. "It knows how to rain up here, I'd almost forgotten." He shivered as icy droplets found their way down the neck of his collar.

Kate was shivering too and not just because of the rain. Part of her past, the one she'd tried so hard to escape was sitting right next to her. She didn't know what to think as she sat gripping the steering wheel and rested her head on the curve. The shock of seeing his face and hearing his voice brought back painful memories. Unbidden tears started to mingle with the raindrops on her face and merged to spill onto her soaking wet jeans. Next to her, Ryan was rooting around in the glove box looking for a tissue. His hand found an old crumpled pack at the back.

"Here, take this," he offered, shifting around in his seat so that he was facing her as much as he could in the confined space.

Kate took the proffered tissue and wiped her face. Pulling herself together she looked at Ryan fully for the first time. "What do you want Ryan? Why are you here?"

Ryan went on to the explain that he had returned home at his dad's request. "So whatever else you're thinking I am genuinely here to help out at the pub."

Kate listened but was skeptical. Part of her wanted to believe he was genuine. She had always felt a connection with Ryan that she hadn't with Darren. Kate breathed heavily in and out in an effort to try and think straight. Ryan reached for her hand that had fallen into her lap. She let him hold her fingers lightly in his hand. "It's just a bit much to take in Ryan. I don't know what to think."

Ryan, pleased that she didn't pull away, gently massaged her freezing cold fingers. "I knew you'd be shocked, I'm sorry. Meeting you worked much better in my head."

Kate's head snapped up. "What does that mean?"

Realising his mistake, Ryan tried to backtrack. "I didn't know it was you in the car."

"But that doesn't make sense. How long have you known I'm here?"

"Only a couple of days. I heard some regulars at the pub talking about a Yorkshire woman taking over Harbour Café, and though it was chance in a million I asked a couple of questions and thought it might be you. I saw Joe coming out of school and it all just clicked into place."

"You've been watching me?" Kate was incredulous.

"Not watching exactly. I just wanted to make sure it was you."

Kate pulled her hand away. "So you planned this?"

"No. Not like this I promise." Ryan took her hand again. "I promise Kate, but once I knew it was you, I couldn't just walk away. You know what we had together. Wasn't it you that always talked about signs?"

Kate was slowly pulling herself together using the now-ratty tissue to wipe away the remaining tears. She looked up at Ryan, searching his face for... she didn't know what.

"Look, why don't we start again?" he said earnestly. "Why don't you drop me in the village and I'll give you my number? That way you can contact me in your own time, whenever you feel ready?" Ryan rooted round in his pocket and pulled out a scrap of paper that had miraculously stayed dry despite his jacket being soaked. He passed the piece of paper over to Kate and reluctantly she took it from him.

ithout looking at what was written on it she shoved it into the back pocket of her jeans, restarted the engine and didn't speak another word.

5

K ate pulled into the allocated parking space opposite the café and got out of the car. She'd dropped Ryan off in the village and her head was still spinning. She had so many questions, and a complete mix of emotions. She could see through the café window that the lights were still on and Jack was inside. She couldn't face anyone just yet. She had to get a grip on herself and process what had just happened with Ryan.

She felt claustrophobic which, considering she was sat on a bench facing the vast expanse of the loch, made no sense but she could feel it. That familiar feeling; knot in her stomach, clenched fists, toes curling inside fur-lined boots. She tugged her hood up over her beanie hat and leaned forward, breathing deeply. The rain had abated to a steady icy drizzle, each drop feeling like a needle point on her face. The bench she sat on had been damp and her bum felt wet and numb. The wind still whirled around her, finding gaps in her coat, sending shivers down her spine. She shifted her position, turning her back to the café. Behind her, crunching footsteps approached and she knew who it was. Jack sat down alongside her, completely ignorant as to whether he was welcome or not. In truth, Jack wouldn't have cared. They sat in silence for a few minutes, each lost in their own thoughts. After a while Jack made to move.

"Are you coming inside hen? You'll catch your death if you stay out here."

"Just five minutes Jack and I'll be in. Just need to clear my head." She was touched by her friend's concern.

Jack slowly stood up, the icy wind playing hell with his arthritic joints. He gently placed a hand on Kate's shoulder as he turned to walk away. "Whatever you're looking for lassie, you'll no find it out there." He trudged back up to the café and Kate heard the door close behind him.

J ack pondered Kate's mood. It was strange for her to be so distant with him. He admired Kate. She was a determined young woman who clearly adored her son. He didn't know what had happened in Kate's past, and it wasn't really any of his business. She had made it clear that it wasn't up for discussion and he respected that. Kate was a hard worker and he had never regretted offering her a job and subsequent share of the café. He knew she wouldn't let him down. Offering her the upstairs flat had done them both a favour. A pub was no place to raise a young boy in his opinion and he'd been debating what to do with the place for a while so it had all worked out well. It helped that Jack thoroughly enjoyed the company of young Joe and he had found himself getting more attached as time went on. The three of them had formed a close bond and Jack felt protective of them both.

He shrugged out of his coat just as Kate re-entered the café. "Ah, there you are." He helped Kate with her coat and took her over to meet the stranger standing at the counter with a tape measure. "Kate, this is Adam," Jack introduced the two.

"Hi Kate," said Adam. "I think we've met before at The Kingfisher." He reached forward to shake Kate's hand. She started at the mention of the pub and felt the colour drain from her face.

"Ah, right. I thought you looked familiar," she managed to reply.

"Me and Adam have been going through your list and he reckons it will only take a couple of weeks," said Jack.

"Aye, there isnae much that needs doing though the electrics need a bit of an update. When do you want me to start?" He addressed the question to Kate but received no reply. He looked over at Jack. Jack shook his head. Kate had wandered over to the window. "Kate?"

"What? Oh sorry, I was miles away. What did you say?"

"When would you like me to start the work?" Adam asked again.

"Oh, erm... Monday?" She looked over at Jack for acknowledgment that was OK with him.

"Aye," answered Jack. "That's fine with me. Just let me know if you need anything." He walked Adam to the door and they said their goodbyes. Jack went to stand by Kate at the window. "Not having second thoughts are you hen?"

"No. God no, not at all." Kate felt guilty for not giving Jack her full attention. "I've just had a bit of a shock that's all."

"Oh right. Anything I can help with?" Jack wasn't sure what or how he might be able to help but he was always willing to lend an ear.

"No, not really but thank you. I bumped into an old friend today and it's taken me back a little. I'm not sure what to do or think."

"An old friend? Around here? I thought you didn't know anyone around here?"

"No, I don't. He's here helping out in the family business for a short time. I did know he was from around here but I never imagined for second I'd bump into him." Kate sighed and sat on the nearest chair. "It's just a bit of a shock that's all."

"And what's he doing in Gairloch you say?"

"He's helping out in his dad's pub, The Kingfisher?"

"Oh, he's Len Albright's boy then is he?" Jack knew Len from way back, and used to be a frequent visitor to the pub.

"Erm... I think that's his surname. We weren't particularly close friends or anything to be honest." Kate wanted to play down her friendship with Ryan in case it raised too many questions. "Well, anyway." Kate stood up and put her coat back on. "I need to go collect Joe. Thanks for sorting things out with Adam."

Jack took that as his cue to leave also and collected his own jacket from where he'd thrown it over the table earlier. "Right you are then. See you tomorrow," he called cheerily as he left the café.

As he took the short walk back to his cottage he couldn't help but feel something wasn't quite right. He 'had a feeling' as his Annie used to say. He thought back and could remember stories about Ryan Albright. Of course, Ryan had only been a kid back then, but Jack remembered the youngster was a bit of a troublemaker who'd been kicked out of school at 15 and had left for England shortly afterwards. And now he'd turned up in Gairloch and there was no doubt that Kate was thrown with his reappearance. As he trudged along he decided to give it some more thought but he felt unsettled and hoped it was nothing more than coincidence.

6

The tiny square of paper was burning a hole in the back pocket of Kate's jeans. On it was Ryan's mobile number. She hadn't stopped thinking about the chance meeting all night, and although it was mid-morning in the café and building up to the busiest time of day, Kate was finding it really hard to concentrate. There was something about the conversation with Ryan yesterday that she just couldn't shake. She felt certain that Ryan had hinted that he had something to tell her but no matter how many times she replayed the conversation in her head she couldn't quite put her finger on it. She felt sure there was more to it than the fact that he was helping out in his dad's pub. She knew she would only get the answers she wanted by contacting him, but would that open a huge can of worms that she would rather keep locked away. The debate had continued all night in her head, leaving her feeling exhausted and irritable. As she cleared another table, Jack called over to her.

"Kate, can you keep an eye on the till for a second please?"

"Yeah, sure," answered Kate as she made her way through the tables.

"You okay?" he asked when Kate reached the front of the café.

"Yeah, fine thanks." She emptied the tray she was carrying and placed it in the kitchen. Jack followed her.

"You sure cos you seem to be lost in a world of your own?"

"Yeah, yeah I'm fine, honestly Jack," she replied, touching Jack's forearm. "Don't worry."

"Well I do, and I think you should take the rest of the day off and sort your head out."

"But it's almost lunchtime," said Kate in disbelief.

"Aye, and you're no good to me or Gill when you're lost in your own world. Even the regulars have started to notice."

"Aye, that's right," Gill chipped in. Neither of them meant any offence and only spoke out of concern.

"So go make yourself a cuppa and take as much time as you need to get your head straight, and maybe have a wee nap, you look exhausted." As Jack said this, he directed Kate towards the door that led to her flat upstairs. She went along willingly and could hear Gill chuckling away in the background. Raising both hands in mock surrender, she let herself be guided. "Ok, OK, I can take the hint but shout me the minute it starts to get busy."

G rateful for the break, Kate climbed the steep stairs to the flat and flopped down onto the overstuffed three-seater sofa. She reached into the back pocket of her jeans and removed the incendiary note, staring at the number. She twisted the piece of paper around in her fingers trying to figure out what to do. The internal monologue that had been running all night started up again. She pushed her hands through her hair and let out a moan of exasperation.

"What the hell is wrong with me?" she asked the empty room. She stood and started pacing back and forth across the living room. Part of her wanted to ring him and tell him where to go, but she couldn't deny that she was intrigued. Was it true that he was here to help out in his dad's pub? If it *was* true then she knew she would have to stay away from him. She couldn't afford to invest emotionally in a relationship with him; it would leave her vulnerable and she wasn't prepared to go down that road again. But what if his reason for being here *wasn't* so innocent? What could he do that would cause harm?

'Oh, so much,' she thought. Two and half years might have passed by, but she could still remember the day like it had happened yesterday. Just the thought of the decision she had made brought a wave of nausea over her, and she felt her legs go weak. She looked at the number again.

'I could just text him.' She immediately dismissed that thought as ridiculous. It might not even be his number.' Again, she dismissed that thought out of hand. 'Oh for fuck's sake, just ring him.' Decisively she picked up her Nokia and with clammy palms and overactive heartbeat she punched in the number, almost misdialling she was shaking so much. It didn't even finish its first ring before she heard his voice.

"Kate. How's you?" Ryan sounded cheerful and positively happy to hear from her. "I'm glad you rang." He'd only shared his number with two people and one of them was serving time.

She didn't know what to say now that she'd found the

courage to call. Her mouth was suddenly dry, and she had to sit down.

"Kate? You OK?"

She swallowed. "Hi, yes I'm fine."

"Wasn't sure if you'd ring to be honest. Thought you might just ignore me."

"And why would I do that?" asked Kate.

"You seemed shocked, that's all."

"Of course I was shocked Ryan, you were the last person I expected to pick up from the side of the road." Kate could feel her anxiety levels building and was starting to wish she hadn't bothered to call.

"Ah, come on Kate. Don't be like that. This could be a chance of a new start for us, you know without any of the crap."

"I don't think so Ryan. What is it you really want?"

"Ooo, touchy. Come on, you know we had it good back in the day," Ryan laughed. The flirting wasn't working on Kate, and Ryan realised he had his work cut out if he was to win her trust. He changed tack. "Look, I was only joking. I'd really like to meet up, I just want us to be friends whilst I'm here, that's all. Besides, I've heard from Darren."

Kate sat up straight. "What? You're in touch with him?"

"Not in touch exactly but you'll want to hear what he has to say."

Kate couldn't believe what she had just heard. Why on earth was Ryan in touch with Darren.

"So, do you want to meet up?"

"Wait a second," responded Kate, trying to gain some control and recover her composure. She'd be damned before she let Ryan affect her. "I want to know why you're in touch with Darren."

"I can't tell you over the phone. Come on Kate, just a cup of coffee that's all."

"Can't or won't?"

"One cup of coffee plus it would be nice to see you, catch up on old times."

Kate hesitated. It was the catching up on old times that Kate wanted to avoid. She inhaled deeply and closed her eyes. "OK, one coffee but it's today or never. I don't have much time."

"Busy lady with your new life, eh?" Ryan teased.

Kate knew better than to rise to the bait.

Ryan carried on regardless. "How about 2pm today then?" If he was offended by Kate's silence he didn't let it show.

Kate quickly ran it through in her mind. She had to collect Joe at 3:15pm so she had the perfect excuse to get away after an hour. "Yes that's fine."

"Right, I'll come to the café then," suggested Ryan.

"No!" said Kate. "I'd prefer somewhere neutral. What about Poolewe? Bridge Café."

"Yeah, I know the place. See you there at 2pm then. Looking forward to it."

The call ended and Kate let out a breath she didn't know she was holding. She replayed the conversation in her mind and she now had more questions than her brain could handle. Annoyed with herself for not being firmer with him, she cursed out loud and threw her phone across the room.

Kate arrived at Bridge Café early, hoping to beat Ryan to it and find a table first so she could get her thoughts together. The café was only small; four tables downstairs and three upstairs. She had deliberately chosen it as she knew it would be quiet at that time of day: the hill walkers would have been and gone. She was gutted when she pulled into the car park to see Ryan sat waiting on a bench. Steeling her resolve, she stepped out of the car and crossed the road.

"Hey, you came then?" Ryan greeted her, moving forward to kiss her cheek. Kate took a swift side-step and headed into the café without saying a word. They both ordered coffee and Kate led the way upstairs. Silence descended. Unable to bear it any longer, Ryan broke the frosty atmosphere.

"So how have you been?" he asked, looking at her.

"I've been doing fine, thank you."

Ryan realised this wasn't going to be as easy as he thought. "Kate, look. I don't want it to be like this."

"Like what exactly?"

"This. Cold, frosty, defensive. It's not like you. Well, not like the Kate I used to know anyway." He watched Kate's face closely for a response.

"I'm not the Kate you used to know, that's why." She picked up a sugar packet and tore off the top, pouring it into her cup.

"I know, I get that. How did you end up here of all places?"

Ryan didn't know about Witness Protection so Kate was cautious with her answer. "Seemed as good a place as any." She stirred her coffee, avoiding his gaze.

"Really? Well I'm glad you did." He reached his hand forward to stop her constant stirring and felt her shake. "Hey, what's with the shakes?"

"It's all just a bit of a shock Ryan, can you blame me?" Finally, she met his eye but pulled her hand away.

"No. I understand, really I do."

"So what did you have to tell me? You've spoken to Darren? I'm amazed you had the guts."

"I didn't 'speak' to him exactly. More like I had a message delivered from his cronies." Ryan paused. "He proper screwed me over Kate." Ryan adopted a semblance of being the wounded party.

"Is that right?" Kate asked warily.

Ryan carried on. "It is pure chance that I'm here at the same time as you, but it couldn't have happened at a better time for me to be honest." He looked away, staring out of the window.

"Go on."

"Darren and his little cronies played a right number on me. Tried to grass me up but when that didn't work he got some of his 'gangster' mates to start spreading shit around about me." Ryan shifted in his seat and looked back at Kate. She was staring at him and he could see the uncertainty on her face. "Some really nasty rumours involving kiddies and that."

Kate was stunned into silence. She looked at him questioningly. "What? You mean…" Kate couldn't quite form the words to finish the sentence.

Ryan nodded. "Yeah. Exactly. Course it doesn't take long for mob mentality to kick in where we live does it? It was a blessing when Dad rang and asked me to look after the pub. Gave me a reason to leave and I couldn't get away fast enough."

"Shit Ryan, that's awful."

"I know, right? You don't believe them do you?"

"No, no of course not. How awful. And what a bastard Darren is. God, I'm glad I got away when I did." She reached over and took Ryan's hand. "I'm sorry you've had to go through that."

"Huh, it's not your fault. Just a bit shit, know what I mean?"

"Yes, yes of course. So what will you do? How long are you staying?" asked Kate, concern written all over her face.

Ryan didn't answer immediately, framing his response in his head before he opened his mouth. "Erm, not sure. Dad goes in hospital for a knee op shortly, but it's the recovery that takes longer so who knows? Definitely over the summer anyway. After that, who knows?"

They let the sentence hang between them until Kate realised the time. "I have to go. I need to pick Joe up from school." She pushed her chair back and pulled her coat on. Ryan stood and helped her with it.

"Look, Kate. I know this is all a bit sudden but can we at least keep in touch?"

Kate looked at Ryan, studying him. She knew what it was like to be forced out of your own home. She knew Darren was a nasty vengeful bastard but he really had gone too far this time. She knew that Ryan had been used as a punching bag, and looking at him she could see that he was putting a brave face on the situation. "Let's keep in touch and see how it goes, OK?"

"Thanks Kate. It's nice to see a friendly face. I imagine things haven't been easy for you either." He took one of her hands in his.

"Oh, I'm fine now but yeah, it's been a bumpy road. No one knows anything about my previous life around here so let's just say we're friends from way back if anyone asks?"

"Well, that is true really isn't it?" Ryan smiled at Kate and she found herself smiling too in acknowledgement. She turned to leave him, and he pulled her back towards him when she didn't pull away. He kissed her gently on the forehead and said goodbye. He didn't follow immediately, claiming he had to use the facilities.

He watched from the window as Kate's car disappeared off into the distance. 'What's one more secret between us Kate?'

7

H arehills Lane, Leeds 1997

R yan pushed opened the door to the Dog and Gun and stepped inside. It wasn't one of his usual haunts so there was little chance of him bumping into anyone he knew. The place was a dump. Sticky carpets, nicotine-stained walls and less than welcoming bar staff. It was still early doors so the place was empty, but the smell of body odour lingered and last night's beer dregs added to the slickness across the bar top. A barmaid wandered through, half-heartedly wiping a filthy cloth across the pumps. Ryan could see directly into the tap room where his counterparts were already seated and slurping pints of bitter. As he waited for his own pint to be poured, he studied the motley crew he had unwillingly become a part of. Three of them huddled around a small table, and from his vantage point he studied each of them.

As usual, Jon was banging on about his days as a rally driver. If Ryan could be arsed, he would love to know how much of this were true. Having seen Jon's driving, it wasn't so much that he had a lead foot but he had absolutely no spatial awareness on the road: forever clipping mirrors and scaring pedestrians with his erratic driving. The bloke was harmless enough, just a bit of a knob in Ryan's opinion.

Suddenly the three roared with laughter and Ryan assumed Clive had said something random as always. For the life of him Ryan couldn't figure out why Charlie had even brought him in on the deal. At 52, he was older than the others, and a bit gormless but he had also been a long-time associate of Charlie's. Hilariously Clive had been told to be the lookout but with one eye pointing east and the other west, he really was a standing joke.

Finally, with his pint in hand Ryan made his way through to the back room. "Alright?" he asked, dragging a stool over.

"Brighty! Good to see you pal," said Jon, reaching over to shake Ryan's hand which he ignored.

"Now then," said Clive. "Was starting to think you'd bottled it son."

Ryan hated being referred to as 'son'. He chose to ignore the dig and Charlie jumped in.

"So we all set for tomorrow then?" he asked, lowering his voice unnecessarily. There was a nod of consent from around the table.

Clive rubbed his hands on the thighs of his already shiny jeans. "Yeah mate, looking forward to it."

Ryan looked at him and shook his head. *'Prick,'* he thought.

"Ready as we'll ever be," chipped in Jon. "Got the motor all lined up. Lovely Beemer 3 series, runs as sweet as a nut."

Ryan rolled his eyes waiting for the next predictable sentence.

"When I was a rally driver..." The rest of the lads flipped beer mats at him and told him to shut up.

"So what's the plan then Charlie?" asked Clive for the hundredth time.

"Oh for fuck's sake man, how many more times?" Ryan blew out a huge breath of frustration.

"Hey, come on. It's OK to ask." Charlie grabbed Clive's shoulder in reassurance.

Ryan shook his head and stared at Charlie. 'What the fuck has he got on you?' He wondered. He knew Charlie had done some time inside for breaking and entering. Hardly Brinks Mat standard though.

Originally from the East End of London, Charlie had built himself a bit of a reputation when he'd shown up in Leeds years ago. Someone not to be messed with, a bit of a hard man. He was handy with his fists after he'd had a few and often regaled newcomers with his glory stories. He was the living cliché of an East End nutter. He definitely had the build at over 6ft tall with a shaved head and prison-made tattoos. But, he'd started to lose his edge. The once grid iron stomach had softened to a rounded belly that had started to flop over his waistband. He reckoned this job would be his last, which is why he was determined to take as much as they could.

Charlie ran through the plans again: he knew them by rote. He'd been working on this for over 18 months and he was damned if anything was going to go wrong now. He knew they made a motley crew but he had relied on Ryan for much of the job. Ryan had the contacts after all, and Charlie felt he could trust him.

"Right. We meet here tomorrow night at 8pm. The tills

and safe will be loaded after the punters bets on the National," he explained. "Stuart doesn't lock up until the security van's been at 8.30pm so we need to get in at 8.15pm." He looked around, "Jon, make sure the car's full and running to order."

"No worries boss, I'm on it."

"Clive, Jon will drop you at the crossroads. From there you'll be able to see traffic in all directions. Any sign of the cops, you give the signal over the radio."

"Erm, I ant got a radio." said Clive.

"No dickhead, you'll get it tomorrow," answered Charlie.

Ryan shook his head. 'What the actual fuck.'

"Ryan. Me and you will jump out of the car, kick in the front door, and make it clear we're armed. I'll head into the back office and kick the staff round to the front. Stuart's bound to come out then, if he's not there already, so I'll take care of him and get him to start emptying the safe. Your job Ryan is to keep any punters under control. If you need to fire, aim at the ceiling. I don't want anyone to get shot. Got it?"

Ryan nodded his consent.

"Once we're clear I'll radio Jon. We leave, pile in the car and head to the change-over point. Right, has everyone got it? Any questions?" Charlie looked at each of them in turn. No, no questions.

"Right then, see you all tomorrow." Ryan finished his pint and stood up to leave. He was glad to get outside and into fresh air. He'd listened to what Charlie had to say but he didn't trust it would go as smoothly as he reckoned. Just in case it all went tits up Ryan had sussed out an alternative escape route.

.   .   .

Following Day 8.15pm

"Get the fuck down!" screamed Ryan as he kicked his way into the shop. He glanced quickly around, adrenaline soaring through his veins. "Get down on the floor and don't fucking move!" He could hear Charlie issuing orders to the two cashiers and instructing the shop owner Stuart to fill the holdalls. Suddenly the radio crackled into life. It was Clive "COPS!" he shouted across the radio.

"Fuck this," said Ryan. He fired off a quick shot, kicked on the fire exit door and pelted over the wall. He could hear the sirens in the distance, and he didn't stop until they were far behind him.

8

I t was 10am in the Harbour Café. Kate often worked the Sunday shift on her own whilst Joe was happy to wander around the harbour with Jack. They were never really busy on Sunday mornings. It was usually the end of people's holidays and they called in for a coffee before setting off on their trips home.

She took an order for a couple of lattes and went around the counter to start prepping the coffee machine. She heard the door jingle and shouted over her shoulder that she wouldn't be a minute.

"No rush," came the reply. It was Ryan.

Her stomach lurched and she turned around quickly, almost spilling the milk she had in her hand.

"Oh, hi," she said. "Just give me a minute." She was unnerved to see him so unexpectedly but was determined not to let it show. She made the coffees and handed them to the couple before turning her attention to Ryan. "What can I get you?" she asked, trying to be nonchalant.

"Erm, just a black coffee with sugar and maybe a bacon butty?" he asked, looking a bit worse for wear.

Kate started the prep, "Wow, heavy night?"

"Yeah, just a bit. Don't usually drink on duty but had a rowdy crowd in on the whisky so you know how it goes."

Kate knew exactly how it went with Ryan. Never one to say no, especially if someone else was paying.

"And you just couldn't resist?"

"Yep, that's the one."

"Back in second, I'll bring you your butty."

A few more customers came in after that, so Kate didn't have a chance to speak to Ryan until it went quiet. She noticed he'd finished his coffee and sandwich but still hung around. Kate felt a little tingle of... she wasn't sure what, excitement, nerves? She cleaned the last of the tables and made herself a cup of tea, topping Ryan's coffee up at the same time. The café was empty now, so she grabbed the chair opposite and sat down.

"So, what plans have you got for the rest of the day?" he asked.

"Not much. Joe's out with Jack at the minute but they'll be back soon so probably lunch and a walk to the park I would have thought. Why do you ask?" she replied.

"Wondered if you fancied going for a walk or something?" he asked. Kate hesitated and looked at him,

"With Joe?" asked Kate.

"Of course with Joe. Be nice to see him again, he was just a bairn last time I saw him properly."

"Uh, I'm not sure." Kate picked at an imaginary stain on the table.

"C'mon, you said yourself you've nothing else planned and it would be nice to spend some time with a familiar face."

Kate thought for a second, and that familiar 'sod-it' feeling came over her. The feeling that she got when she was about to do something she really shouldn't. 'What the hell.' she thought.

"Yeah, why not? Where did you have in mind?"

"Um, dunno, didn't expect you to say yes to be honest."

Kate laughed, "Well, I like to keep you on your toes."

"Yeah that's true," said Ryan laughing along. "What about Flowerdale Falls? It's a bit of a trek but lots for Joe to explore?"

"Sounds good. I'll just clear up here and Joe should be back in a second."

"Cool," said Ryan.

It was another 10 minutes before Jack and Joe returned to the café. In that time Ryan had filled Kate in on the previous night's antics, having Kate in fits of laughter with his imitations of the people in the bar. Kate was just wiping tears of laughter from her face when the door jingled and Joe burst in.

"Mum, we saw him. Ollie came right up into the harbour and sat there for ages. He's massive. Jack reckons he's about 30 years old! Do seals even live that long? I'm going to look it up." Joe dashed over to the kids' corner where the animal encyclopedia was. If Ryan's presence registered with him, Joe didn't acknowledge it. Jack did though. He hesitated as he walked over to the table,

"Ah, you've got company I see?" inquired Jack, looking straight at Ryan.

"Yes, sorry Jack – this is Ryan, Ryan – this is Jack," said Kate quickly making the introductions.

Ryan stood up to shake hands with Jack.

"Ah, you must be Len's eldest lad?"

"Yes, that's right. I'm helping out whilst he gets his knee fixed."

"I'd heard," said Jack, turning away and making his way

into the back. "I'll just collect a few bits Kate then I'll get out of your way. Don't forget Adam's here tomorrow to start work." Jack grabbed what he needed, which in truth was nothing but he wanted to take a good look at Ryan. He remembered him now as a youngster. Jack still had an uneasy feeling that he couldn't quite put his finger on. 'Probably best left alone, none of my business,' he thought as he headed towards the door. "See you tomorrow," he called, and the door slammed shut behind him.

"See you... Oh, he's gone. That was quick, he didn't even say goodbye to Joe," said Kate wondering what had gotten into her friend. She shrugged it off, knowing that if there was a problem Jack would let her know in his own way.

"Mum, it's true seals really do live longer than 30 years, it says so here," shouted Joe excitedly as he dashed over with the book, pointing to the pictures and the paragraph.

"Hahaha, so they do," laughed Kate, pulling Joe into a cuddle after he thumped the heavy book onto the table. "How do you fancy going to see a waterfall today?" she asked, knowing he'd jump at the chance to go off on an adventure.

"Yes please, can we take a picnic?" he asked, stomach first – always.

"Not really the weather sunshine, but we can take a drink and a few snacks," replied Kate, getting up from her seat and making her way into the kitchen.

"Is it OK if I come with you Joe?" asked Ryan, tentatively.

"Who are you?" questioned Joe, as if seeing Ryan for the first time.

"Joe! Don't be so rude," admonished Kate. "This is Ryan and he's a friend of mine."

"But you don't have any friends," said Joe.

Ryan laughed as Kate blushed, "From the mouth of babes," he said.

"Joe, that's rude and I do have friends so don't be cheeky," said Kate, ruffling Joe's hair as she returned with a handful of wrapped biscuits and a bottle of juice. "How about you go get your boots on before I change my mind."

Kate turned to look at Ryan, "Sorry about that, he's usually quite polite."

"No worries, kids eh?" said Ryan.

Joe didn't seem at all fazed that Ryan would be joining them, and Kate felt herself relax a little as she locked up the café and watched Ryan and Joe walk on ahead, chatting away. She caught up with them just past the post office and the three of them crossed the road to begin their walk.

Flowerdale Falls was one of the first places she and Joe had explored when they moved to Gairloch. They had been staying at The Old Inn and the entrance to Flowerdale was just opposite. She'd learned that it was private land, owned by the Mackenzie family who owned much of the land in and around Gairloch, as well as the ancestral home, Flowerdale House, that was along the route. It was a beautiful walk as long as you didn't go without midge protection in the summer months, something she discovered too late last year. In spring it was fine, with lots of the wild plants starting to come to life. They'd seen a few small animals too, much to Joe's delight.

"Yeah, and we saw a skunk," he declared to Ryan. Ryan looked at Kate quizzically.

"No, it was a stoat Joe," laughed Kate, swinging him by the arm.

"Now that makes more sense," said Ryan, holding Joe's other arm and together they started to swing him back and forth.

"Ooff, you're a big lad, aren't you?" commented Ryan when they'd swung Joe for the fifth time. "My arm needs a rest," he said, shaking it as Joe ran ahead.

"You've got a smashing wee boy there Kate," said Ryan with a nod of his head towards Joe.

"Thanks. I don't think he came out of the whole ordeal too badly. He was a bit confused at first but over time the questions stopped, and he just got on with it. I'm glad he wasn't any older or I think it would have been harder for him to adjust," Kate replied, picking up a stick and poking the ground as they walked along. She hadn't meant to open up to Ryan like that, but it had been a long time since she'd had anyone to really talk to, and it just spilled out of her.

Ryan reached over and took hold of Kate's hand. "You've done a grand job Kate, all things considered," he said giving her hand a gentle squeeze of reassurance.

"Thanks, I try my best," she said, not taking her hand away.

They carried on walking past the horse pastures and Flowerdale House onto the dirt trail that started the path towards the breathtaking waterfall.

"Have you been here before?" she asked Ryan, very aware that they were still holding hands but not truly wanting to break the connection.

"As a kid, yeah, but it's changed a hell of a lot since then. The path was never this good, I'm not even sure there was a path to be honest. But we'd fish in the stream and chase dragonflies down the path, not sure why. My sister always used to believe they were fairies and was desperate to catch one." Ryan chuckled at the memory of him and Molly escaping their mother for the day and having wild adventures in the glens.

"And did she?" asked Kate.

"Ha, no. Have you ever tried to catch a dragonfly? They're fast little buggers!"

"What's a dragonfly?" Joe came hurtling out of the woods towards them.

"You know what a dragonfly is Joe, you've seen them before," said Kate, catching Joe in a bear hug that he wriggled frantically to get out of. "They hover over water and are brightly coloured."

"And very fast," chipped in Ryan.

"Oh, I know what you mean. Mum, can we stop at the bridge please?"

"Course, wanna play Pooh sticks?" she asked. She'd been playing this childhood game with him since he was old enough to walk.

"Race you!" called Ryan, setting off at a slow jog until Joe caught up with him

"You might regret that Ryan; the bridge is a fair way yet! You two run ahead and I'll catch you up!" called Kate, but already the boys were yards ahead.

Kate stopped a moment to catch her breath and look around her. The beauty of the glen and the landscape never failed to lift her spirits. It felt so good to share her surroundings with someone familiar. The anxiety that had seemed to be a constant companion over the last couple of years was replaced with an optimism she once believed to be impossible to feel again. The struggle, the holding-it-together, the game face she'd worn every day didn't feel false or fake. For the first time in a long time she felt a lightness in her step. Could she finally be finding some peace? She sincerely hoped so, not just for her own sake but for Joe as well. She wanted him to grow up feeling loved and secure; that he could talk to her about anything. They had an impenetrable bond after all they had been through, but she needed more than a seven-year-old as her best friend. Joe had been right back at the café, she didn't have any friends, apart from Jack but she couldn't be truly honest with him either. She couldn't confide in him about her innermost thoughts and feelings, and she didn't dare strike up a friendship with any of the Gairloch community for fear that they would want to know about her past and that was something she wasn't willing to share. She could see Ryan and Joe just up ahead; they'd already reached the bridge and were searching the path for sticks. It was good to see Joe enjoying himself with Ryan. If she had any worries about how they would get on they were put to rest. Joe hadn't asked any questions and clearly didn't remember Ryan, but it had been a long time ago.

"Here!" shouted Kate, "I've found a couple of good ones for you." She hurried forward, thrusting two sturdy fallen twigs at them.

"Great stuff," said Ryan, taking them from her. "Just need a couple of good-sized leaves now."

"What for?" asked Joe inquisitively, looking up at Ryan.

"For sails of course! Don't tell me your mum doesn't make sails for your wee boats?"

"No, we just throw them in," said Joe. "How do you make sails?"

Ryan scouted around and found a couple of large leaves and threaded them onto the twigs. "Here, like that." He handed one to Joe and the other to Kate. Joe dashed over to the wooden railing.

"Hey, wait for me," said Kate, going to stand next to him. "Ready? 1-2-3, GO!" she shouted and they simultaneously dropped their sailboats into the stream, dashing over to the other side to see which came through first.

"It's mine, it's mine!" cried Joe, pointing over the rail at the first one to make it through.

"So it is!" exclaimed Kate. "You always win!" She grabbed Joe around the waist and spun him round, laughing.

"Funny, that," said Ryan, raising an eyebrow at Kate and joining in the conspiracy.

With the excitement of Pooh sticks being over, Ryan challenged Kate and Joe to a game of hide and seek.

"You two go run and hide, I'll come and find you," said Ryan, turning his back.

Kate and Joe separated and went in different directions.

"Not too far Joe!" she called out, but her son was already off.

Ryan counted to ten, then set off in search. It didn't take long to find Kate. He stealthily moved around a big old, solid tree trunk and spied on her as she was looking the other way.

"Boo!" he called out softly, not quite loud enough to give the game away to Joe that he'd already found his mum.

Kate jumped, turned, and playfully slapped Ryan on the chest. He caught her up in his arms and held her to him. For once Kate didn't wriggle or struggle to get free.

"Not letting you go this time," he whispered into her ear.

She pulled her head back, still in his embrace and gently laughed, "Do you see me struggling?" she said with a huge grin on her face, and felt her heart skip a beat.

They looked at each other for a minute, until Ryan moved away.

"C'mon, best find Joe," he said, taking hold of her hand and leading the way. Kate could feel herself blushing. She allowed herself to be tugged along, a glow of happiness building inside her.

9

J ack started to read the news story again for the fifth time but try as he might he just couldn't settle. He threw the newspaper down and grabbed his well-worn wax jacket from the hanger in the hallway and headed out of the door of his beloved cottage.

Something about this Ryan bloke just didn't sit well with Jack, and he was dammed if he could place his finger on exactly what it was. Knowing that they'd gone out for the afternoon, Jack made the decision to visit The Kingfisher.

"W ell, hello stranger!" called out Janice from behind the bar as Jack walked through the double doors of the pub. He blushed, not wanting to draw attention to himself. He'd hoped it was someone else behind the bar, Janice was an old gossip and pretty much part of the furniture of the pub. His Annie always used to say 'never trust a gossip unless you want to know a secret' which was wise advice he'd always thought.

"Hello Janice, how are you?" he asked as pleasantly as he could, "not many in today" he commented, taking a look around. Apart from 2 locals in the corner, the place was empty.

"Sunday isn't it? They'll all be down at The Old Inn getting their Sunday lunch," said Janice. "Told Len we'd lose trade when he stopped serving food but he wouldn't listen to me. What can I get you Jack?" she asked.

"True, true... I'll have a pint of Bitter please hen." Jack pulled up a bar stool, figuring Janice was his best chance as any to get information from about Ryan.

"I hear Len's going to be out for a while?" he asked in what he hoped was a conversational tone as he waited for Janice to pull his pint.

"Aye. Shouldna be too long in the hospital, it's the recovering that takes time. He reckoned a couple of weeks in all, but I think it'll be much longer. When Mary got her knee done..." She handed over the pint and kept talking whilst she took his money and sorted out the change but he'd switched off, taking a big gulp of his drink and feigning interest in her tittle-tattle.

"I see he's got young Ryan running the place," he commented, wiping off his beer 'tache.

"Oh, don't get me started on that," she said. Jack braced himself for the onslaught of whinging he knew was headed his way. "Why he thinks we need a bairn to run the place is beyond me," she fumed.

"He's hardly a bairn Janice, he's 27."

"Well, you know what I mean. Age is just a number Jack. You should have seen him in here last night, carrying on like an eejit! Nearly drank the bar dry of whisky, the lot of them. It's no way to behave. He'll drink the profits if I let him. No surprise that Len didn't really want him here."

Jack thought he had misheard her, "What do you mean, Len didnae want him? I thought he asked him?"

"Dinna ken where you heard that but no, fair bullied his way in here, so he did. Told his poor da some sob story about how hard his life was in Leeds, that some nasty things were being said and he needed to get away for a while. Course, Len being the soft wee bugger he is, he opened his doors and handed over the cellar keys." Janice folded her arms across her chest and made a harrumphing noise. "Huh, I'll tell you this for nothing Jack, if there's any more carry on like last night I'll no be hanging around."

At that, thankfully a group of walkers entered the bar and ordered their drinks. As Janice went over to serve them, his mind wandered back over her tirade, wondering what to make of it all. Janice finished serving and propped herself in the corner behind the bar, a bit too close for Jack's comfort.

"Now you know me Jack," said Janice in a partial whisper, "I'm not one for gossip." Jack nearly spat his beer all over her. "But all I will say is that it was something to do with kiddies!" With that last statement she pulled a conspiratorial face and winked at Jack and waited for his response. It took a few seconds for him to register what she meant, and when realisation hit him it made his blood run cold.

"That can't be true Janice, where did you even hear that?" he asked, incredulous.

"Straight from Len! I think he was in shock, and I only overheard part of the phone call," she confirmed.

'You mean you listened in nosey bugger,' thought Jack but didn't say anything, Janice was in full flow.

"Oh aye, heard it from the horse's mouth. Course, none of its true I'm sure but what do you have to do to upset someone enough to start those kinds of rumours? No smoke without fire some might say." Janice looked at him with eyebrows raised, expecting him to chip his own thoughts in, but he knew better than that. He took a final swig of his pint and handed her the glass.

"Aye well, none of our business really is it?" he said, trying to end the conversation. "I'd best be off, see you later and give my best to Len." He headed straight for the door and gulped in the fresh air. He wasn't much of a beer drinker at the best of times and he'd fair downed that pint to get away from Janice and the unbelievable gossip she was famed for sharing.

But what should he do now that he had that information? Was it true? He felt his skin prickle at the thought of Kate and Joe on their own with Ryan. He had to tell Kate, but what if it wasn't true? And how did Kate know Ryan in the first place?

10

I t wasn't that Jack was ignoring her exactly, but he was definitely 'off' with her. So far that morning Kate had asked him a couple of questions regarding the electrical work that Adam had started, and his answers had been short and snappy. She knew Jack well enough to know when something was wrong but for the life of her she couldn't figure out what she had done to upset him. Or maybe it was nothing to do with her at all. All this was going around in Kate's head whilst she served customers, made sandwiches, and generally kept the café running. She knew Jack would tell her in his own time if it bothered him that much.

"Bread delivery is due shortly Jack, will you be around to help out?" called out Kate to Jack who was in the kitchen at the rear of the café.

"Aye, where else would I be?" came his snapped reply.

Kate was shocked. Should she say something? There was clearly something on Jack's mind but with the café filling up and with so much to do, now wasn't the time. She put his reply to the back of her mind and carried on with her duties. Finally, 3pm came around. Kate removed her apron and set off to collect Joe from school, leaving Jack in charge for the 30 minutes it would take.

Jack was feeling bad for the way he'd spoken to Kate, but he just couldn't shake the uneasy feeling he had about Ryan. He knew he should say something to Kate but not being one to gossip or share hearsay he wondered if he should stay well enough alone. Just as he thought that the café doorbell rang, and Ryan came in.

"Take a seat, I'll be with you in a minute," said Jack as Ryan approached the counter.

"No bother, Jack, is Kate around?" asked Ryan.

"No, she's away to pick the bairn up from school, shouldn't be too long."

Ryan took a seat farthest away from the counter and a few minutes later Jack came over to get his order.

"What can I get for you?" asked Jack, with obvious disdain.

"Just a black coffee please Jack." Ryan had picked up on Jack's tone and though he didn't know Jack well he could sense some form of animosity.

"Everything alright? " ventured Ryan.

"Aye. I'll bring your coffee over." Jack walked away.

Deciding that he'd done something to offend Jack, Ryan approached the counter as Jack prepped the coffee. "Have I done something to offend you, old man?" asked Ryan.

Jack flinched at the term 'old man'. His hackles raised, he turned to face Ryan. "What makes you think that?" he asked as politely as he could.

"I just get the feeling something's bothering you?"

Jack couldn't hold back. The knowledge of the trouble in Leeds had sat heavily on his shoulders all night, and he couldn't see another time when he'd get the chance to have the conversation without Kate around. "Why are you here?"

Ryan was completely taken aback by the change in character. "For a coffee?" he put forward.

"No, not that. Why are you really here, in Gairloch?"

"Helping the old man out, you know that Jack."

"That's not what I heard."

"Oh, yeah. You visited the pub yesterday didn't you? Been listening to the old whingebag, have you? Wouldn't believe a word she says."

"She made some pretty wild accusations, heard it from Len by all accounts."

"Nosey bitch, she should keep her nose out of other people's business. She's just feeling pushed out cos dad asked me to take over."

"From what she said, he didn't want you here at all."

"Yeah well," said Ryan, "she's wrong."

"Really? Well, let me tell you this laddie, if you hurt Kate or go anywhere near Joe then God help you. I might be an old man but there's plenty around here that have taken to Kate and wee Joe, you'd be out on your arse in a second." The fury in Jack's voice was unmistakable, but if Ryan was shocked he didn't show it.

"Calm yourself down old boy, you'll give yourself a hernia. Me and Kate go back a long way, and I think you'll find she actually wants to spend time with me." Ryan was cocky with his response, leaning over the counter to intimidate Jack.

Jack took a step back, shaken with the venom of Ryan's tone. "So, my advice to you, old man, would be stay the fuck out of it."

Jack was shocked, he hadn't been spoken to in that way in a long time, and even then it was only in a heat of the moment spat. Ryan's anger and volatile personality came across in spades.

"What's going on here?" Kate entered the café and went straight over to the pair. She thought Jack looked pale and was visibly shaking.

"Nothing, just some friendly banter, isn't that right Jack?" said Ryan, staring Jack down, willing him to go against him.

"Aye, aye," stammered Jack. "Just having a wee chat. I'll get off now you're back Kate," he said, taking off the apron that was tied around his waist and handing it to Kate.

"Oh, OK well I'll see you later then," said Kate, a bit taken aback at Jack's abrupt departure. He would usually hang around until closing and help with Joe and the clearing up. She thought back to how he had been this morning and wondered if her old friend wasn't well? She made a mental note to call into his cottage later and check up on him.

Ryan was furious. He should sack that bitch Janice or teach her a lesson in keeping her mouth shut. He thrust his hands deeper into the pockets of his jacket as he walked back to The Kingfisher at a furious pace. Who the fuck did she think she was anyway? Just some washed up old hag of a barmaid that had nothing better to do with her time. He'd show her, he thought. No one stood in his way. His mind raced with the possibilities. If it wasn't for his old man, he'd have her out on her arse, maybe make her disappear. But Jack, well that was a different problem altogether. He knew the bond that Kate had with him, and with Joe for that matter. Keeping the interfering old bastard out of the way posed a bit of problem. He slowed his pace as he pondered how to deal with this dilemma. He somehow had to drive a wedge between the bond they'd developed.

He was pleased with how things had gone so far. He thought back to their walk at Flowerdale the previous day. Winning Joe round was always going to be the easy part; kids are so trusting. He hadn't expected Kate to drop her defences so easily though, she must be starved of affection he thought, smiling to himself. He knew she'd expected him to kiss her, which was exactly why he'd pulled away and changed the subject. Slowly does it, he thought, too much, too soon would have her running for the hills. But there was a timeline he had to work to, and interference from Jack was something that he just didn't need – or could be arsed with. Maybe it would be easier to make Jack disappear.

Reaching the pub, Ryan decided to have a quiet pint and give it some thought. He knew there must be a way, and he looked forward to the challenge.

11

———————

Ryan accepted the charges and greeted his old mate. "Now then, how's it going?" he said cheerfully into the mouthpiece. He'd stepped outside as soon as he'd seen the blocked caller ID. Only two people had this number and one of them was currently toying with bacon rolls and tea-making in the café.

"How do you fucking think? Only got 10 minutes, what's happening?" asked Daz.

"Not much to be fair. Weather's shit as usual," replied Ryan, knowing damn well that wasn't what Daz meant.

"Stop being a twat and tell me what's going on," demanded Daz, his voice rising.

Ryan moved out of the wind and stood in the sheltered doorway of the pub. "Like I said, not much." He thought back to the walk at Flowerdale and wondered if he should tell his mate that he was making inroads again on Daz's former missus. Probably not a good idea if he wanted his payout, though he was quite sure Daz wouldn't care.

"Taking time, aren't I? Got to build up trust and that," he

settled on; the less information shared over the phone the better.

"What about Joe?" asked Daz, his voice softening on his son's name.

"Yeah, sound little lad, always up to mischief, takes after his old man." Ryan laughed at his own joke.

Daz was quickly losing his patience and not for the first time wondered if Ryan was the right person for the job. "And what about the plan?" asked Daz, careful not to say too much knowing that all phone calls were monitored. It had been hard enough getting a new number added to his allowable phone call list.

"It's all under control pal, don't worry," Ryan reassured him.

"For sure?" asked Daz.

"Fuck's sake man, yes I'm sure, I'm not some fucking amateur," spat Ryan.

Daz backed down, not something he did very often. "Right, well keep me up to speed. I'll get my release date next week," he said and hung up.

"Prick," they both said as the call ended, without the other hearing.

12

G airloch, Late Spring 2000

"Come here buddy, let's fasten that shoelace before you trip up," called Ryan as Joe went tearing along the harbour. Joe stopped and looked at his feet. He knelt down, determined to tie his own shoelace. He made the bunny loops with his little fingers and tried to cross them over each other, failing miserably, getting too many fingers involved. Ryan caught up with him and tied it for him instead. As soon as he was done, Joe was off again.

"Does that boy ever stay still?" wondered Ryan, shaking his head. He offered to take Joe off Kate's hands for a while, mostly to stop him from getting under her feet. It was a Friday afternoon and there had been a sudden rush in the café. With school holidays just around the corner, Joe had finished at lunchtime and worked his way through copious amounts of food and most of the books in the book corner.

Ryan had called in at the café on the off chance that he'd catch Kate alone but no such luck. When she complained about Joe getting bored, he saw the perfect opportunity to build his friendship with Joe and offered to take him off for a walk. Kate had been extremely grateful, as long as it didn't inconvenience Ryan too much. Ryan had almost laughed in her face, then remembered himself and assured her it was no big deal.

"Why do you like the harbour so much Joe?" asked Ryan, taking hold of the little one's hand.

"Cos it's always different," replied Joe. "And when I come with Jack, we look at the birds through bidoculars," he said matter of fact, clearly peeved that Ryan didn't have any with him.

"You mean binoculars," said Ryan, laughing at the slip-up. Joe looked up at Ryan, unaware that he'd said it wrong, and tried to wriggle free from Ryan's hand.

"Hey, what's the matter? Don't you want to hold my hand?" asked Ryan, feeling the little fingers pulling away. Having not spent much time with seven-year-olds he'd assumed you were supposed to hold their hands but maybe not.

"No, I'm a big boy. I only hold hands when I'm crossing the road," pronounced Joe.

"Is that right? Well, I don't want you to run away," said Ryan, letting go. He didn't want the boy to feel uneasy in his company. 'Slowly, slowly catch a monkey', thought Ryan as he watched the lad run to the head of the harbour. Ryan caught up with him.

"Have you ever been on a boat Joe?" asked Ryan, pointing at the pleasure boats in the harbour.

"Yes, mum once took me on the glass-bottomed one. We saw all sorts, lots of jellyfish too," replied Joe, recounting the story. Ryan let the child ramble on, not really paying attention. His thoughts were miles away when he heard a scream coming from Joe's direction. He scanned around and couldn't see Joe anywhere. Other people along the harbour had heard the scream too. Ryan set off running towards where the sound had come from. He pushed through the crowd that had gathered and saw Joe laying on the seaweed-ridden slope that led down to the jetty.

"Out of my way," he demanded, forcing people to let him past. A couple of men had started to make their way down, and Ryan raced passed them all. "It's alright fella, I've got you," he said as he reached Joe and pulled him into his lap. "Are you hurt?" he asked, concerned. Joe sat up and rubbed the back of his head.

"No, don't think so," he said, with tears starting to form. "I slipped." He looked up at Ryan. "I'm sorry," he said, blinking away the threatening tears.

"Hey buddy it's OK, it was an accident I'm sure. You shouldn't be so clumsy though should you?" said Ryan, gently setting the boy back on his feet. "You can all clear off now," he shouted to the onlookers, sending them away looking suitably shamefaced that they'd stood by to watch a little boy cry. "Come on you," he said, "let's get you back to mum."

"Don't tell mummy, will you?" pleaded Joe. "I'm not supposed to go on the jetty, but I thought I saw a crab."

"OK, I won't say anything. It can be our secret," answered Ryan, only too happy to collude with Joe and keep something from Kate. "We all know mummy loves a secret after all," he muttered quietly under his breath.

. . .

By the time they had made their way back to the café it was somewhat quieter, and Kate and Jack were in the kitchen catching up with the washing up. Joe went straight to the chilled cabinet and pulled out a carton of orange juice whilst Ryan stepped behind the counter and started to prep the coffee machine. Jack popped his head round the door to see what was going on, and who was helping themselves to coffee.

"We don't let customers help themselves," commented Jack. "I'll do that," he said, trying to grab the grinder from Ryan's hand.

"Ryan's hardly a customer Jack," laughed Kate. "Besides, they've got one of these at the pub, so he knows how to use it." Kate rolled her eyes at Ryan, dismissing Jack's comments out of hand. Jack shrugged his shoulders and headed back to the washing up.

"Did you two have a good time then?" asked Kate, ruffling Joe's hair and pushing the straw into his drink carton.

"We did, didn't we Joe?" said Ryan.

Joe took his drink off Kate and stuck the straw in his mouth, sipping furiously to avoid having to answer the question outright. Instead he just nodded his head quickly and headed to the book corner.

"Aww it's lovely to see the two of you getting on. And thank you Ryan, I'm sure you've got better things to do than hang out with a seven-year-old." Kate reached onto her tiptoes and kissed Ryan on the cheek.

"I've told you, it's no bother. I'm happy to help," he said, smiling at Kate.

· · ·

Having made his coffee, he headed over to Joe who was sat on the floor looking through a picture book of sea animals.

"You did well there, Joe," said Ryan, squatting down so he was level with him. "Mum didn't suspect a thing! See how easy it is? Sometimes mum doesn't need to know everything, does she?"

"No, I guess not," said Joe, not really sure what he was supposed to say. He hadn't actually lied to his mum, had he? He just didn't tell her so that was OK he thought. And he knew Ryan wouldn't say anything or he'd get into trouble too for not holding Joe's hand when he was supposed to.

13

Leeds 1998

"C'mon Kate, it's just for a couple of days till I think of somewhere better."

"Throw it in the canal for all I care Ryan. I do not want that in my house."

"It's not loaded, I just don't want Sean to find it in the flat."

"Oh, it's alright if Daz finds it, is it?"

"He won't, c'mon, just while the heat dies down."

"Ryan, it's been used in an armed robbery. Why the fuck would I even consider it?"

"For old times' sake?"

"Oh, fuck off, that was over when you went to Sheffield." Kate emptied the washing machine into the laundry basket. She couldn't believe that Ryan had just turned up out of the blue expecting favours.

"Yeah but it was good though wasn't it?"

Kate blushed at the memory, "Stop it Ryan."

"Aww you know it was the best sex you've ever had," said Ryan, grabbing Kate round the waist as she bent over to pull the last bits out of the machine and grinding against her. Kate shot up, almost knocking Ryan over.

"For God's sake Ryan, no!"

"All right, sorry. I wonder what Darren would say if he knew about us." Ryan leaned back against the kitchen table, grinning.

"Ha that's a laugh, blackmail? He's your best mate, you wouldn't dare say a word. He'd floor you with one punch, probably worse. As for me, I've taken my share of punches over the years, what's one more." Kate heaved the heavy basket and opened the back door. Stepping into the back garden, she headed for the washing line. Ryan followed her out, slamming the door shut behind him, not willing to give up just yet.

"Come on, I'm desperate, and I swear it will only be for a few days." Ryan held the handgun in front of him and proffered it to Kate. She pushed it back towards him and bent down to take a t-shirt from the laundry basket.

"No Ryan, for the last time..." She heard the back door slam, and Ryan threw the gun into the basket just as Darren came out into the garden. Without thinking she bundled the gun inside the damp t-shirt she was holding and buried it under the pile of the remaining laundry.

"What's going on here then?" asked Darren.

"Alright mate, just popped in for a brew," replied Ryan, turning his back on Kate.

Kate was seething, what was she supposed to do now. She watched them go back into the kitchen. Her heart was all over the place, and she felt herself break out into a sweat.

She scoured the garden, looking for somewhere to put the weapon, at least for now. She could hardly go back into the house with a gun wrapped up in a t-shirt. She didn't care if Darren knew about the fling she'd had with Ryan, but she did care about losing custody of Joe and she had no doubt in her mind that Darren would use it against her. She stepped onto the patio and heard one of the flags make its familiar 'thunk' as she walked over it. She stopped and lifted it up. The sand underneath had all but worn away. She retrieved the offending bundle, lifted the loose flag, and stuffed it underneath. It wasn't brilliant but it would do for now. She hung the rest of the washing out and headed back into the house with every intention of telling Ryan to get it back later that night.

"Where's Ryan?" she asked Daz as she walked into the kitchen.

"Dunno, was just about to put the kettle on and he said he had to be somewhere and fucked off. What was all that about outside?"

"All what about?" replied Kate, turning her back to Darren and reaching to grab a mug from the cupboard.

"That, out there in the garden –- with him?"

"Don't know what you mean. I was hanging the washing out."

"Seemed to me something was going on. You both looked as guilty as chuff." Darren slammed his hand on the worktop, stopping Kate in her tracks. She looked up at him hoping the guilt didn't show on her face.

'Oh, here we go again,' she thought, bracing herself. Darren moved forward and grabbed Kate's wrist.

"So what's with the guilty look?" Darren twisted her wrist tighter.

Kate flinched and tried to pull away from his grasp. "Nothing. He came looking for you."

"So why were you outside?"

"I was hanging the washing out, I've told you." She looked Darren dead in the eye, holding his glare. Eventually he backed down and threw her wrist away from him. It clashed with the freshly boiled kettle which fleetingly caught Kate's hand. She winced out loud and thrust her hand under the cold water tap. "What was that for?" She was fighting back tears.

"Just watch your fucking step, I'm getting tired of your shit." Darren made his way out of the kitchen.

"My shit? That's rich." Kate thought she had said it quietly enough not to be heard by him but he had walked back in.

"What does that mean?"

"At least I'm working."

"What the fuck has that got to do with anything?" raged Darren.

"Maybe if you had a job you wouldn't be hanging around here all the time and having to put up with 'my shit'."

"Someone has to be around here to take care of my son. God knows, you're a shit mother."

Nothing could be further from the truth but at the mention of their son Joe, Kate backed down. She knew where this argument would end. Darren would take Joe and leave him with his mum again, stopping Kate having access.

"Anyway, I've got some work so that should stop your constant whining," retorted Darren when it was clear that Kate wasn't going to react.

"Really? Running drugs again? Look where that got you last time."

"Oh fuck off." Darren had had enough of her smart mouth and left the kitchen, slamming the door behind him.

14

_____

G airloch, Summer 2000

L en took a look around the pub, making sure everything was as it should be before he departed for the hospital. He'd left instructions with Janice to keep an eye on Ryan, not that it would do much good he thought, that lad was a law unto himself.

"Where are ye?" he shouted down the stairs.

"Alright, I'm here for God's sake," answered Ryan, already impatient. "I was just checking there was enough petrol in the car."

"Well hurry up, I've to be there for 9am."

Ryan would be glad to see the back of his old man. The last couple of weeks had been fraught and with so much still to do, getting him out of the way would make life easier. Every time Ryan set foot in the pub or showed his face behind the bar there was Len; interfering, asking questions, challenging him on everything from where he'd been to how many fags he'd smoked. Still, 'just one more hour,' thought Ryan. Len came downstairs into the bar.

"Don't forget the brewery deliver on a Monday. You need to put the order in on a Sunday."

"Yeah dad, I know. You've said." Ryan sighed and snatched the overnight case from Len's hand. He made his way across the rear car park and opened the battered Vauxhall Vectra that was on its last legs. Len followed slowly behind, shouting instructions to Janice as he climbed into the passenger seat. Ryan started the engine on the third try and reversed out, Len already complaining about the speed and gear changes.

'Not much longer,' thought Ryan. 'Not much longer at all.'

O ver in Harbour Café the day had started on a very different note. Kate was trying to get ready to open the café but a very excited Joe was skipping and jumping around the flat, a bundle of excitement.

"Do you think I'll need my binoculars?" he asked, stuffing them into his backpack without waiting for an answer.

Kate laughed. "Probably but if you don't hurry up then you'll miss the coach." She grabbed his coat and tugged the backpack from his hands. "Finish your breakfast while I go put everything in the car."

It was finally the day for the school trip to Applecross. It was only across the way but anyone would think Joe was going on a week's holiday with the amount of stuff he'd shoved into his bag. As she turned the lights on in the café she took the chance to go through his bag and removed anything that he didn't need. It felt incredibly heavy and she didn't want him lugging it around. She unfastened the draw-strings at the top, and saw that he'd packed all his nature books, from bird watching to sea mammals. Smiling at his enthusiasm, she took the heavier books out and left them on the table. Joe came hurtling down the stairs and wasn't too pleased to see his mum had removed his things. He started to complain when Kate reminded him that he still needed to add a drink and his packed lunch. Placated by the thought of taking food Joe shrugged his backpack on to his shoulder and fidgeted, willing his mum to get a move on.

"Mum, we're going to be late."

"No we're not, and I just need to do a couple of things then we'll be off, I promise."

The workmen were due that morning to replace a couple of kitchen units that were in desperate need of repair. Adam had convinced Jack to have them replaced instead of just fixed and Kate was delighted to be having cupboards that didn't need to be held closed with tape. She unlocked the rear exit door so the workmen could let them-selves in then turned to Joe.

"Right you, come on. Let's go." They left by the front entrance and headed to the car. Thirty minutes later, with Joe safely on his way, Kate returned to the cafe and found that the workmen had already arrived.

"Morning Kate. On your own this morning?"

"Gill's off today but Jack should be in at lunchtime. Coffee all round?" she asked them. She received a round of grateful acknowledgement and fired up the coffee machine. She set about her usual routine of cleaning and making sure all the tables had the full set of condiments. The café was quite large, with twelve tables, each seating up to six people. She'd reconfigured the layout not long after she had first started working there so that more tables could be fitted in, increasing the number of seats and the result had been an increase in takings. She'd added high stools by the panoramic window that looked out over the loch so people could sit and sip their coffee whilst watching the ever-changing view. Adam had suggested a couple of additions to the place that Kate hadn't thought of; a display cabinet to sell Gill's amazing cakes, and he'd even suggested adding a computer for customers and holidaymakers to use. Jack had been resistant until Kate pointed out that the longer people stayed the more drinks and food they would have. There was no question that Kate had brought the café kicking and screaming into the 21st century. She was just about to grab her own coffee when the café telephone rang. It was Morag from Gairloch Museum reminding her about the event that day, and asking if the sandwich order was ready to collect or would Jack be delivering it? Kate was thrown. She didn't know anything about an order for the museum. They didn't take many outside catering orders but the museum occasionally held visitor days and today was one of those days.

"Sorry Morag, Jack's not here at the minute. What was your order again?" Morag ran though it, Kate's shoulders dropped and she knew that she definitely didn't know anything about it. Rather than admit her ignorance, and risk losing the income, she promised Morag it would be ready for 12pm and she would drop it off for them.

"Shit!" she said out loud. "Why today and why didn't I know anything about it?" She was furious with Jack. Morag had placed the order a week ago. Kate didn't even know if they had all the stock they would need. In a blind panic she went into the kitchen and was confronted with cupboard doors and workbenches. Dodging around the workmen she went through what she would need to fulfil the order. She could feel her anxiety rising and just as she was about to make a start the little bell above the cafe entrance tinkled. Wiping her hands down the front of her apron she went through to the seating area.

"Morning Kate, how are you?" It was Mr Wheeler.

"I'm good thanks, a bit stressed but what can I do for you?"

"I was just wondering if our hiking group could have lunch here today? The Old Inn have let us down."

Before she knew what she was doing she agreed to a party of 15 for lunch. "Why? Why?" she said to herself as she walked back into the building site that was supposed to be a kitchen. 'It's two cupboard doors, how can it take so long,' she thought. She went outside to find the workmen who were taking another break. "Do you think it will be much longer? It's just that the café is about to get busy and I've got orders to make up."

"Nae, another 15 minutes or so and we'll be out of your way." Thankfully they had moved the work bench outside. Good job health and safety weren't due to call in. They'd visited last month and the café had received glowing reviews.

"Good stuff, thank you." She went back inside and took a moment to assess what she had to do. She really needed Jack to come in earlier but he'd worked so much recently and had been fighting off some kind of cold for the last couple of weeks which might explain his recent moods. She had positively encouraged him to take a day off, and now she was regretting it.

'Think, think,' she thought, 'Who else can help out?' The first name that sprang to mind was Ryan but she was loathe to lean on him again, no matter how much he protested that he was happy to help out. He'd been such a lifesaver recently; helping with Joe, serving coffee when they were busy. She was sure he wouldn't mind. She looked at the time. It was now 9.30am. Steeling herself, she dialled his mobile.

"Hey."

"Hey Ryan, are you busy?"

Ryan looked around the hospital car park, trying to remember where the clapped-out banger was. "Erm, why?" he asked absently.

"I could really do with a hand at the cafe. I hate to ask but do you think you could help?"

Ryan closed his eyes and swore under his breath. He had other plans for the day, something that would take him closer to his goal but he also knew that for it to succeed he needed Kate to trust him. He sighed. "Yeah sure. Be there as soon as I can." He hung up, found his car, and battered the hell out of the steering wheel, cursing out loud.

15

It was over an hour before Ryan showed up at the café. Kate was frantically working her way through the outside catering order when Ryan popped his head around the kitchen door.

"Kate, there's people waiting to be served," he said. He looked at Kate and saw that her face was glowing from the heat of the ovens and her hair, which was always a mass of frizzy red curls, had fallen out of the headband she used. She had butter across one cheek and a smudge of God only knows what over her forehead. She looked frazzled and it took all of Ryan's effort not to laugh. He saw her inhale deeply and knew that look on her face, he'd seen it once before.

"Yes Ryan, thank you. Any chance you could take their orders?" She was trying really hard to keep her anxiety – and temper – under control.

Ryan took his jacket off and grabbed an order pad. "Thank you for helping out Ryan. Hey, thanks for pulling me out of the shit Ryan." Sarcasm rolling off his tongue. Kate stopped what she was doing and looked at him.

Kate sighed, instantly realising how ungrateful she must have sounded. "Oh God. I'm so sorry." She walked over and kissed him on the cheek. "It's just been such a stressful morning. The museum phoned and I didn't even know there was an order for today. Then Mr Wheeler…"

Ryan stopped her mid-sentence with a kiss on the lips. "Hey, shush. It's fine, I was only taking the piss." He pulled her to him and squeezed. "I'll sort the customers out, you crack on with whatever you were doing." He released her and, as she turned back to her task, he smacked her on the bottom. Kate turned, blushing, and shooed him out of the door. The rest of the morning carried on in a similar vein, with Ryan serving and Kate doing the cooking and orders in the kitchen. At 12pm she finally emerged with several trays of sandwiches, sausage rolls and quiches. After loading her car, she stepped back into the café just as Mr Wheeler and his hiking group were arriving.

"I'm just headed out, but Ryan is running the café for the time being. He's expecting you so just go in and find yourself tables," she called as she slammed the boot shut.

"Sure thing Kate. Thank you." The hiking group pushed tables together and rearranged chairs so that they were all sat together. Once they had all decided what to have they waited patiently for Ryan to take their order.

At the museum, Kate unloaded the food with the help of volunteers and was just about to leave when Morag called out to her.

"Thank you Kate. I wasn't sure if he had passed the order onto you to be honest so I'm glad it was no bother."

"No problem Morag, I think Jack must be getting forgetful in his old age," laughed Kate.

"Jack? Oh no dear, I left the order with that young man of yours. Ryan is it? Len Albright's wee boy. Well no so wee these days but you know what I mean."

"With Ryan? You left the order with Ryan?"

"Aye, you'd gone to pick the wean up from school when I popped in."

"Oh right. Well, no bother. It's all sorted now."

"Well thanks again anyway." Morag waved Kate off as she drove back to the café.

'Ryan had taken the order. Why hadn't he told me about it,' she thought. She wondered what day it had been. Maybe he'd just forgotten or been busy. It was an easy mistake to make she reconciled but it didn't stop her from feeling guilty at railing at Jack about it in her head all morning.

Back at Harbour Café, the place was packed to the rafters. Apart from the hiking group, it appeared that every parent in Gairloch had taken the chance to go out for lunch whilst the kids were away to Applecross. She looked around for Ryan but couldn't see him anywhere. She headed into the kitchen, expecting to find him knee deep in orders. He was nowhere to be seen. The rear exit door was open a crack where the workmen had left so she popped her head out. Ryan was leaning up against the wall sharing a cigarette with Adam.

"Ryan! What the hell..."

"Ah you're back. Just grabbing five with Adam here."

"Have you seen the café, it's mobbed and there are people waiting." Kate was on the verge of exploding. What the hell was wrong with him?

"Aye, and I've no stopped since I got here. Keep your hair on."

Fuming, Kate went into the kitchen, threw an apron on, and headed into the fray. Within twenty minutes she felt like she was back in control. Ryan had finished his unofficial break and pulled his weight eventually, but Kate was still silently seething about the museum order. As she finally said goodbye to the last customers, she closed the door and sat heavily in a nearby chair.

"Wow, that was a busy one."

Kate looked at him and shook her head. "I've never known it be so busy. Thanks for all your help." She was grateful, and she didn't want to piss him off by accusing him of not passing on the catering order, but she had to mention it. "Did you take an order last week?" she ventured tentatively.

"Erm, nope don't think so," he replied as he carried two cups of tea over to the table and joined her.

"It's just that Morag mentioned she gave you the order?"

"Me? No, she must have it wrong."

"Really? She seemed quite certain it was you she passed it to."

"I've said No Kate, I don't know what else to tell you."

Kate didn't want to push it any further. She was tired, her feet were aching and all she wanted was take a shower and sit down before she had to collect Joe from the school gates.

"Yeah, maybe, -" she said. They drank the rest of their tea in silence. "Well, I'm heading upstairs for a shower and change of clothes before Joe gets back." She was hoping that Ryan would take it as his cue to leave. Instead, he walked round to her side of the table and started massaging her neck and shoulders. She felt a tingle down her spine and relaxed into the feeling. Despite her initial resistance Ryan had wormed his way into her affections over the last few weeks, and she hated to admit it but those old feelings for him had resurfaced. He reached down and took her hand, leading her upstairs into the flat.

"What the hell," she thought. "It's another hour before I need to pick Joe up." And she let herself be led away.

16

"Did you have a good day then?" Jack asked Joe as they walked from the school gates.

"Aye, it was amazing. We saw all sorts, there was a boat trip and everything..."

Joe continued with tales of the day as Jack walked alongside him. Jack had no idea where Kate was which was most unlike her. She had encouraged Jack to take the day off, so he'd taken the chance to visit Len in hospital. Len had been pleased to see his old pal and they'd spent a happy couple of hours catching up and playing cards. Len was due home in a few days, something to do with his irregular heartbeat had kept him in longer than expected. Len had quizzed him about Ryan but Jack really didn't have much to tell him. Ryan had been spending a lot of time at the café and although Jack tried to avoid him, Kate was clearly enjoying his company. Jack figured it was her business so he'd kept out of it. He'd been to The King-fisher a couple of times but Janice had the place running like clockwork so he had filled Len in on the pub antics rather than the developing relationship between Ryan and

Kate. Where Kate was right now, he had no idea. He'd been walking to the café when the coach had pulled up and the school kids had tumbled out. He looked around but hadn't seen Kate anywhere so took it upon himself to collect Joe.

"I'm staaaarving," bemoaned Joe as they reached the café steps. All the lights were out, and when Jack tried the door it was locked. He dug around in his pocket for his own key and let them both in. He flicked on the lights and looked around. The place was in disarray. Clearly it had been a busy day he thought to himself as he shouted for Kate. 'Not like her to leave the place in a mess.' Joe made his way into the kitchen at the rear but there was no plate of food waiting for him: just a pile of dirty plates and cups. Jack joined him and looked around. He was starting to get worried. This really wasn't like Kate at all. He shouted again.

"Kate!" No answer. He headed towards the door that led up to the flat, telling Joe to stay where he was, not knowing what he was going to find. "Kate?" he called as he reached the top step and opened the door to the flat.

"Jack! Shit, what time is it?" Kate appeared looking dishevelled with her dressing gown wrapped around her, a flushed face and hair all over the place. "I was just..."

"Hey Jack, we were just having a lay down." Ryan appeared outside Kate's bedroom door. Not knowing where to look, Jack backed away and started to head downstairs.

"Wee Joe is back from his trip. He's in the kitchen. I'll fix him his supper." He couldn't get away quickly enough, embarrassed and more than a tad annoyed. As he descended the stairs he could hear giggling behind him.

"Stop it." A soft noise of a hand being slapped away. "Thanks Jack, I'll be down in a minute," Kate shouted after him but he'd already closed the door.

Fifteen minutes later Kate came into the kitchen just as Jack was plating up Joe's supper.

"Sorry about that Jack, we were just..." blustered Kate, clearly uncomfortable.

"Nothing to do with me," came the reply.

"It's just that it's been such a busy day, what with Gill being off and the museum order, then the hiking group wanted lunch and you weren't here so..."

"I wasn't here because you talked me into taking a day off. And it's a good job I was passing the school when I did." He paused, trying to keep his voice level.

"Thank you Jack. I'm really grateful." She went to squeeze Jack's hand in a thank-you gesture but he'd turned away. Ignoring the slight, she carried on waffling. "And Ryan has been such a help. I don't know what I would have done without him."

"You should have called me. I would have come in."

"I know, but it didn't seem fair, and you've been getting over that cold and everything..."

"It's about priorities Kate. I would have come in." He hadn't meant for his words to be so cutting but Kate almost flinched with their sharpness. An atmosphere developed between them just as Ryan walked into the kitchen. He ignored Jack and went over to where Joe was eating.

"Alright wee man, have a good day did you?" he asked.

"Aye," said Joe with a mouthful.

Ryan turned and spoke to Kate. "Right, I'll be off then." He leaned over and kissed her fully on the lips. Jack turned away, embarrassed by the show of affection.

"OK, I'll see you tomorrow?" she asked.

"Maybe, I'll call you."

Kate turned back to Jack, "I'm sorry I wasn't there to collect Joe."

"Aye well, no harm done I guess," Jack answered gruffly as he started to clear the dirty pots and pans from the work surfaces.

Kate joined him. "You don't have to do this Jack, I'll clear up."

"It's no bother." Another gruff response.

They spent the next hour clearing up and wiping down until the café and the kitchen were spotless. Joe had finished his tea and Kate had roped him in to help, hoping it would lift the mood. No such luck. Jack had carried on in silence and no matter how hard Kate tried she couldn't coax a smile out of him.

"Will you join me for a cup of tea Jack?" she asked as Joe headed upstairs to watch cartoons before bed.

"No, I'll get off."

"Please Jack. I'd like to talk to you."

Reluctantly Jack sat down and let Kate pour him a cup of tea. After a few awkward minutes Kate started talking, trying to explain her relationship with Ryan but Jack cut in.

"It's none of my business hen, you've got your own life to live."

"But I don't understand what you have against Ryan. He's been so helpful of late and we've grown quite close."

"Aye, I can see that." Jack fiddled with the spoon at the side of his cup, wanting the conversation to end.

"So what is wrong then?"

"He's bad news Kate. Always has been."

"But that's when he was a kid. He's changed Jack."

Jack huffed. He couldn't say anything else. Kate was right. Ryan seemed to be helping and he had definitely put a smile on Kate's face, but all Jack had right now was feelings of wrongdoing. He couldn't put his finger on it or start making accusations.

"Please Jack, just give him a chance?" pleaded Kate. She couldn't bear the thought of upsetting Jack when things were going so well with Ryan. She knew Jack felt a responsibility for herself and Joe. "And I can look after myself you know." She reached over and placed her hand on top of Jack's. Jack sighed heavily.

"Aye hen, you're right. I'm just looking out for you both, that's all." He finished his tea and took his cup into the kitchen. Kate followed him, feeling a little better.

"Right, I'll be away then. See ye after wee man," he called upstairs to Joe as he headed to the door. Joe waved after him.

"And thanks again Jack for you know, school and everything."

Jack nodded and closed the door behind him. How could he get Kate to see sense he wondered, or was he overreacting? He rubbed his bristly chin and headed home. That was enough for one day he thought.

17

Ryan was pissed off, thoroughly pissed off. The hospital had phoned and Len was due home. He knew that once his father was back in the pub he'd end up playing nursemaid and he'd had enough of running around after other people. Over the last week Kate had seemed to think that he was at her beck and call. He was all for keeping her sweet but she was starting to take the piss. He seemed to have become some sort of childminder for young Joe, which wasn't that bad to be fair but he was knackered. Why couldn't he just get on with his own plans and fuck everyone else and their needs?

He kicked the barn door that stood at the rear of the pub, someway off the entrance and tucked away around the corner. It had stood there for as long as he could remember. Years ago his dad has used it for storage, and at one point as a garage, but the building was so dilapidated Len had been convinced it would collapse at any moment and stopped parking his car there.

The wood splintered where Ryan had kicked it but didn't give way. He removed the rusty old padlock easily by breaking the door handle it was connected to and heaved it open. After much pushing and shoving it finally gave way. Once inside Ryan could see why he'd had so much difficulty. Years of neglect had left part of the wooden roof beams to collapse and they'd fallen just behind the door, leaving the inside entrance open to the elements. Leaves, branches, and debris had made their way inside and collected behind it. He kicked the crap out of the way and looked around. The first thing he noticed was the smell; a dank, musty smell of rotting leaves and animal faeces, probably rats. He walked over to the interior wall and gave it a kick: solid. He did the same on the other three and apart from loose bits of timber falling in, the structure was sound. Right at the back there were three stalls that once upon a time had stabled horses or cattle, not that he could ever remember. He pulled one of the doors and the top half fell off its hinges, the weight dragging the rest of the door with it. He jumped backwards out of the way as the whole thing crashed at his feet. Moving onto the next one he tried the same, ready this time for any falling debris. The door was purposely split in two, so the top half could be opened separately, allowing horses to poke their heads out. He unfastened the bolt that was holding it closed and with a bit of force it finally moved from its resting place. Swinging the door wide, he peered inside. The smell was foul. The leaking roof had encouraged rain to create a constant puddle and the stench of stale, stagnant water was overpowering. Covering his nose and mouth with the crook of his elbow, he moved onto the third stable. There was only the lower half of the stable door on, and at first glance it appeared to have avoided the neglect of the others, being reasonably dry and draft-free. Clearly someone else had thought so at some point as there were the remnants of a sleeping bag and empty tins of Tennants lager strewn across the chalky floor. Ryan walked in and kicked the stuff to one side. A rat ran right across his foot, giving him a fright and only just missing out on getting a kick up its arse. He looked up and saw that the roof was more or less intact in this stable. The sleeping bag was covered with dust and cobwebs, and he tentatively picked up one corner, shaking it out. Relieved that no rodents had made their home there he stuffed it into a corner, kicking the empty beer cans alongside it. He double-checked the half door again, pulling and pushing it closed a few times from the inside. Certain that it would suit his needs, he did the same from the other side and saw that, although the bolt was rusty, it still worked and held fast when pushed into place.

'Hmm, maybe a padlock as well,' he pondered. He walked back through the barn, noting the abandoned pieces of worthless brewery machinery; long-forgotten empty barrels and broken pumps. Nothing he could sell or use he thought. He walked outside and closed the huge entrance door behind him, this time much easier than before without the collection of nature stopping it.

"Definitely need a new padlock on this," he muttered. Just as he turned to leave his mobile rang. Fishing it out of his pocket he looked at the caller ID. Kate. 'What now?' he thought, wondering whether to answer it or not. He reluctantly accepted the call.

"Hey."

"Ryan, hey. Oh thank God you answered. It's Joe. He's missing." Came the frantic voice of Kate on the other end.

Ryan's heart skipped a few beats and it was a few seconds before he answered. He fleetingly wondered if Daz had double-crossed him. "What do you mean 'missing'?"

"Just that. I had a call from Miss Watson just after

lunchtime. Joe didn't go back to class after lunchbreak and no one can find him."

"OK, OK. Calm down. Tell me exactly what happened."

Kate explained that once Joe hadn't turned up for afternoon registration his teacher had sent the school caretaker to check the playground and playing fields to see if there was any sign of him. One of the other children had said they'd seen Joe wandering off towards the school gates so it was assumed that Joe had a dentist or doctor's appointment and his mum had forgotten to collect him again so he'd set off home on his own.

"Only he hadn't, and now no one knows where he is." Kate was in tears.

Ryan could hear a commotion in the background. "Where are you?"

Sniff. "I'm at the café. Jack sent me back here in case he shows up. Ryan, please help. I don't know what I'd do..."

"OK, I'm on way. I'll see you soon."

As Ryan drove towards Harbour Café he could see hordes of locals out searching for Joe. Some had sticks and were poking the gorse bushes that bordered the road. Every so often he'd hear a call of "Joe." "Joe." He pulled up just outside the café as Joe's schoolteacher arrived.

"Have you found him?" he asked Miss Watson abruptly.

"No. No. Not yet. I was just on my way to see Kate."

"You had better hope nothing's happened to that wee boy," he spat, seeing all his own plans fading by the second. They walked into the café together. Kate was sat with Mr Wheeler who was doing his best to comfort her and force tea on her. She stood when she saw Ryan and fell into his arms, sobbing on his shoulder.

"Oh Ryan, what if something's happened to him?" She lifted her head, searching his face for answers.

"It will be OK, we'll find him. I promise." He led her back to the table and asked Mr Wheeler about the search efforts. He mentioned that the whole of the small community had been rallied and were out searching.

"I don't understand why he would have run away. It doesn't make sense." Kate was desperate for answers.

Miss Watson finally spoke up quietly from her position by the door, "I think I might know why."

Kate noticed her for the first time. "Oh, often lose pupils do you?" Miss Watson flinched at the remark, feeling it was somewhat out of order considering.

"I understand you're upset with me and you've every right to be, but I think I know why he might have taken off."

"Go on," said Kate, arms folded defensively across her chest.

"Some money went missing from school last week, the day before the trip to Applecross. It was part of the collection box that we've had in the classroom. I asked the children about it, but they said they didn't know anything. It was only afterwards, when we arrived back at school, that I thought about it and realised that Joe had been buying his friends ice creams and he bought books from the gift shop." She looked at Kate. "It wasn't a lot of money that was taken, about ten pounds, but as you know we only allow the children to take two pounds on any school trip. Joe seemed to have more money than most so the next day I asked him about it."

"You did what?" exclaimed Kate. "Why didn't you speak to me?"

"I was certain it was a misunderstanding. I asked him if you had given him more than two pounds. He said no but couldn't give me a reason why he had so much money on him. Kate, I'm sorry. This is all my fault. I should have spoken to you first." Miss Watson stood wringing her hands, tears forming in the corner of her eyes.

Kate made a move towards the teacher, and Ryan thought she was going to slap her. He quickly stepped in between them and thinking fast he spoke next. "It was me," he said. Everyone turned to look at him.

"What do you mean?" asked Kate. "What was you?"

"It was me that gave Joe the extra money. I didn't want the kid to go without..."

"Ryan! You shouldn't have done that." Kate looked at him affectionately, all the pieces seemingly falling into place. "I did wonder when I emptied his backpack where the new books were from."

Miss Watson visibly let out a huge sigh of relief, all the attention being taken from her.

"I'm sorry Kate, I just wanted the boy to have a good time."

Kate was torn between being furious at Ryan for not telling her, understanding his affection for Joe, and desperation to know where the hell he had got to.

"Kate. Leave it with me. Let me look for him and I promise I'll bring him back to you." He held Kate to him, feeling her shaking and kissed her on the forehead before heading out of the door.

18

'Well this wasn't part of the fucking plan,' thought Ryan as he made his way along the harbour path. He called Joe's name every so often but to no avail. Part of him did wonder if Daz had somehow double-crossed him but dismissed it as unlikely. He didn't have a release date yet so what would be the point. He pulled his fags out of his jacket pocket and lit one as he sat on the bench, trying to figure out his next move.

If he found the boy Kate would be eternally grateful, and he might even be seen as a bit of hero. 'I could live with that,' he thought, stretching his legs and crossing his ankles in front of him. For once it wasn't bloody raining, in fact it was quite a pleasant day. If it wasn't for the fact that his entire future depended on the lad being found he would have sat there longer, enjoying the sun on his face. He sat up and flicked the remains of his cigarette into a nearby plant pot. He started to give some thought as to where the boy might be. He figured he wouldn't have gone far and was probably just doing it for a bit of attention; God knows Ryan had done it often enough when he was seven. Where was

Joe's favourite place? The place where he spent loads of time with Jack? It hit him like a bolt of lightning. The Harbour. Everyone else was looking up by the main road and around the park, so Ryan walked in the opposite direction. He picked up his pace and headed towards the moored boats. As he got closer he slowed down and quietly called Joe's name.

"Joe?" No answer.

"Joe, it's only me." Still no answer. Ryan wandered over to the pleasure boats, the ones used to take eager tourists out to see the dolphins and whales. He lifted a couple of tarpaulins as he passed them, until he reached the glass-bottomed boat.

"Joe? Are you hiding in there?" Ryan bent down and looked under the covering. A small figure moved forward, and a little face appeared; tearful and scared.

"Ah, there you are. Good hiding space. Are you OK? I mean, you're not hurt or anything?"

Joe shook his head. "Am alright," he sniffed, climbing further out until he was level with Ryan on the edge of the boat. Ryan made no attempt to move. Instead he opened his arms and Joe moved in for a hug.

"Everyone's looking for you, you know."

"I'm sorry," he whispered.

"You don't have to be sorry. You're safe and that's what matters but Joe, why did you run away?"

No answer, just a fresh onslaught of tears.

"Hey, come on. You know you can tell me and I won't tell anyone. Was it something to do with the trip to Applecross?"

Joe nodded slowly.

"Did you take the money out of the money box?"

Hic. "Yes."

"Why?"

"Mum was really busy and had forgotten to give me any spends and I wanted ice cream."

"Ah Joe. You know you shouldn't have done that, right?"

A slow nod of the head.

Ryan hunkered down so he was face to face with the seven-year-old. "It's alright pal, I've covered for you."

Joe looked at Ryan. "What do you mean?" Sniff.

"Well, I said that I gave you the money."

"Why?"

"Well, I didn't want you to get into trouble and we're mates right? That's what mates do."

Joe looked confused. "But won't mum go mad with you?"

"Don't you worry about that, it can be our secret, yeah?"

Joe nodded and wiped his nose on the sleeve of his coat. "OK."

"Right, shall we go back home now?" Ryan stood and took Joe's hand. "And not a word to mum, right? We'll just say you thought it would be fun to hide in the boats."

Joe took Ryan's hand and walked alongside him. They saw a couple of locals along the way back to the café who were relieved to see the little boy safe and sound. They congratulated Ryan wholeheartedly with handshakes and slaps on the back.

By the time they had reached the café word had got back to Kate, and she threw herself at Joe as they came through the door.

"Joe, where have you been?" Joe would have answered but his mum was smothering his face with kisses. She released him and knelt down, brushing hair away from his face and wiping his tears away with her fingers.

"I'm sorry mum," came the quiet reply.

"You're home and you're safe that's what matters." Kate

stood up. "Ryan, how can I ever thank you enough? Where was he?"

"Hiding in the boats. Thought it would be fun apparently."

She wrapped her arms around him and kissed him deeply. "Thank you so much."

He gave her a quick hug, eager to make his escape now that his plans could continue. "No bother, as long as the lad's fine." He ruffled Joe's hair. "I need to go." He said his goodbyes and left the café.

Kate turned to Miss Watson, "Thankfully he's safe. I'm sorry if I snapped at you."

Miss Watson had never been so relieved to see one of her pupils in all her twenty years of teaching at Gairloch Primary. "It's fine. I'm just glad he's safe and home. Are you OK Joe?"

Joe nodded, a bit overwhelmed with all the attention that was being paid to him. He wished he hadn't taken the money now. He knew it had been wrong, but he didn't want to miss out and it had seemed to be the only way. He wouldn't do it again, that was for sure. Ryan had confused him. Why hadn't he been mad? Why did he say he had given him the money? Joe liked Ryan a lot. He was good fun, had taught him all sorts of new games, and was always showing him new places to play, places that mum would definitely not let him go. Suddenly he felt very tired. All he wanted was to go to bed, or even better eat crisps and watch cartoons.

As everyone left the café one by one, there was only Kate and Jack left. Kate sent Joe upstairs whilst she locked the café early.

"Thank God Ryan found him," said Kate, rinsing the

cups and passing them to Jack to place them in the dishwasher.

"Aye, stroke of luck that," he said as he took a cup from Kate. Kate caught the disparaging tone in Jack's voice.

"Jack, will you give it a rest. What is wrong with you?"

"Nothing. I just said it was a stroke of luck, well it was wasn't it?"

"It was the way you said it."

"Ach, Kate. Look I don't want to fall out with you. I think we'll have to agree to disagree where that Albright lad is concerned."

"You still don't trust him?"

"It's not that. I remember him as a kid, and he was always out for himself. Even Len, his own father, doesn't trust him."

Kate shrugged her shoulders. "Do you know what. I'm too tired for this right now. You're right. We'll agree to disagree." She stormed off and left Jack to lock the doors behind him.

Not knowing what else to do, Jack grabbed his coat and headed off. He was too long in the tooth, too old and battle-scarred, to not know trouble when he saw it and he was convinced that Ryan Albright was just that – trouble.

19

"About fucking time. Where the hell have you been? I've been waiting ages for you."

"Nice old man, nice way to greet your son that."

"Oh, get to feck. Just get me home."

Ryan took the handles of the wheelchair and wheeled his dad over to the car. With much huffing and puffing and moaning from Len he finally manoeuvred him in. Ryan stood back and looked at him, lain prone across the back seat, completely helpless. He couldn't help but chuckle to himself.

"What the fuck are you laughing at?" growled Len. "I'm in pain here."

"Aye. That you are. Here." He passed his old man the painkillers and a bottle of water. "Take these for the journey."

"I'm not taking jack shit from you." But he took them anyway, knowing he was in a position of weakness and didn't have the strength to argue.

Ryan watched him swallow two of the pills, collapsed

the wheelchair into the boot and climbed into the front driver's seat.

Twenty minutes into the journey and the painkillers had clearly kicked in.

"What have you been up to?" came the slurred words from the back seat. Ryan adjusted his rear-view mirror so he could see his dad's face.

"What was that? What have I been up to? Who says I've been up to anything?"

"Aye. I know you lad."

Ryan shook his head and concentrated on the road. Len had closed his eyes and Ryan hoped he would sleep for the rest of the way. He'd almost made it when Len roused.

"Where are we going?" he asked.

"Home. Where else?" Len drifted off again. Ryan pulled into the Kingfisher car park and drove around the back. He'd given Janice the day off so he had no worries about being seen. He trundled down the dirt road that led to the barn, pulling up just in front of the door. He'd fitted new locks and a sliding bolt for extra stability and security. As the car halted, the jerky movement woke Len who did his best to push himself up and see what was going on. With his knee heavily bandaged his movements were restricted, and the painkillers had made him drowsy. Just the effort of lifting his head exhausted him so he collapsed back against the passenger door. Ryan walked round the back of the car, unlocked the barn then turned and opened the car boot. He assembled the wheelchair and opened the car door that Len was leaning against. He tipped backwards, almost hitting his head on the hard ground. Ryan found something really comical about it and had to pause whilst he stopped laughing. The air was blue with Len cursing his son and every sinew of pain that ripped through his body.

"What the fuck!" he yelled. Ryan pulled himself together and made an attempt to sit Len upright. "What the hell are you doing?" demanded Len.

"Shut up old boy and help me out. I'm trying to get you in your bloody wheelchair." Ryan hooked his hands under his dad's armpits and pulled. Len objected to being hoisted like a sack of coal, and he screamed as his legs hit the floor unceremoniously with a sickening thud.

Len screamed again. "Get the fuck off me." He thrashed about as Ryan dragged him to the chair then thrust him into it.

"Come on old man, give us a hand."

"I'm no giving you anything. What the hell are you playing at?"

"Shut up." Ryan was losing his patience and realised that he hadn't really thought this through. Len was a tall man at 6ft 4in but he'd lost weight and his muscle mass was zero. He continued forcing his dad into the chair as Len struggled against him. Ryan drew back his fist and thumped his dad square in the face. Len's head snapped backwards and hung there. Thankful for the silence, Ryan began taping his hands to the arms of the wheelchair with industrial strength duct tape. He extended the footplates and bound his legs tightly, avoiding the bandaged knee.

Dazed, confused and in pain, Len lifted his head and tried to move. He was well and truly secured to the wheelchair, and Ryan was pushing him towards the old barn. Every bump and rock they hit sent a jolt of pain through him and he continued to cry out. He was scared. He knew his son was dangerous but this was a whole new level of danger.

"What are you doing son, what's all this about?" Len's voice wavered.

Ryan continued to push and drag the wheelchair until it was in the middle of the barn. Len looked around him. He hadn't visited the barn in years and was surprised to see it still standing. He could smell the years of decay hanging in the air. His nose throbbed where Ryan had punched him, but he could still move his head. Nothing had changed apart from the gaping holes in the roof.

"Ryan. Please. Stop. Think about what you're doing." Sweat broke out on his forehead.

"I have, and you're best here for now." Ryan retreated and went back to the car boot. He carried bottles of water and energy bars. He stacked them on a stool next to Len.

"I've got shit to do and I don't need you interfering." Ryan twisted the top off a 2-litre bottle of water.

"But I wouldn't get in your way son. I promise. It's none of my business." Len was pleading with Ryan now.

Ryan had to admit he was getting quite a thrill out of his old man being so reliant on him. For years he'd taken the verbal and often physical abuse. It was payback time and he delighted in telling his dad so.

"When? When have I stopped you doing what the hell you want? You always would anyway."

"All. The.Fucking.Time," Ryan emphasised his words. His patience was nearing its end. He dug the bottle of pills out of his pocket. "Now, I need to disappear for a while so you're going to take these before I go and you can have a nice sleep." He spoke to him like a five-year-old child, "Are you going to be a good boy and take them?" It wasn't really a question. Ryan walked to the back of the chair, forced Len's head backwards and popped four of the tablets into his mouth. He followed it swiftly with a blast of water from the bottle. Len choked but finally swallowed. Once Ryan was sure he had swallowed them he pulled off another strip of duct tape and pressed it over Len's mouth. He withdrew a knife from his jacket pocket, ordered his dad to keep still and made a slit just wide enough for a straw to fit through. He placed the water bottle in Len's lap with the straw bobbing in the water. Ryan stood back to assess his handiwork. Satisfied that he could do no more, he turned and left.

"Sweet dreams old man," he said as he secured the barn door and climbed into the car.

20

J ack couldn't understand it. He'd made the trip to see Len in hospital only to be told that he had discharged himself a week ago. After much to-ing and fro-ing with the unhelpful administrator on Len's ward Jack had finally seen the discharge papers. By all accounts, his daughter Molly had been the one to collect him and her home address was on the discharge sheet. Jack was perplexed. He was certain that Len had told him he would be returning to The Kingfisher, and he had a vague recollection of Janice saying the same thing. He'd puzzled over it for the last couple of days and vowed that the next minute he wasn't needed in the café he'd take a trip over to The Kingfisher to find out what was going on. As it was, he barely had time to lift his head up from the day-to-day running of the café. Joe had broken up from school for the summer holidays and Kate had reduced her hours to part-time, as was usual in the school holidays. This left himself and Gill running the show most days, and it just wasn't working. Thanks to Kate's two-for-one promotions and local marketing efforts they were busier than ever. He decided he was getting too old for this caper and that they should look at getting someone else in to cover the holidays. He'd passed that job on to Kate, and she was currently interviewing potential candidates in the café. He briefly poked his head around the kitchen door and saw that Kate was making her way over to him in the back.

"Any good?" he asked, not holding out much hope from the look on Kate's face.

"Nope. No previous experience and never used a coffee machine." Kate was frustrated with the quality of people who had applied to the advertisement in the post office window. Usually these kinds of positions were filled word of mouth by the locals, but they had left it late and most of the local students had taken summer work in Inverness.

"So, what next?" asked Jack.

"I've no idea Jack, to be honest. I'll sort something out."

Jack went back to his work in the kitchen whilst Kate shouted Joe and told him to put his shoes and coat on. They said their goodbyes and headed off to the local park for an hour's fresh air and to burn some energy off the overactive seven-year-old.

Kate had heard nothing from Ryan all weekend. She'd tried his mobile a few times, each time it went to answerphone. Typical, she'd thought, remembering his past record of disappearing for days on end. She'd hope to catch him today and maybe they could all go into Inverness to the cinema and go for pizza afterwards. Perhaps she'd do that later, for now she was just glad that Joe had bumped into some of his school friends and they had started a game of football. As she sat idly passing the time, her mind wandered back to the last few weeks. Ryan had become such an intrinsic part of their lives that she couldn't remember a time without him. She was grateful for the friendship and they had easily resumed the playful nature of their earlier time together. She didn't believe Jack when he shared his thoughts that Ryan had an ulterior motive for being there. She had asked Ryan outright and he'd answered her honestly. God knows, she'd been lied to enough in the past to spot a player when she saw one. No, Ryan's reasons for being here were genuine and his feelings toward her, and Joe, came with no hidden depths. She acknowledged to herself that he could be snappy at times, but couldn't everyone? Especially when he had the added pressure of running The Kingfisher and keeping Janice in order. She was perfectly aware that Ryan sometimes came across as a bit sharp, a bit rough and ready, but his heart was always in the right place. Jack's fears and worries were completely unfounded and based on a Ryan he knew from years ago. Life and all that entailed had softened him, and her ex-husband had played no small part in that. She didn't believe for one second the lies that Darren had made up and spread around about him. The very thought of Ryan being wayward with kids was laughable. She shook her head and sighed. Shouting lifted her out of her reverie, and she left the park bench to wander over to the impromptu football match. Even though it was summer Joe was still covered in mud, had grass-stains on the knees of his jeans and his little face was bright red from all the running around. She had been scared senseless when he went missing. For those few hours her whole world had stopped, and she was right back in the house in North Leeds. The worry, fear, and anxiety every time Darren had taken Joe away from her, wondering when or if she would be able to see him again. She knew that Darren had used Joe as a weapon to get to her and it worked every time. She would rather take several more beatings than lose her son. He was her life, her reason for being, the reason she had had to break the cycle and escape the nightmare. She would have risked anything, everything, to create the happy life they now had.

She jumped up and down and cheered as Joe's strike hit the back of the net and he was lifted onto the shoulders of his fellow teammates. She was so proud of how he'd coped with everything and relished the freedom that she was able to give him. There had been none of that down in Leeds. Darren had insisted on knowing where they both were, every minute of every day. Joe hadn't had many friends, only his cousin Ted. Thinking of home made her realise, not for the first time, how much she missed Fiona. With only eighteen months' age difference, they had always been close, and Fiona had been distraught when Kate left, even though she knew some of what Darren had put her through.

'Maybe it's time to reach out to her,' thought Kate. They'd kept in touch with Christmas and birthday cards, and she knew Fiona would love to see them both again. Kate had hesitated in inviting her to stay until she felt herself and Joe were settled. Her thoughts were interrupted with an over-excited Joe, as he came tumbling over to her.

"Can I have a drink please?"

Kate passed him the bottle of water she kept in her bag. "Are you winning?"

"Haven't you been watching? We're 3 nil up!"

"Of course I've been watching. I saw your goal, well done," she congratulated him.

"Thanks," said Joe, thrusting the water bottle back into her hand as he tore off down the pitch again. She felt a hand snake around her waist.

"Oh hey, where have you been?" She turned and kissed Ryan.

"Oh you know, out and about." He returned the kiss half-heartedly.

"What are you doing later? I was going to see if you fancied a trip to the cinema and maybe pizza after?"

"Can't tonight. Got plans."

"Oh, OK. Anything interesting?"

Ryan tapped the side of his nose. Kate took that as the end of that conversation and knew not to ask any more.

"Joe scored earlier. You should have seen it."

"Oh yeah?"

Kate took her eyes from the pitch for a second and looked at Ryan, but he was busy with his phone. He waved Kate away as it started ringing.

"Need to take this. See you later," he said, turning his back and walking away.

"Nice to see you too," she called after him, laughing as he over-exaggerated blowing her kisses before climbing into his car.

"Now then mate, how's it going?"

"Got a release date. Four weeks today."

"Good stuff. Plans are all coming along nicely here."

"Cool."

"And the money?"

"As agreed. Paid on delivery."

"Sweet."

End call.

21

J ack waited at the bus stop for the 700 service to Inverness. It had been a long time since he'd used public transport, yet here he was using it twice in as many weeks. He had considered telling Kate where he was going but she was so prickly and defensive when it came to anything to do with Ryan that he had decided against it. He hadn't been able to shift the niggling doubt he had about Len being discharged from hospital – he felt sure he would have heard from him. He'd managed to wheedle Molly's address from Janice without giving anything away. She'd made it clear that Len was expected to return to the pub which only heightened Jack's concerns. He had thought about phoning Molly, but he figured that if Len really was recuperating at Molly's he'd kill two birds with one stone.

As Jack boarded the bus he noticed it was practically empty, but he knew it would fill up as it made its way through Poolewe, Aultbea, Laide and Dingwall. It was a long trip, just over two hours so he knew he would be gone for the day. As he settled into his seat, he let his mind wander over recent events. He couldn't understand why Kate

couldn't see Ryan for what he was; controlling and manipu-
lative. He'd witnessed it first-hand with the way he spoke to
Kate and some of the regulars in the café. At times it raised
Jack's hackles. Part of him thought it was Kate's life to do
with what she would, but he also knew Kate wasn't a fool.
Maybe he'd never understand women, he thought as he
rifled through his pocket for a mint.

When he finally disembarked at Inverness bus station,
he checked the address that Janice had given him and
figured it was close enough to walk. Thirty minutes later,
much longer than he expected, he arrived at Annefield
Road. He knocked on the door of number 21 and patiently
waited. He looked around the neat suburban semi-
detached, noting the well-kept gardens and hanging
baskets. There was no car on the drive, and he began to
wonder if anyone was home. He knocked again, hoping it
wasn't a wasted a trip. He'd considered phoning but what
was he supposed to say? "Is your dad there?" What if he
wasn't? What if there was a perfectly simple explanation
and he'd let his imagination run away with him.

Finally, he saw someone approaching through the
frosted glass panel. His heart began beating at an alarming
rate. The door opened slightly and a harassed-looking
middle-aged lady peered out.

"Yes? Can I help you?"

"Oh, hello. Sorry to bother you. You don't know me…
well you do but you might not remember…" Jack knew he
was waffling. He hadn't given a great deal of thought as to
how he would explain his sudden appearance. The door
began to close.

"I don't buy from the doorstep, sorry."

Jack thrust his arm forward and pushed the door
gently back. "Sorry, this is about your dad, Len?" he blus-

tered. The door opened fully as Molly looked at Jack askance.

"My dad? Len? Is everything OK?"

"Well, that's why I'm here." Jack took off his cap, sweat forming on his brow. He took his hanky out of his pocket and wiped his face. "I've made a bit of a hash of this. My name's Jack Bruce, I run the Harbour Café in Gairloch..." He hoped the mention of his hometown would bring some recognition to Molly.

"OK, and what's that to do with my dad?"

"Well..." Where to start? "I wonder if he's still here? He was recently in hospital and I was led to believe he was recuperating with you?"

"Sorry, I'm confused. Isn't he at the pub?"

"That's just it, he isn't there, but I know he's been discharged from hospital." Jack's shirt was damp with sweat under his coat and having walked quite a way his knees were aching. Right on cue, Molly invited Jack in. He thanked Molly and followed her into the kitchen. It was as neat and tidy inside as it was outside. He could hear voices of children playing upstairs. Molly pulled out a chair for him to sit on, and he gratefully rested his legs.

"Shall we start again?" asked Molly, busying herself with the kettle and cups.

"Aye, that's probably a good idea. I hadn't really planned what I was going to say."

"Right, start at the beginning." Molly joined him at the table and poured tea.

Jack explained how he came to be there and his suspicions that all was not as it seemed with Len and Ryan. Even as he spoke the words, he knew he must sound like an hysterical old man.

Molly was quiet whilst she digested the information.

"Well I can tell you that dad was in hospital but only for five days. He discharged himself and headed back to the pub as far as I know. I did give him the option to recover here but he's a worrier and insisted on going back to the pub. It was a while ago since I spoke to him, he's a stubborn so and so and I figured that if he needed anything he would call. I have no idea why Janice would say he was here. I thought he was getting extra help whilst he was recovering."

"Janice can be a bit of gossip as you know, and Ryan has been helping out, but I just wondered if maybe there had been a change of plan."

Molly's head lifted at the mention of her younger brother. "Ryan? What's he got to do with any of this?"

"Ryan showed up in the spring. He's been running the pub, didn't you know?"

"I had no idea. I thought he was still in Leeds."

"Well that's another reason for my concern. Ryan."

"Oh God, what's he up to now?"

"To be honest, I'm not 100% certain, and forgive me, I know he's your brother, but I just don't trust him and I don't think Len does either."

"Ha, you're right not to. He leaves a trail of havoc behind him for everyone else to clear up." Molly was shocked and concerned by Jack's appearance. She too shared his worries about Ryan.

"Jack, I'm sure there must be some simple explanation for all this. Let me speak to Janice and see if she says anything different." Molly reached over for the handheld phone and walked into the hallway to make to the call. She returned a few minutes later, looking pale.

"You were right, he's no there."

"Do you have Ryan's mobile number? He might tell you what's going on?"

"I've already tried it but it went to answerphone. I've left a message with Janice to get Ryan to ring me as soon as he returns. I'm not sure what more we can do."

"It's all very strange I have to say. How can someone just disappear?"

"Do you think we should just call the police?" asked Molly, voice full of concern.

"Nah, I wouldn't just yet. Let's see if Ryan will tell you more than he told me."

"You're right." Molly stood up and rinsed the pots. "Will you stay for some lunch Jack?"

Jack looked at the time and worked out he had a couple of hours before making the return journey so he said he would gladly stay. The children joined them at the table and they all spent an hour listening to Jack's stories of their mum growing up in Gairloch.

As 3pm approached he bid everyone farewell and thanked Molly for her hospitality. Walking back to the bus station he reflected on his conversation with Molly. He felt somewhat lifted that she had taken him seriously, and for the first time in days, the heavy weight he had been carrying, lifted off his shoulders slightly.

22

The whole trip had taken a lot out of Jack. By the time the bus pulled into Gairloch he was exhausted and wanted nothing more than to get back to his cottage and have a wee dram before heading to bed. He resolved to catch up with Kate the next morning, and share what he had learnt once he heard back from Molly.

As he disembarked, pain shot through his arthritic legs and took his breath away. He leant against the wall, waiting for the pain to pass before setting off. Finally, he reached his front door and fumbled in his pocket for the key, and let himself in. After removing his coat and hanging it up, he made his way into the small living room and antique dark wood sideboard where he opened the liquor cabinet and poured himself a healthy measure of whisky. He slumped into his well-worn armchair and rested his feet on the foot stool. He closed his eyes and was just drifting off when there was a knock on his front door. Somewhat reluctantly he placed his glass on the side table and heaved himself up to see who was outside. Opening the door, he was taken aback to see Ryan Albright standing on his doorstep. Before Jack could say anything, Ryan pushed the old man backwards and walked into the house. Jack had just about recovered and pulled himself together when Ryan turned to speak to him. He was clearly angry. Ryan's whole demeanour was intimidating.

"Where are you been old man?" snarled Ryan, getting right up into Jack's face.

"Wh...What... I..." Jack stammered, trying to back away and put some space between himself and Ryan. He was right up against the living room wall and had nowhere to go. He could smell Ryan's ashy breath he was that close.

"Lost for words? You weren't so dumbstruck earlier were you? " Spittle landed on Jack's face as it flew from Ryan's mouth.

"I...I..." Jack was really struggling and could feel adrenaline pumping through his veins.

"Been to see our Molly, haven't you? Concerned for Len by all accounts?" Though they were posed as questions it was clear that Ryan wasn't looking for answers. Refusing to be bullied, Jack summoned his courage and pushed back at Ryan.

"Aye, that's right I did. Someone has to know where your dad is, that he's gone missing."

"Gone missing? Ha, don't make me laugh. Missing? Really? How did you get to that conclusion OLD MAN!" Ryan emphasised the words 'old man', lurching towards Jack again. Jack ducked out of his way and headed toward the galley kitchen.

"Well where is he then?" Jack made a show of getting cups out of the cupboard and putting water in the kettle. He fumbled in the drawer for a knife or something to defend himself with.

"It's got nothing to do with you. You need to stop inter-fering in other people's business. I thought I'd got the message through to you but clearly you can't take a hint." Ryan stood menacingly at the kitchen entrance.

"You don't scare me Ryan."

"Really? Why are you shaking then?"

Jack ignored him and pushed Ryan to one side to enter the larder and retrieve the milk from the fridge. Ryan followed him into the narrow space. As Len straightened up, he was face to face with Ryan, and saw the gleam in his eye.

Ryan started pushing Jack, poking him as he issued his threat. "Stay out of my business old man..."

Jack stumbled backwards, foot slipping on the concrete floor. The steps leading down to the cellar were right behind him and one more push would send him flying. He dropped the carton of milk and lost his footing. His arms flailed wildly as he tried to grasp a hold of something to stop the fall. Ryan pushed him again, this time much harder. As Jack fell from the top step, he felt a kick in his ribs and knew he was hurtling downwards with no way of stopping himself. A scream escaped from his lips as his head bounced off the bottom step and landed with a dull thud.

"FUCK!" shouted Ryan as he watched Jack's body bounce from one step to the next before landing with a sick-ening crunch on the concrete floor. Ryan stood staring at the crumpled heap for a few seconds, with his hands on his head deciding what to do. He backed into the kitchen slowly and looked round him.

"Shit, shit, shit," he mumbled, spinning around as he took in his surroundings. "That wasn't supposed to happen."

It had been an accident, he hadn't meant to push Jack so hard. He didn't even know the stairs were there. After pacing up and down for a couple of minutes he realised he would have to do damage limitation. Had he touched anything? Would anyone know he'd been there? He didn't think so. He opened the front door and poked his head out, making sure no one was around to see him. He quickly closed the door behind him and headed back to The Kingfisher.

'I t had been his own fault,' he reasoned as he sat on his bed. 'If he hadn't riled me so much it wouldn't have happened.' He stripped off his clothes and headed into the bathroom. 'Well, at least he's out of the way now.' He had no idea if Jack was dead or alive, and didn't care much either way. His plans were progressing and he almost had all the pieces in place. He stepped into the shower, washed his hair, and turned the temperature to freezing for the last thirty seconds. Walking back into the bedroom he reconciled himself with the fact that it had been an accident. The old boy could have fallen down those steps at any time. What mattered now was not letting on that he knew anything about it. He looked at himself in the mirror, adjusting the collar of his t-shirt and rubbing wax into his hair. Happy that he didn't have 'guilty' written all over his face, he went downstairs into the bar.

23

"Nice of you to show your face," commented Janice as she served the punters.

"Mind your own," he snapped back, taking a tumbler, and helping himself to a whisky from the optics.

The bar was busy, but last orders were being called in an hour. He moved to a corner of the bar and stood people-watching. Janice was full of herself; chatting to the regulars, flirting with anyone that gave her the time of day. It made his skin crawl. He had to keep her sweet, knowing that she'd spoken to Molly earlier. He'd already warned her about keeping her nose out of family business but she never listened.

Janice called last orders and thirty minutes later the bar was empty. She walked round the empty tables collecting the ashtrays and empty glasses, and wiping the tables.

"How's Molly doing then?" she called out as Ryan loaded the pot washer, clearly fishing for gossip.

"Fine as far as I know." His response was short and terse, hoping to discourage her from asking any more.

"And your dad, how's he getting on? He's staying with

her isn't he?" She knew damn well he wasn't, but he had no idea exactly what Molly had said to her.

"Why don't you call it a night Janice? I'll finish up here."

Janice looked at Ryan and did a double take. Ryan never closed up but she wasn't about to turn down the chance of an early finish. Ryan called her a cab and waved her off, relieved to see the back of her. After locking the front doors, he made his way through to the back and down the dirt trail leading to the barn.

Len felt woozy and wondered what had woken him. He slowly opened his eyes, blinking as they adjusted to the light. It was dark and there was a constant cold draft that blew right through the barn. He shivered and felt something being pushed against his lips. As his vision became sharper, he saw Ryan leaning over him. He ripped the tape from his mouth and forced water down his throat. Len started to choke. Every cough sent his body into spasms, and he threw up any liquid as it reached his stomach. The water was taken away and he heard a laugh from somewhere in the barn. He blinked again rapidly and tried to move but it was hopeless.

"Funny, thought you'd be desperate for a decent drink." The bottle Ryan had left was almost empty.

"What the fuck Ryan." Len's words came out in a rasp, barely audible. "Let me go," he pleaded.

"No. Still got stuff to do but it won't be for much longer." Ryan circled the wheelchair and leant in close to Len's ear. "Jesus, you stink." Ryan recoiled and realised that Len was sat in his own filth.

"Please son, what... why..."

"Told you. Keeping you quiet while I do a bit of business." Ryan walked over to the outside tap and filled a bucket of cold water. He carried it back across and tipped the contents over Len's head. As the sudden onslaught of freezing cold water hit him, he yelped and tried again to move. Ryan took a step back and laughed. Len started to shiver, bone-deep shivering that caused his teeth to chatter and shake uncontrollably.

"P...p...please Ryan, stop. Help me. What have I done to deserve this?"

"What have you done? You're joking right? Len the big man, pillar of the community. Didn't stop your bullying though did it? Didn't stop you punching mum and me. Not Molly though, eh? Golden girl Molly?"

"B...but... that was years ago. Why this, why now?"

"Cos for once I've got a chance of escape. A real chance of pissing off and never coming back and I don't want you or anyone getting in the way."

"I don't understand." Len's head fell forward onto his chest, exhausted.

Ryan dropped to his knees so he could look his dad in the eye. "You're a fucking joke." Ryan pushed himself away from the wheelchair in disgust, turned, walked out of the barn and locked it securely behind him.

H oping for a few quiet snifters, he pulled a bottle of whisky from the bar and headed up to the flat. No sooner had he sat down and poured a drink than his mobile rang.

"For fuck's sake! Yeah?" he snapped into the phone.

"Ryan? You OK?" It was Kate.

"Yeah, fine. Sorry, just locked up. Long day."

"Sounds like it. Sorry to ring so late but I wonder if I could ask a favour?"

'Again,' he thought but didn't say. "Sure, go on."

"On your way over tomorrow could you call in and check on Jack. He didn't show up again today and I can't get a hold of him. I'd go but Fiona arrives tomorrow, so I'll be tied up for most of the day."

"Yeah, no bother." He ended the call and sank further into his seat. It was turning into a shit show. He knew he had to pull plans forward, but he needed Daz to do the same. He'd worry about the whole Jack situation later. Maybe checking on him would give him the perfect excuse for finding his body. Having settled it in his head, he leaned backwards, downed his drink and refilled his glass.

24

Kate felt she was losing her mind. Three days had gone by and there was still no word from Jack. At first she thought it might be down to the cross words they'd had over Ryan but it had gone on too long, and Jack wasn't one for sulking – as far as she knew anyway. They had never had an argument before, but Kate felt she knew him well enough to know that much.

"Joe! How many times do I have to tell you, no climbing on the furniture." The café hadn't even opened yet and Kate already felt her stress levels going through the roof. Kate had managed to recruit a local student in the café and Mairee was starting today. On top of all that, Ryan still hadn't shown to pick Joe up. She finished applying her make-up and corralled Joe downstairs. After switching all the lights on, unlocking the door, and starting the ovens, she reviewed the bookings that were due in. Thankfully Gill was also due any second so she could at least offload some of the work. She left the list as she heard the familiar tinkle of the bell above the door. Tying her apron around her waist she went into the front of the café.

"Hi Mairee, hope you're ready for a busy day?"

If Kate was truly honest, Mairee had been the best of a bad bunch but she had come across well in her interview, chatting away as though they had known each other for years. Mairee was young, well eighteen, which in Kate's view was young but she was keen and enthusiastic, so Kate took a punt and decided to give the student a chance.

"Aye. I'm all ready. Bring it on," said Mairee with a beaming smile and a spring in her step.

'Let's see if you're still so cheerful by the end of the day,' thought Kate. "That's great to hear. Come on and I'll show you round."

The next hour was taken up with introductions and Kate passed Mairee over to Gill to learn about the inner workings of the kitchen whilst she started to take the few breakfast orders. It was 10:30am before Ryan showed his face, looking worse for wear.

"What happened to you?" asked Kate as he greeted her with a kiss. "You smell like a brewery."

"Aye, too many last night." Ryan rubbed his face and ran his hands through his hair. He felt like shit and had woken later than he intended. He'd wanted to check on Len but had no time.

"Here, you look like you need this." Kate poured him a coffee. "Did you call in to see Jack?"

'Shit,' thought Ryan. It had been his first thought on waking but he'd totally forgotten to call into the cottage. "Aye, no answer when I chapped the door." Kate followed him as he went to sit over by the bay windows.

"This is so unlike him. I just can't understand it. I'll take a walk up later. Mairee started today and Gill's in so I should get time. What are your plans with Joe?" She waved him over.

Joe left his books scattered on the floor and came running. "Ryan's looking after you today sunshine. I was just asking him what he's got planned." Kate ruffled Joe's hair as she spoke. He pushed her hand away and smoothed it down with a look of disgust.

"Ach, well I'm needed at the pub so I thought a day of gaming?"

Joe nodded enthusiastically. Kate looked perplexed. "Ryan. You know I don't like him at a screen all day. We've had this planned for ages."

"Aye, well things happen. Can't help it." He finished his coffee and passed the cup to Kate. "And this one doesn't mind, do you wee man?"

"Err... No. Can we play Sonic? I've got a new high score."

"Sure, sure. Go get your coat." Ryan made his way to the door. Kate kissed them both goodbye and turned her attention back to the café. Mairee was in amongst the tables, taking orders and chatting away with the customers.

'At least that's one less thing to worry about,' she thought as she headed to the kitchen. "Gill, I'm just popping out before it gets busy. Mairee seems to have everything in hand, you don't mind do you?"

"No hen, you go ahead. Are you off to see Jack?"

"I thought I might. Ryan said he went this morning but there was no answer. I'm worried to be honest."

"Ach, he might just have gone away for a few days. You never know." Gill pulled a tray of fresh-baked sausage rolls out of the oven. The smell made Kate's tummy rumble, reminding her she hadn't yet eaten breakfast.

"True. I won't be long." Kate grabbed her coat and headed for the door. It wasn't a long walk, and it was a pleasant day with just the loch breeze blowing her hair gently. Approaching the cottage, she looked around to see if

anything was out of place. She couldn't see anything unto-
ward but noted that the curtains to Jack's bedroom were still
closed. She knocked several times but no answer. Next
door's cottage door opened, and Mr Wheeler came out onto
the doorstep.

"Morning Kate. Everything all right?" he asked.

"Not sure. Have you seen Jack recently?"

Mr Wheeler scratched his chin. "Come to think of it, no,
haven't seen him for a couple of days."

"No, I haven't either and I'm just a bit worried." Kate
walked over to Mr Wheeler's garden wall that separated the
two houses.

"Hold on, let me ask the wife." He disappeared inside.
"No, she has nae seen him either."

"I don't suppose you have a spare key to his house do
you?"

Mrs Wheeler came out and joined them on the garden
path. "We do as a matter of fact. Let me go get it." She trotted
off and returned a couple of minutes later. The three of
them walked around the short path that led to Jack's front
door, and Kate let herself in. She turned back to the couple
and gave what she hoped was a reassuring smile.

Entering the house, she called out his name but there
was no answer. His coat and hat were hanging in their usual
place, and his boots were by the front door. She walked into
the living room, calling his name again. She spotted a
tumbler of whisky on the small side table and an icy finger
of fear crept along her spine.

"Everything alright hen?" called Mr Wheeler from the
doorstep.

"Not sure, give me a minute." Seeing the remains of the
glass of whisky had freaked Kate out a little. 'There's no way
Jack would waste a drink,' she thought. She looked around

but didn't see anything out of place or disturbed. She crossed the room and entered the galley kitchen. It looked as though someone was making a cup of tea. The teapot was on the worktop, along with two cups. She lifted the kettle. It was full. As she turned around her eye caught the ever so slight gap in the door to the larder. Sensing that something was wrong, she shot over and pulled the door open. She saw the trail of congealed milk and flicked on the light. She looked down the cellar steps and saw Jack's crumpled form lying at the bottom. She screamed his name and raced down the stairs.

Alerted by the scream, Mr Wheeler dashed inside the house and followed the sound of Kate's cries for help. He reached the top of the cellar steps and saw Kate looking up at him, face strewn with tears whilst she cradled Jack to her.

"He has a faint pulse, call an ambulance," she shouted up.

Mr Wheeler used Jack's landline and dialled 999. He turned to his wife.

"What's happened?" she asked, twisting a hanky round in her hand. He took hold of her, feeling her shaking.

"I'm not sure but it looks like Jack's taken a nasty tumble down the cellar steps."

25

K ate followed the ambulance in her car. She swore as she struggled to find a parking space and ended up ditching it in the drop-off bay, vowing to move it once she knew how Jack was doing. She raced into Accident and Emergency, giving his name to the receptionist.

"He's in resus' and the doctors are with him at the mom..."

She didn't get to finish her sentence as Kate quickly looked around for the resuscitation area. She began making her way over when Mr Wheeler stepped in front of her, blocking her path.

"He's OK, he's OK," he said. "They're taking a look at him now. Here. Sit down, you've had one hell of a shock."

Kate fell gratefully into a seat. Mr Wheeler sat alongside her and took her hand. "They haven't said too much but it looks like he fell down the cellar steps."

"How long had he been there?"

"I have no idea. I'm sure the doctors will be along to update us soon."

Kate had never felt so guilty. Why hadn't she checked on him sooner. She had known something wasn't right. Had she really been so busy that she couldn't have spared ten minutes to check on her old pal. What had been so important that she couldn't find the time to just pop her head in and see that everything was alright. All these thoughts whizzed through her mind. With her head in her hands she let out a sob.

"I should have checked on him."

"Now come on. Don't go blaming yourself. It was an accident. He's not getting any younger and a slip is easy enough on those stairs." Mr Wheeler rubbed Kate's hand reassuringly.

"But when he didn't turn up at the café I should have known," Kate continued to beat herself up.

"Why? We live next door and we didn't think to check. And you've had all that business with Joe as well as keeping the café open. I'm sure Jack would rather you kept the business open than running around after him."

Kate figured that was probably true, but it didn't take anything away from the regrets she had. Jack had been so good to both of them. She owed him so much. Had she really been so self-absorbed that her only friend might die? She let out another sob and rummaged in her pocket for a tissue.

"Jack Bruce relatives please?"

Kate and Mr Wheeler stood up and approached her. She greeted them and showed them into the family room.

"Can I ask how you're related to Mr Bruce please?" she asked, clutching a clipboard.

Kate looked at Mr Wheeler. "We're not relatives, just close friends and neighbours."

"Oh. OK then. Does he have any family?"

Kate again turned to Mr Wheeler. "There was a brother once but I have no idea where he is now," he replied.

"That's OK. Well just to keep you up to date. As you know, Jack had a nasty fall. He's been left with a broken leg, a couple of cracked ribs and a nasty bump on the head."

"But will he be OK?" asked Kate, leaning forward.

"I don't see why not. The injury we're most concerned with at the moment is the bump on the head. Jack's still unconscious but that's to be expected. We're taking him down for a CT Scan. You can wait in here until there's more news if you prefer?" The nurse made to leave the room. "Do you have any more questions?"

"No. I don't think so. Thank you. Thank you very much." Mr Wheeler followed the nurse to the door. "I'll go fetch us a wee cup of tea." He left Kate alone and wandered off to find the vending machine.

Kate tried to pull herself together and get her head around what was going on. She felt useless. She should have insisted on making time to visit Jack. She should have *made* Ryan check on him sooner. She needed to speak to him and let him know what had happened.

Mr Wheeler returned with two cups of tea. "I've put sugar in it, didn't know if you had any but it helps with the shock." He passed the insipid-looking brew to her. She placed it on the little coffee table and stood up.

"I need to move my car and let Ryan know what's happened." She felt a twinge of guilt at leaving for even a short time. "Are you OK to stay here?"

"Aye, of course. You go do what you need to."

Kate left the family room and headed to the car park. As she sat in the driver's seat she saw the yellow ticket on her windscreen. "Great, a parking ticket." She got out and tugged it from the window, scrunching it up and putting it in her pocket. She reached into her bag and pulled out her mobile phone, Ryan's number was at the top.

"Hey, it's me," she said the second the call was answered. "There's been an accident."

"Hey, what kind of accident. Are you OK?"

"Yeah, it's not me. It's Jack."

"Oh no. What's happened?" asked Ryan, hoping the concern sounded genuine.

"Not sure. Looks like he fell down the cellar steps. He's broken a few bones and has a bump on his head but that's all they know at the minute. We're just waiting for the CT scan results." Kate started to cry. "I feel so responsible. I should have checked on him the other day. God knows how long he's been down there."

Ryan let go of the breath he was holding. "So will he be OK?"

"I've no idea. Oh Ryan I feel like such a shit friend."

"Hey, come on, you weren't to know." Ryan walked outside and lit a cig. "Where are you now?"

"I'm at the hospital. I don't know how long I will be. Are you OK to keep Joe for a while?"

"Yeah, yeah that's fine. Don't worry about us. Janice is fussing over him."

Kate's tears started falling again. "If only I'd checked on him. What happened when you called round?"

"Me?" Ryan had flashbacks to the moment he saw Jack tumbling. "Oh, there was no answer so I didn't hang around to be honest." He paused. "Maybe I should have done."

"Oh Ryan, don't go blaming yourself," Kate sniffed.

Ryan smiled to himself at the irony in Kate's words. "Yeah, you're right. I guess it could have happened at any time."

"I guess so. Look I need to get back inside, I just wanted to let you know, and to hear your voice."

"No worries. Will you let me know when he's awake?"

"Yes. Yes of course." Kate was touched by Ryan's concern.

Once she was back inside, she rejoined Mr Wheeler in the family room and waited for more news.

"ingfisher."

"Ryan, it's Molly."

'Great,' he thought. "Hi, what can I do for you?"

"I rang yesterday about dad, you didn't ring me back."

"Yeah, been a bit busy."

"So where is he?" Molly had very little time for Ryan. He had caused nothing but hassle for their parents over the years and she could never forgive him for walking out when he was 15.

"Who?" Ryan loved goading his sister. She thought she was so high and mighty with her stuffy husband and clutch of brats. Her lack of ambition pissed him off.

"For God's sake Ryan, cut the crap. I've had Jack from the café visiting, thinking Dad was recovering here, and Janice didn't seem to know much about it. What is going on?" Barely controlled anger crept into Molly's voice and he pictured her pacing the floor of her posh kitchen.

"How would I know?" He'd rehearsed this but knew he couldn't play it too cool.

"Seriously Ryan. I KNOW you picked him up from the hospital. Where the hell is he?"

"He's fine, calm down. He didn't want to come back here because of the stairs. It's not the ideal place to recover is it?"

"Stairs? What..."

"He can't get up and down the stairs can he? I would have thought that was obvious. Even if I could get him upstairs he wouldn't be able to do anything would he and I'm not taking him for a piss or giving him a bed bath."

Molly paused. "So where IS HE!" Molly was shouting now. Ryan suppressed laughter and wondered how long he could keep winding her up for.

"Calm down silly cow. He's at Sheildaig Lodge. What did you think I'd done with him?"

"Sheildaig? The convalescent home?" Molly was taken aback. It had been the last thing she'd expected him to say.

"Yeah. I had a word with Hamish and he had a ground floor room available so agreed to take him. They go back years so it's fairly cheap but if you want to chip in don't let me stop you."

She ignored the question. "Why the hell didn't you just say that then instead of causing all this hassle. You really haven't changed have you?"

"What, miss the chance of winding you up? Where's the fun in that?" Ryan laughed.

"You really are a first-class prick, do you know that?"

"Thanks sis, love you too."

Molly ignored the jibe. "Seriously though, is he alright? Should I go visit him do you think?"

"Nah, he's fine. In his element actually. Lots of his cronies around him, playing cards all day. He's having a grand old time." Ha, God he was good at this.

"Well if you're sure? We're so busy here what with the

girls breaking up from school and Michael working away, it's been crazy."

Ryan was bored of the conversation now. "He's fine, I've told you. I'll get him to call you, eh? Would that make you happy?" He was sure he could convince Len to put on a convincing show. Anything to keep her away.

"That would be great Ryan, thank you."

He let out a sigh of relief and quickly ended the call.

ack had been moved into Intensive Care, and finally
Kate had been allowed to see him, just for a short
time. She pulled up a chair to his bedside and
tenderly took his hand in hers. Bruises gave his
pallor a yellow tinge, and Kate thought he looked much
older than his years. She stroked the back of his hand gently
and tears splashed onto his lifeless skin.

"Mrs Ward?" She turned in her chair and saw the doctor
stood in the doorway.

"Yes?" She couldn't be bothered getting into the seman-
tics of Miss/Ms.

"Would you like to follow me?"

She followed the doctor into a side room and sat down.

"OK, so we have the majority of the results back. The
bump on his head was our biggest concern. It's led to
swelling on his brain, and we're not sure at this point if
there's any permanent damage."

Kate's hand flew to her mouth, and the tears that never
seemed far away collected in her eyes, threatening to spill
over. "Oh God, just how serious is it?"

The doctor passed Kate a tissue. "We're not sure at this stage, and we won't know until the swelling subsides so for the time being we're keeping him in an induced coma. It's common practice for suspected brain injuries."

"Oh gosh, that all sounds dreadful." She wished Ryan was here for support.

"Yes I know, but the thing to remember is that the brain heals better and faster when it rests, and sleeping which is what he's doing in effect, means he stands a much better chance of a full recovery."

"And how long will it take?"

"How long is a piece of string? It's hard to say, and with Jack being an older gent the body heals slower but let's focus on the positive. He's breathing on his own, and his other injuries are all treatable. He was very lucky to land the way he did. It could have been a lot worse."

Kate knew the doctor was trying to be helpful but the thought of losing her friend was too much to bear, and she slumped forward, placing her hands on her head.

"Is there anyone here with you?"

Kate blew her nose. "Yes, another of Jack's neighbours. He's in the family room."

"OK, well I'll get him for you. Just take as much time as you need." With that and a reassuring pat on the arm the kindly doctor directed her back to Jack's room where she was eventually joined by Mr Wheeler. The two friends sat side by side where they held vigil until visiting hours had finished.

. . .

Exhausted, Kate pulled into The Kingfisher car park. She checked her reflection in the mirror. She looked dreadful; pale, drawn, tired. She wanted to collect Joe and head back to the flat for a bath and a good night's sleep, though she feared the sleeping part might not be so easy. Ryan was just walking up the dirt trail at the back of the pub as she got out of her car.

"Hey," she called out to him. His mind was clearly elsewhere.

He looked up and walked over. "Hi, how's Jack?" He took a step closer and held her to him.

Kate rested her head on his chest. "Oh I wish you were there with me, he's so frail."

"What was the verdict from the scan?" He took her hand and they walked into the pub together.

"They're keeping him sedated until the swelling on his brain subsides."

"That doesn't sound too good?"

"They don't know if there's any permanent damage. Oh Ryan, he looks so old."

Ryan guided her over to a corner table and sat opposite. "Well from what you've said it was one hell of a fall."

"I know, it's awful to see him laid there like that."

"You're not still beating yourself up over it are you?"

"Yes... no, I don't know. I feel so guilty. I should have done something sooner."

Ryan stood up and went to get them both a drink. "Well all we can do is hope for the best I guess." Why hadn't the fucker just died? He'd have to keep this charade up now until he left, for fuck's sake. He turned back to Kate, hoping his face was showing the right amount of sympathy. "When are you going to see him next?"

"Tomorrow. Could you watch Joe again for me please? I don't want him to see Jack looking like he does."

"Sure. So is it just his head then?" Ryan needed to know exactly what he was dealing with.

"Gosh no. He's broken his leg and has cracked ribs but that's all treatable. It's the head injury that's the worst thing." Kate sniffed and Ryan could sense a fresh onslaught of tears.

He turned his back, calling out, "I'll just go get Joe for you."

Five minutes later the two of them came downstairs. After much fussing they finally left. Relieved to see the back of them, Ryan helped himself to a double whisky and headed upstairs to the flat. He needed to speak to Daz but he wasn't due to call until the end of the week.

'Fuck's sake,' he thought as he sat in the dark, nursing his drink. How had he got himself into this mess? It had all seemed so straightforward. Befriend Kate and Joe, hire a car, bundle Joe into the back and deliver him to Daz for a 10k payout. How had it got so fucking complicated?

28

Kate sat by Jack's bedside as often as she could. Slowly, underneath the heavy bruising, the normal pallor had started to return to his face. As she observed her friend, she thought he had aged twenty years in the week he'd been in hospital. The swelling on his brain had gradually reduced and two days ago he'd been moved from ICU onto a general ward. The doctors had kept Kate up to date with his condition on a regular basis and the general feedback was that he would make a full recovery. Only time would tell if he would suffer any short-term memory problems but doctors were confident that if he did it would be temporary.

Kate shifted in her seat and turned the page of the newspaper that she had taken to reading out loud to him. She had no idea if he could hear her but one of the staff nurses had assured that he could so she had carried on, plus it helped to pass the time. As she settled to read the local weather report, she felt the bedsheets move underneath the newspaper. She looked up at Jack and saw his eyelids flicker then flutter open. Kate jumped out of her seat, dropping the newspaper to the floor. She leaned over Jack and whispered his name. As his eyes slowly became accustomed to the bright light she reached down and took his hand.

"Jack? It's me, Kate."

"Kate?"

"Yes, Kate. Do you remember me? Do you know where you are?"

Jack coughed, his throat sore and mouth stale after so long asleep. He tried to sit up but winced at the pain. Kate reached over to the bedside locker and poured a glass of water. She held it to Jack's lips, supporting his head as he took tentative sips.

"You're in hospital Jack. Do you remember?"

Just as she asked, a passing nurse saw that Jack was awake and approached the bed. "Now then Mr Bruce. How are you feeling?" She fussed around his bedding, readjusted his pillows, and started to take his blood pressure. "Do you know where you are?"

"Aye," croaked Jack. "In the hospital and I'm awfully thirsty."

"That's to be expected. You've had a long sleep." Kate helped him take another sip of water.

"Aye, that's right. But your friend here has been visiting every day. You're very lucky." The nurse filled out his chart. "I'll send the doctor along, then you can have a cup of tea." The nurse bustled away and Kate retook her seat, pulling her chair closer to the bed.

Jack eased back into the adjusted pillows and closed his eyes. Kate wasn't sure if he'd slipped back to sleep so she sat back and waited. She felt tears of relief trickle down her face, and she wiped them away with the back of her hands. She blew her nose loudly with the remnants of the tissue in her pocket.

"Well, that's lovely," mumbled Jack, the corners of his mouth turning up into a flicker of a smile.

Kate laughed, pleased to see Jack still had his sense of humour. "I thought you'd gone back to sleep. How are you feeling?"

"Sore," came the one-word answer. Jack swallowed and attempted to lift his hand to his face, not realising he was connected to an IV line.

"Steady, you're on a drip. It's just to keep your fluids up."

Jack tried again, this time slowly. He rubbed his hand across his face, feeling the beard growth on his chin. "How long have I been here?" He turned his head to Kate.

"A week."

"What?"

"You were brought in by ambulance last week. Do you remember what happened?"

Jack dropped his hand to his side and closed his eyes whilst he tried to recall his memories. "I canna remember."

"It's OK. The doctor said you might have short-term memory problems but it will come back eventually." Kate tried to hide her concern. "What's the last thing you remember Jack?"

Silence whilst Jack thought. "It's all a bit fuzzy to be honest. I remember being in the café."

"Can you remember who was there?"

"You, Joe. I think we were in your flat?"

Kate blushed at the memory, realising that the last time Jack had been in Harbour Café was when she and Ryan had sneaked upstairs. "OK, well that's only a day or so before you went missing."

"Missing? What do you mean, missing?"

"I didn't see you for a couple of days, but let's not worry about that now. You do remember Joe then?"

"Aye I remember the wee lad, where is he?"

"He's with Ryan, who has been an absolute Godsend to be honest with you."

At the mention of Ryan's name Jack felt something like a bolt of lightning shoot through his entire body and he stiffened. "Ryan? Who's Ryan?"

Kate was taken aback, by Jack's obvious physical reaction but also that he couldn't remember Ryan. She knew there was no love lost between them, but Ryan had been around so much she was surprised he had no recollection of him. "Ryan Albright? He's looking after The Kingfisher whilst Len, his dad is in the hospital. Ring any bells?"

Jack looked flustered and confused. Kate noticed beads of sweat breaking out on Jack's forehead and his complexion had paled. Concerned that she had pushed Jack too far she decided he needed a rest. "Look, why don't I grab a cuppa and let you have a bit of rest?"

Jack nodded and watched her as she walked out of the ward. He tried to think back. The name Ryan seemed familiar to him but he had no idea why. Just the mention of it had sent shivers down his spine. No matter how hard he tried, he just couldn't pull the pieces together. He reached his free hand up to feel his head and touched the swathe of bandages wrapped around his skull, poking here and there to see what hurt. Slowly moving his hand, fingers shaking, he touched his face and grimaced as he felt the swelling on his cheek and under his eye. His vision was clearing but was still a little hazy around the edges.

"What a mess," he thought. He lifted his head and peered down at the cast on his left leg. He tried to wiggle his toes and winced as pain shot up his leg. He turned to see Kate returning with a vending machine coffee.

"What happened Kate?" he asked, choking back tears.

"It looks like you had a tumble down the cellar steps."

Jack looked scornfully at Kate. "Cellar steps? What, in my house?"

"Yes, it looks that way. When we found you, you were laid at the bottom of the steps." She hesitated to say he'd been there for who knows how long before being found.

"But... I don't understand." Jack looked confused. "I've been on those steps hundreds of times, why would I fall?"

"I honestly don't know Jack. It looked as though you were making a cup of tea. Maybe you took a step back and lost your footing?"

Jack closed his eyes once more. She could tell he wasn't convinced with her explanation. She sat quietly by his side, sipping the vile coffee, lost in her own thoughts. She was snapped out of her reverie when she felt a hand gently on her shoulder.

"Kate?" She looked up and saw the doctor who had been overseeing Jack's care.

"Yes. Sorry." She realised she was crying again and wiped her tears away with her hand.

"No need to apologise. How's he doing?" Doctor Mackintosh removed the notes hanging from the end of Jack's bed.

"He's a bit confused I think," she spoke quietly. "He doesn't seem to be able to remember what happened. I haven't told him about all his injuries yet."

There was a moan from the bed and Jack woke, trying to sit up.

"Mr Bruce. We thought you were sleeping. How are you feeling?"

"Aye, ye know...a wee bit sore."

"Yes, that's to be expected. You've had a mighty fall. Are you in much pain?"

"A little but I'll be fine," replied Jack. Kate smiled. 'Stubborn as ever,' she thought.

"No need to be brave, I'd expect a few aches and pains. Now, would you like me to go through your injuries?"

"Well there's a bandage on ma heed and a cast on ma leg so I think I've worked it out."

Kate hid a smile behind her hand. Dr Mackintosh adjusted awkwardly in his seat before catching Kate's eye and noticing the smile.

"That's all very true but I'd like to talk to you about your head injury. Good news is that there is no permanent damage. Any memory loss is purely temporary and should return in a couple of weeks. We'll have you back in for regular scans just so we can keep an eye on it." The doctor paused and looked to see if Jack was taking it all in. After consulting his notes, he continued, "As for your leg, it was a clean break so the plaster cast can come off in a few weeks then you'll need physio..."

Jack interrupted, "Aye, when can I go home?"

"It will be another couple of days, just until your blood pressure comes down and we'll give you another CT scan now you're awake."

Kate, who had been clutching Jack's hand felt relief for the first time. "See, told you it was all fixable." Jack nodded his head.

"Do you have someone to look after you when you get home?"

Jack looked at Kate, not knowing how to answer. He didn't want to stay in any longer than he had to. Kate jumped in.

"I'll be staying with him." She squeezed his hand. "Plus there's plenty of friends who want to help."

"That's great stuff. Right I'll get the scan booked in and

let's see about getting you home." The doctor stood. "Once you're home, you must rest." Dr Mackintosh said his good-byes and Kate and Jack were once again on their own.

"Well that's good news Jack. Home in a couple of days."

"Aye, but you're no staying with me!"

Kate laughed. "Who'd run the café if I did that? No, it's all covered. Everyone's been worried about you. We're all keen to get you home. You'll have so many homemade soups and casseroles you won't be able move!"

"Humpf, well I don't want people making a fuss." Jack folded his arms across his chest like a defiant teenager but he was secretly pleased.

"You won't have a choice. Right, I need to go and collect Joe. I'll bring him with me at some point, he's missed you." Kate leaned over to kiss Jack's forehead. Jack blushed at the intimate gesture and waved her away.

"Be off with ya lassie." He brushed her away.

Kate left the hospital feeling lighter than she had in days. She couldn't wait to tell Ryan and Joe the news that their friend was on the road to recovery.

29

P ain ravaged his body. When he lifted his head, his reduced world span in nausea-inducing revolutions. His torso was encrusted with bile. Consciousness came and went with the fever that raged.

This wasn't right, he didn't deserve this. He knew he needed medical attention. He couldn't remember when he'd first had the pungent whiff of infection but now it was all he could smell. In rare moments of lucidity he could see the wound left by knee surgery was oozing yellow pus. The bandage was torn and puckered skin surrounding the scar was livid red. Rats were frequent visitors, even foxes had dropped by, paying more attention to him as the foul odour grew stronger.

He tried shouting but the tape only allowed so much movement. Besides, he was tired. Bone-deep exhausted. Was this how it would end?

"Wakey wakey."

A drenching of ice-cold water snapped him back to reality. Ryan stood in front of him, laughing. He walked round to the back of the wheelchair and released the brakes. "Taking you somewhere nicer."

The words barely registered with Len. "Son, please," he croaked.

"Not long now." Ryan dragged the chair to the far corner of the barn and undid Len's bindings. He threw him on the floor of the stable, aiming roughly for the rotten sleeping bag in the corner. "Not like you're capable of running away is it?" He manhandled Len into a sitting position then squatted down to face him.

"OK, so here's what going to happen..." Ryan recoiled. "Jesus, what's that smell?" He looked down and saw the infected wound. "For fuck's sake!" He stepped away, unable to bear the smell. Once he'd regained his composure he took a closer look. "Shit, that's not good." He turned and raced up the dirt track back to the pub. Once inside he raided the bathroom cabinet in search of a first aid kit or something to treat the wound with, swearing under his breath constantly. Finding nothing of any use in the flat he entered the bar and grabbed some towels. It was the only thing he could think of.

"You alright?" Janice asked.

"Fine. Where's the first aid kit?"

"What?"

"FIRST. AID. KIT. Where is it?" He closed in on her, making it clear not to mess with him.

Janice, shaking, walked slowly backwards and reached under the till. She grabbed a green synthetic bag and thrust it at him without a word. Snatching it from her he exited through the back door and stomped back down to the barn. He tore the kit open and looked for bandages or something that would help. His hand found a bottle of antiseptic liquid. He unscrewed the cap and made his way to the stable. Len was unconscious again. 'Not for long,' thought Ryan.

Approaching Len, he poured the fluid directly into the fetid wound. A raw guttural scream escaped from Len, ripping the tape from his mouth in the process. Ryan thought he was having some kind of seizure as his body jerked violently. He forced his hand across Len's mouth and held it there until the screaming subsided to a low moan. Unravelling the bandages, he wrapped one tightly around the knee. He stood back to admire his handy work. Satisfied, he went to his car and retrieved the water he'd brought with him, along with energy bars and painkillers. He sat and patiently waited for Len to rouse.

"Here, take this." He forced tramadol down his dad's throat and passed him an energy bar, insisting he ate it whilst Ryan watched. The smell still hovered but intermingled with antiseptic, vomit and human waste. Realising that his old man would be there longer than expected, and no longer strapped into the wheelchair he pulled an old bucket into the stable.

"Use this," he instructed Len, having no desire to sit with him any longer.

Heading back to the bar, he checked his mobile phone. No missed calls. He had planned on getting Len to ring Molly but clearly that wasn't going to happen with Len in his current state. He'd try again tomorrow. He dialled Kate's number, hoping for an update on Jack. Why that fucker couldn't have just died was beyond him. He couldn't risk Jack revealing everything but wasn't sure what to do about him. He couldn't go finish him off now, could he? Would it raise too much suspicion? Right now it all looked like an accident. Hadn't Kate said something about short-term memory loss? That would buy him a bit of time.

"Hey Ryan." Kate sounded tired.

"Hey, just wondering how you're holding up?" He was getting good at this.

"Oh, not bad. Hoping Jack comes home today."

"Aye? How is he?"

"He's OK, considering. Still can't remember what happened."

'Yes, get in ya beauty.' "Oh that's sad. Do you think it will come back to him?"

"Not sure, time will tell I guess," Kate sighed. "I'm really sorry to ask this but do you think you could mind the café when I go pick him up?"

'Can't do any harm to be there when he gets back, can it?' he thought. "Aye, course. No bother."

"Brilliant Ryan. Thank you. I don't know what I would do without you."

"I'll be by shortly."

Ryan ended the call. There wasn't much more he could now but wait for Daz's call anyway, and he couldn't bear to be around Janice. He grabbed his jacket from the bar and headed to the door.

"You away again?"

His hand stalled on the handle. "Aye, not that it's any of your business."

"We need a new first aid kit, do we?"

"Aye, I'll pick one up while I'm out." He left as quickly as he could to discourage any further questions. "Nosey bitch," he muttered as he drove off. About time she was taught a lesson.

· · ·

R yan arrived at the café and saw Kate already had her coat on.

"What's going on?" he asked.

"Jack's just phoned, he can come home!" Kate was clearly over the moon.

"Great. Off you go then, tell him I'll pop up and see him soon."

Kate left with a quick kiss to the cheek and hurried out of the door. Ryan hung his jacket up and headed into the kitchen.

30

Kate held the door open as wide as she could for Jack to hobble through on crutches. Finally his blood pressure had dropped to a reasonable level and he had been allowed home with strict instructions to rest.

The close-knit community had rallied around, and Jack's little cottage had been rearranged to include a makeshift bedroom downstairs. The fridge was packed with home-made meals and someone had even left a bottle of his favourite tipple. Jack felt overwhelmed as he limped through the front door. He caught Kate staring at him.

"What's the matter?" he asked.

"Nothing. I just wondered if coming back here would trigger any memories?"

"Not so far but give me chance to take ma coat off!"

Kate stepped back. "Sorry. You're right. Here, let me help you." She stepped forward again to help him but he was having none of it.

"Away with ya lassie. I can take my own bloody coat off! "

Kate laughed and stepped into the living room. Jack

slowly followed her, still getting to grips with his sticks as he called them.

"Mr Wheeler has set up a camp bed in the living room, just until you can get up and down stairs, and the fridge is packed with food." Kate passed the living room and into the galley kitchen. She opened the door to the larder and pulled a casserole out of the fridge. "All you need to do is heat it up in the microwave."

Jack nodded, and sat heavily on the couch, propping his sticks at the side of him. He had been nervous at the thought of coming home but he was also ready to start his life again. He needed routine, and to be back in the community he loved. Like Kate, he wondered if returning would help with his memory. He glanced around the room and everything looked just as remembered, as far as he could tell. He suddenly felt inexplicably tired. Maybe it was the journey from the hospital or the drugs working their way through his system. He could feel his eyes closing, and his head started to drop forward.

Kate watched on from the kitchen door and saw him nodding off. Quietly, she walked back into the living room and placed a blanket across his knees before creeping out of the front door.

Jack woke with a start a couple of hours later, stiff from the awkward position he'd fallen asleep in. It took a few minutes for him to come round completely. He stretched the best he could, triggering pain in his leg and ribs. Reaching for his sticks, he heaved himself up and headed to the kitchen. He set about making a cup of tea, clumsy and awkward with his sticks. He opened the larder door and stepped in to get the milk out of the fridge. He paused, glancing down the cellar steps. He felt an icy chill run along his spine but he still had no recollection of his fall. Frustrated, he took the milk carton and slammed the larder door shut. He left the carton on the worktop, not wishing to tempt fate. Once he'd figured out how to carry the cup of tea and manage the crutches he headed back to the couch, painstakingly slow and spilling more tea as he went along. Kate had left painkillers on the little coffee table, and there was just enough tea left to rinse down a couple of tablets. Dragging his legs onto the couch, he sat back and tried to think back. He must have dozed off at some point, and he woke with a start. He tried to sit up, the painkillers taking the edge off the pain in his ribs, and swung his legs onto the floor. Grabbing his crutches he stumbled to the hallway and rummaged in his coat pocket. He'd had a fleeting thought on waking that he'd been on a bus. He pulled out a crumpled piece of paper. Limping back into the living room, he smoothed it out as best he could.

"Now why would I go to Inverness?" he wondered out loud as he read the ticket. He looked at the wall calendar and tried to work out the dates. He'd gone there the day of his accident. But why?

He couldn't figure it out, and sat staring at the ticket, willing memories to come back to him. "Think, damn you." He knew getting annoyed wouldn't find the answer, but he had to make sense of his confused thoughts. He felt as though he had some of the right pieces but just couldn't get them in the right order. He reached over to the drawer underneath the coffee table and pulled out a pad and pen. He only ever used it to write his shopping list or racing bets. At the top of a clean page he wrote 'Inverness' along with the dates and times. Moving down he wrote the name 'Ryan'. He still didn't have a clear recollection of who he was but he could remember his reaction when Kate first mentioned his name. Hadn't Kate said something about him being Len Albright's son? Did she mention he was helping out whilst Len was in hospital? He added 'Len' and 'hospital' to the list. He'd ask Kate when he saw her next. He was exhausted again with the effort and tried desperately to fight off sleep. He had a sense of unease that he could feel in the pit of his stomach. It felt familiar yet strange. He closed his eyes and took a deep breath.

Before he knew it, he had drifted back off to sleep, notepad slipping from his fingers and tumbling to the floor.

31

Ryan unlocked the padlock and slid back the crossbar. Despite his best attempts it was still rickety and wouldn't take much effort to kick it in. Not that Ryan was bothered. The charade would be over in a matter of days, and no one was looking for Len. He entered the dusty space and walked to the rear of the building where Len was still safely ensconced in one of the dilapidated stables. Len was just where he'd left him; shivering in a corner but for once he wasn't unconscious. He looked dishevelled and forlorn, like a broken man. He unfastened the stable door and stood looking at his father. He was disgusted by the sight of him.

Len lifted his head slowly at the sound of footsteps. "Ryan?"

"Now then old man, you're looking well." Ryan laughed, bending down to inspect the leg wound. It looked considerably better, the antiseptic seeming to have done its job. The skin was a natural pink, rather than the livid red it had been previously. Len flinched as Ryan adjusted the bandage over the hole.

"How much longer..." croaked Len.

"I need one small favour old man." Ryan stood and took his phone from his coat pocket. "I need you to speak to our Molly." Ryan scrolled through his phone and pulled up Molly's contact details. "Just a few words, letting her know you're fine and you'll see her soon." Ryan looked at his dad sprawled on the dirty floor. He kicked his good leg. "Did you hear me?"

Len jerked and let out a low moan. "I need a drink."

Ryan pulled out a bottle of water and passed it to him. "Here, and eat this too." He threw an energy bar at him. Len grabbed at them both and gorged himself on the only sustenance he'd had in days.

"So, you gonna speak to Molly then?"

"No."

"Ha, let me rephrase that. You will speak to Molly, and this is what you'll say. Are you listening?" He grabbed Len's hair and pulled his head up, remnants of the energy bar stuck to his chin. Len grunted but didn't answer as he reached for more water.

"I need you to speak to Molly. I want you to tell her that you're at Sheildaig Lodge. You're recovering from your op and that you're perfectly happy where you are. I visit you regularly and you have all your cronies with you." Ryan had sat on the dusty floor and looked straight into Len's face. "Did you get all that?"

Len blinked. "Why would I do anything for you?"

Ryan reached into the bag he had brought with him. He pulled out a cloth black hood, the kind used in kidnaps. "Simple. Do you want to live? Do you want to see daylight again?" He shook the hood and moved to place it over Len's head. "See, I think I've been quite fair until now old man."

Len snorted. "Right."

Ryan pulled something else out of the bag: rope. He ran it between his fingers. "It could all end so differently for you." He saw the fear pass across Len's eyes. Finally the message was getting through. He pulled the hood down and looped the rope around Len's neck, tugging slightly. Len started to struggle but was weak and exhausted. Ryan let it go and removed the hood. "So you gonna play nice and speak to Molly?"

Terrified, Len nodded. "Wh...what... what am I saying?"

Ryan repeated his message. "And don't even think of saying something I haven't told you to say." Ryan ran the rope through his fingers again. He passed the phone to Len.

"Hello... hello?"

"Molly? It's Dad."

"Oh thank God, how are you?"

"I'm fine hen, fine. " Len glanced up at Ryan who continued to run the rope through his hands.

"Are you still at Sheildaig or are you back home now?"

Len paused. What had Ryan said? That he was at Sheildaig? "Yes I'm at Sheildaig but don't worry about me. I'm fine." He let the sentence hang, willing Molly to pick up on his tone of voice. He could hear his grandchildren playing in the background. "How are you?"

I'm fine dad, just been worrying about you."

"Oh I'm alright, don't worry." He swallowed, trying to generate some moisture in his mouth.

"I was going to drive through and see you at the weekend."

Ryan shook his head vigorously, pulling the rope tight in his hand.

"No! I mean no, there's no need to do that. I think I'll be home soon. Why don't you call around then?"

"Only if you're sure. Michael's away again and the girls..."

Ryan swiped his finger across his neck, indicating that Len should end the call.

Len interrupted Molly as she continued to tell him about her busy life. "Listen hen, I need to be off. Don't worry about me. I'm fine." Tears started to pool in his eyes and his voice almost gave way.

"It's so lovely to hear from you dad. Thanks for calling and I promise to come through and see you when you get home."

Len cleared his throat. "OK hen, speak soon."

Ryan snatched the phone from his dad's hand and hit the disconnect button.

"Happy now?" asked Len.

"Yep. That's all I needed."

"There'll be more than Molly looking for me."

"That's where you're wrong old man. No one is looking for you, no one." Ryan squatted down. "How does that make you feel? All those years serving behind that bar and not one person is wondering where you are."

"Molly must have been wondering."

"Interfering more like, just like the rest of you."

Len looked Ryan in the eye, hoping to see some trace of his son, the one he knew from years back. There was nothing on his face but hatred. "So what now?" It was useless begging for release, he accepted that, but he didn't want to die. He didn't want this to be the sum of his life.

Ryan stood and laughed. "I'll be gone for a few days so I'll leave you some water and food." He upended the carrier bag. More energy bars fell out and he kicked them towards Len. "There's water here too." He lifted a couple of bottles closer. "There's no use shouting or trying to escape so don't even think about it."

Len doubted he had the energy anyway, and pain was still coursing through him.

"Ryan..." he croaked at his son's receding back.

"What?" Ryan pulled the lower part of the stable door closed and re-attached the padlock. He leaned over the door, bored and tired of the stench.

"I just... I..." Len had forgotten what he was going to say. "Doesn't matter," he said dejectedly. Even his own mind was failing him.

Ryan laughed and walked away, making sure the barn door was firmly locked behind him.

32

I t had been such a long time since she'd seen her sister that Kate was filled with a rush of love as Fiona closed her car door and came running across the road. The two sisters hugged and jumped up and down like giddy teenagers. They both started talking at once.

"How are..."

"So good to see..."

They collapsed in fits of giggles. Kate hooked her arm through Fiona's and escorted her to the café.

"Joe, look who's here!"

Joe was playing with his Game Boy. He looked up and his face lit up when he saw Aunty Fi. He hurtled across the café and received the biggest hug.

"Gosh, you've grown!" exclaimed Fiona.

Joe pulled away, smiling. "I didn't know you were coming." He couldn't believe it. Aunty Fiona was one of his favourite people and wrote to him all the time.

Kate stepped in. "I thought it would be a nice surprise," she laughed. "Here. Let Aunty Fi sit down, she's had a long drive."

"God no, I've been sat down for hours. I need to stretch my legs."

Gill and Mairee came out from the kitchen, watching the family reunion. Kate made the introductions then ushered Fiona upstairs to the flat. Once inside, the sisters hugged again and Kate went to put the kettle on. Once the excitement had died down slightly, and Joe had stopped bouncing between them, they finally had some time on their own.

"Tell me everything," said Fiona, assessing her sister and noticing how much weight she seemed to have lost. "See you've still not tamed that hair."

Kate smiled and ran a self-conscious hand over her red curls. "No chance of that up here, the weather plays havoc with it."

"So come on, how is everything?" asked Fiona again.

"Oh it's just perfect Fi. Joe is completely happy, Jack has been such a good friend and I finally feel settled." Kate adjusted herself on the sofa so that she was facing her sister.

Fiona was grinning. "That's so good to hear. I know we write and phone but it's not the same is it?"

"No. I'm so glad you came, and I'm sorry I haven't asked you before. It just never seemed the right time."

"Hey. It's OK." Fiona patted Kate's leg. "I get it. Don't apologise." She took a sip of her tea and realised that Kate was holding something back. "So who's the one that's put the twinkle in your eye?"

Kate blushed. She hadn't wanted to let Fiona know about Ryan straight away. She had never told her about her fling with him, and thanks to Ryan's reputation in Leeds she wasn't sure what Fiona knew about him. "Oh there's plenty of time for that. How long are you staying?" she asked, deflecting the question.

"Not sure. I'd planned a week or so but to be honest

there's not much going on at Uni until the new year so I can stay longer if you need me."

"How's the studying going?" Fiona had qualified as a nurse years ago and had recently decided to study further and specialise in Pediatrics.

"Yeah fine, wish I'd have done it years ago but you know how it is. But I don't want to talk about me, what's your news? How's Jack?" Kate had told Fiona about Jack's accident the other day and although they had never met, Fiona knew what Jack meant to Kate and Joe and was shocked to hear about his fall.

"He's home, so that's something but he still has no memory of the fall."

"That's understandable, it will come back in time," said Fiona, reassuringly. Joe came tearing into the room clutching his artwork books.

"Aunty Fi, do you want to see my drawings?" He plonked himself in between them on the sofa.

"Of course I do."

Joe opened his books and introduced each drawing with a detailed explanation of what each bird was and where it lived and Kate knew he would ramble on for hours if she let him.

"Joe, Aunty Fi might be tired after her long drive. Why don't you leave it until later? "

Joe looked sloughed.

"No, honestly it's fine Kate, I'd love to see them. They're really very good." Joe had developed a close eye for detail and it came out in his pencil drawings. His schoolteacher had even suggested that he sell them in the café, something Kate wasn't too keen on, thinking it might be a distraction from the rest of his school work.

She left them to catch up and headed back down to the

café. She felt guilty at throwing Mairee in at the deep end but she seemed to have coped well and Gill had no complaints.

"Gosh, doesn't your sister look like you?" commented Mairee as she cleared tables.

"Haha, yes it has been said. I got the curly hair from dad though." She helped her carry the full trays into the kitchen. It had quietened down somewhat so she took the chance to have a quick chat with Mairee.

"How are you settling in? I'm sorry I haven't been around much."

"Ach, it's no bother. Gill's been great and I think I'm doing OK?"

"Oh yes, I'm delighted to be honest. Gill?"

Gill looked up from the bread she was currently making. "Aye, you'll do far me lassie."

"That's great then Mairee, as long as nothing is bothering you?"

Both women went silent and started making themselves busy with other things. Kate picked up on the atmosphere straight away. "What is it?"

Gill spoke. "It's probably nothing, and I really hate to bother you with it." She fidgeted awkwardly with some dough that was stuck to her fingers.

"Go on." Kate folded her arms across her chest as she braced herself.

"It's just that the till's been a wee bit short a couple of times."

"The till?"

"Aye. I've been doing the cashing up and on the odd occasion it's been anywhere between ten pounds and fifty pounds short," Gill said, almost apologetically.

"But how?"

"No idea. As you know it's been me and Mairee most days recently and I know it's not either of us."

"Hmm, that's interesting. Leave it with me and let me have a think. I know I haven't touched it, and Jack's been off the scene. How odd. You're sure it's not just a miscount?"

"Certain," said Gill.

Kate didn't know what to say. How could the till be short? She thought fleetingly of the trouble with Joe and money missing at school but quickly dismissed it as Ryan had solved that mystery.

"Can you make a note of the days you've noticed and keep a track if it happens again? One of the regulars might be helping themselves."

"Aye, maybe so." Gill didn't sound convinced, but Kate was the boss.

Having finished the tidying up and seeing the last of the customers out of the door, Kate called it a day and sent the two women home. She was just about to head upstairs when there was a tapping on the window. She turned to see Mairee waving at her.

She unlocked the door and let her back in. "What did you forget?" laughed Kate, but she quickly saw that Mairee was close to tears. "Oh goodness, what's wrong?" Kate guided her to a chair.

"I didn't want to say anything when Gill was there, but I think I know who's been taking the money."

Kate was taken aback. "Really? Who?"

"Promise not to go mad?"

"Mairee, when have I ever gone mad, at you or anyone for that matter?"

"It's Ryan." The words came out in a rush, and Mairee looked up at Kate warily.

"Ryan!"

Mairee nodded.

"Oh, I think you're mistaken Mairee. Why would Ryan take from the till?"

"I noticed the days that money was going missing seemed to be when he was either helping out in the café or keeping an eye on Joe. I didn't want to get the blame, what with being new and everything so I kept watch and a couple of times I saw him help himself." She started crying. "I'm really sorry."

Kate was shocked, certain that Mairee was wrong. "What are you sorry for?"

"He caught me watching him and threatened me if I said anything to you."

"Threatened you? Don't be ridiculous."

More tears. "Oh gosh, I shouldn't have said anything. I just thought you should know that's all."

Kate was stunned into silence. She let the news wash over her for a minute or two, then pulled out a tissue for Mairee. "Look, I appreciate your honesty, really I do but I'm sure there's some misunderstanding. Let me talk to Ry..."

"No! You can't!" Mairee bolted up out of her seat. "He'll get me sacked and I really need this job."

Kate stood and went over to her employee. "Come on, calm down. There's only me that can sack you, and until I've looked into it you're going nowhere, trust me."

"Oh Kate, I am sorry."

"Now stop that. It's important I know but I still think there must be a mix-up so leave it with me and I'll look into it, without a word to Ryan. I promise."

Once Mairee had calmed down, and after several more assurances from Kate she finally left and Kate locked up behind her.

Thank God she had a bottle of wine chilling in the fridge –- she needed it.

33

"Is that release date definite?" asked Ryan.

"Yeah, why?"

"We need to pull plans forward."

"And how do you suggest we do that?"

"I don't fucking know, it's your kid. You work something out."

"You've fucked up haven't you?"

"No. I've just got better things to do than sit in the arse end of nowhere waiting for you to get out of fucking prison."

"What have you done?"

"Nothing! I've told you."

"For God's sake. You had one job. How could you have possibly screwed it up?"

"I've told you. I haven't. I just need to move on with my life."

"If you bail now you'll not get a fucking penny from me."

"I'm not bailing. Just want it done sooner, that's all."

"Yeah well, it is what it is."

"Christ I wish I'd never got into this."

"Yeah? Well I'm wishing I'd never fucking met you."

Ryan jabbed the disconnect button and swore loudly. Two more frigging weeks. Everything was such a mess. God knows what was happening with Jack. He hadn't seen him yet, avoiding him at all costs. His own father was falling apart in front of his eyes, and if he had to spend any more time with Janice he wouldn't be responsible for his actions. 'Scratch that,' he thought. 'I'm in enough shit.'

He had been stood outside, at the back of the pub, somewhere he seemed to be a lot recently. Between the pub, the barn, and the café he wondered why he ever thought the plan was a good idea. All for ten grand. Sure, it would buy him a plane ticket out of there but the stakes had become too high. He had to figure out a way of restoring some order, some kind of calm, but he was damned if he knew how.

34

J ack reached for his crutches and heaved himself off the couch. Tired of being stuck indoors he decided to try and make his way to the café. Stepping outside, he was pleased to see that although there was an autumn chill in the air, the day had been blessed with sunshine. It felt good being out in the bracing fresh air, and it reaffirmed his determination to make the short walk. He felt much better; stronger inside and out. The bruising had finally faded and his ribs had settled, unless he moved too quickly. He was even getting to be a dab hand on his sticks though he had high hopes that from tomorrow they would be a thing of the past. The journey would have been much quicker but for the few friends he bumped into wishing him well. The small community had really pulled together and Jack would be eternally grateful.

Having finally arrived, he pushed opened the door, the familiar jingling of the bell letting everyone know he'd arrived. He was greeted with calls of hello and very nearly landed on his back when Joe spotted him and hurled himself at his legs.

"Steady on there wee man," Jack laughed, thrilled to see his wee pal again. Joe went bounding off towards the kitchen, no doubt to let his mum know that he was there. Sure enough, Kate came out of the kitchen wiping her hands on her apron.

"Jack! How did you get here?" She was grinning from ear to ear.

"I walked. Well, limped anyway." He sat gratefully in the chair Kate had pulled out for him.

"You must be exhausted. You're supposed to be resting," she scolded, but was secretly thrilled to see her old friend up and about. "Here, let me fetch you a cup of tea."

As Kate hurried off, Joe came over to inspect Jack's plaster cast leg. "Does it hurt?" He asked with the morbid curiosity of a nearly eight-year-old.

"Not anymore but it itches like crazy."

"How long is it on for?"

"Not much longer, I hope. Back at the hospital tomorrow so keep your fingers crossed."

"Do you get to keep the plaster?"

Kate came back over with the tea. "Joe, that's gross. No he doesn't."

Joe looked suitably wounded and sat beside Jack. "Will your leg look funny? Henry in my class broke his leg and it looked weird afterwards."

Jack laughed and ruffled the boy's hair, "I have no idea."

"Joe, why don't you go and let Aunty Fiona know that Jack's here. I'm sure she'd love to meet him."

Joe went tearing off so Kate joined Jack at the table.

"Fiona?"

"Yes. I haven't had chance to tell you but my sister has come to stay for a while."

"Oh aye, I remember you talking about her. That must be nice?"

"It is. I haven't seen her for so long so we've had lots of catching up to do."

Fiona came down the stairs with Joe tugging on her arm. "This is Jack."

The three adults laughed and exchanged greetings. "It's nice to finally meet some of Kate's family."

"I know, but it had to be the right time for Kate," answered Fiona, instantly warming to the old man. "Besides, you seem to have taken good care of her and Joe anyway."

Jack blushed. "Nah, it's a pleasure." He took a sip of tea as the café door opened. He looked up to see who had walked in and felt the blood drain from his face. He didn't need anyone to tell him who it was.

"Ryan!" shouted Joe as he rushed up to greet him. He took a hold of Ryan's hand and pulled him over to the table. "Look who's here," he announced, clearly pleased that all his favourite people were together.

Ryan nodded a hello to everyone and Kate did the introductions.

"Your sister? Now that's a surprise," he said.

Fiona felt uncomfortable as Ryan stared down at her. She stood so that they were almost eye to eye. "Nice to meet you Ryan, I've heard a lot about you."

"All good I hope?"

"Maybe," she answered. Turning her back, she bent down to speak to Joe. "Why don't we go and get your drawing book so you can show Jack your artwork?"

Joe scuttled off, Fiona following. Ryan turned to Jack.

"Now then old man. How are you?" Ryan sat in the vacant chair opposite Jack.

Jack struggled to find his voice, but eventually managed a weak "Fine." Although his memory was still shot from the accident he would have known Ryan anywhere. No one had ever instilled the sense of unease and nervousness that Jack felt the moment he had seen him. He stared into his cup of tea, avoiding eye contact.

"How's the leg?"

"Fine."

"Not up to speaking, old man?"

It was that phrase: old man. Jack had always found it patronising but when Ryan said it, it seemed to take on a new meaning; belittling, sarcastic, nasty. He ignored Ryan's question, judging that it wasn't actually a question at all.

Ryan pushed his chair back without saying anything and walked into the kitchen to see Kate. Lost in a world of confused thoughts, Jack was snapped out of his reverie when he felt a heavy slap on his shoulder.

"Right. I'm off old man. Places to go, people to see." He leaned into Jack's ear, "Take care of yourself, eh? Try not to have any more accidents."

Jack exhaled as the café door slammed shut. He wiped the back of his hand across his mouth, feeling sweat on his upper lip. He took his handkerchief out of his pocket and wiped his face. His heart was still racing. He closed his eyes for a moment, trying to regain his composure. There was something familiar about that slap on the back. It jolted something in Jack's memory, but it was just out of grasp. It had been so heavy it had pushed him forward. His stomach flipped as he saw himself falling down the cellar steps.

'Could it be... no, surely not. Why would he? He'd never done anything to Ryan. He barely even knew him, so why would he?'

35

As Jack recovered his thoughts, Fiona came and sat alongside him.

"Are you alright Jack? You look pale."

"Aye lassie, I'm fine." He wiped his face again and tried to still his shaking hands.

"Perhaps the walk was a bit too much for you?"

"Aye. Maybe." Jack sat back and tried to focus. "So how long are you here for?"

"Not sure to be honest. As long as Kate needs me I guess."

At the mention of her name, Kate, who had been taking orders, joined them at the table. "Talking about me?" she asked jovially until she saw Jack's face. "Are you OK?"

"I'm fine, stop fussing." Jack still hadn't recovered fully and hated looking weak in front of Kate. He couldn't even begin to put into words the effect that seeing Ryan had had on him. He put his hand in his jacket pocket and felt the note that he had wanted to share with Kate. He wondered now if it was the right thing to do, but he had so many unanswered questions.

Knowing Jack, she moved the conversation on. "Ryan just came by to let me know he was away for a couple of days."

"You never mentioned he was up here." Fiona raised her eyebrows at Kate.

"Oh, I'll tell you all about it later Fi. Not that there's much to tell."

"Hmm, OK." Fi was skeptical. She'd seen the look on her sister's face as he'd walked in. She'd noticed Jack's reaction too. "Look, Jack would you like me to take you home?" asked Fiona.

"Aye, that's no a bad idea hen." Jack fumbled for his sticks.

Once they had said their goodbyes, Fiona led the way to her car and had Jack back at home, in his favourite chair, in no time. Though he was loathe to admit it, the walk had been too much. Fiona didn't want to leave Kate's friend until she knew he was going to be alright.

"That better?" she asked, pulling his footstool over so he could rest his leg.

"Aye. Not as young as I used to be."

"Ah, no shame in needing help from time to time, Jack." Fiona sat on the edge of the sofa. "Jack, could I ask you something, if you're feeling up to it?"

"Sure hen, fire away but how about a wee dram first eh?"

Fiona laughed. 'He wasn't that tired then.' She took a tumbler from the sideboard and Jack directed her to the liquor cabinet.

"So, how can I help you?" he asked, taking a sip and relaxing back.

"It's a bit sensitive to be honest. I'm not sure how much you know. I do know that Kate thinks the world of you, Joe does too."

"Well, the feeling's mutual."

"I guessed that, which is why I wanted to ask you..."

"Come on, out with it hen."

Fiona liked Jack's direct approach which was how she preferred to deal with people. "What do you know about Ryan?"

The reaction couldn't have been more dramatic if a bomb had been dropped in the room. It took Jack a few minutes to answer. "Not much. Knew him as a wean, know his dad. Know that Kate is smitten with him," Jack sighed. "Does that answer your question?"

"Yes and no. How long has he been up here?"

"Now you're asking. Must be since spring at least." Jack really didn't want to talk about Ryan, it felt disloyal to Kate, but Fiona pressed on.

"I saw your reaction when he walked into the café. What's going on between you?"

'Now she's opened a can of worms,' he thought. He took a moment to compose himself. "I don't trust him, that's all."

"Can I ask why?"

Fiona had only met Ryan face-to-face a handful of times at Kate's house in the past, but knew he was a friend of Daz's which told Fiona all she needed to know. That he was now in Gairloch seemed strange to her and she couldn't figure out why he was here.

"Why don't I trust him? I can't quite put my finger on it to be honest with you. Something just doesn't seem right."

"Would it help if I told you that I didn't trust him either? I don't understand what he's doing up here for a start, or why Kate has been so cagey about him."

"Oh I can tell you why he's here." Jack was warming into his story after the 'wee dram' had been refilled. He went on to explain everything he knew about Ryan's sudden appearance. She listened intently. As he finished, he pulled the note from his pocket that he had been going to share with Kate. "I've been trying to remember what happened before the accident." He smoothed the paper out on the table and passed it to Fiona. She read through the list.

"I'm not sure I understand?"

"Well I keep getting snatches of memory. Like erm..." Jack clicked his fingers, forgetting the word.

"Like flashbacks you mean?"

"Aye. That's right, flashbacks. Just wee snippets of things but I'll be damned if they make any sense." He paused and took another sip.

"Well that's a good idea and something we recommend to head injury patients." Fiona had no idea where this was going.

"Oh that's right. You're a nurse, I remember now. Anyway, I found this bus ticket to Inverness in my coat pocket but I can't remember why I went there."

"Wait, you caught a bus to Inverness? When?" Even though she wasn't local Fiona knew Inverness was a fair way away, she'd driven it herself only recently.

He pulled out the bus ticket and Fiona read the date and time. "Isn't this when you had your accident?"

"Aye."

"What are you saying? You went to Inverness, arrived home and fell down the cellar steps?"

Now Fiona had put it in such a matter-of-fact way Jack felt a little foolish. She interrupted his thoughts.

"Go through the rest of the list with me. Len is Ryan's dad, right?" She didn't wait for an answer. "And he's been in hospital for an operation. So Ryan is here to look after the pub." It was more of a statement to herself than an actual question.

"Well, yes but he seems to spend more time at the café and flitting about."

"So is he up here for good then?"

"Who knows? I hope not but Kate will be upset if he just ups and leaves."

Fiona rubbed her hands on her jeans, trying to make sense of it. She wasn't sure what to make of what Jack had said. "And where is Len now?"

Jack shrugged his shoulders. "No idea." He felt tired all of a sudden, and he sighed again, closing his eyes. Fiona reached forward and took Jack's hand tenderly in hers.

"I'll leave you to rest Jack and give all this some thought but try not to worry. I'm sure we can work it out between us." She gave him a gentle squeeze.

"Just one other thing before you go." Jack opened his eyes. "Something I haven't added to the list yet. Kate said there were two cups on the counter when she found me."

"OK." Fiona fastened her coat.

"If I was on my own, why would there be two cups?"

36

K ate opened the café as usual, unlocking the front
door so that Mairee and Gill could let themselves in. Her conversation with Mairee had
been going round her head for most of the night, and she
wondered if Gill had the same thoughts about Ryan. She
knew she wouldn't be able to get through a full day without
knowing. She just had to find the right time to talk to her.
The little bell above the door rang and Gill came in.
Hanging her coat on the rack, Kate approached her.

"Morning Gill. No Mairee?" The two women usually met
at the top of the harbour path and walked down together.

"No, not today. Didn't she call you?"

Kate had left her mobile upstairs and the cafe phone
hadn't rung at all. "No. Is everything OK?"

"She's no feeling too well so she's staying at home today.
I said I didn't think it would be a problem as we're fairly
quiet. Sorry, I thought you knew?"

"No, I haven't heard from her." Kate thought it was
strange after their last conversation that she should phone
in sick. "She said something odd last night after you left."

"Oh yes?" said Gill, tying her apron around her ample waist.

"Do you have any thoughts on who might have been taking money from the till?"

Just then Fiona and Joe came downstairs. "Morning," called Fiona cheerily.

"Morning," they both replied.

"So, any thoughts?" asked Kate again as Fiona and Joe went into the kitchen to make their breakfast.

"Do you have any yoghurt?" shouted Fiona.

"Aye hen, I'll be there in a second," replied Gill. "Can we talk about this later?"

Kate took that to mean yes, but let Gill carry on with helping Fiona. The bell rang again.

"Morning."

"Hey you, thought you were going away?" It was Ryan. It was early for him. Maybe he'd dropped by to give her a kiss on his way.

"Hi. Yeah, lots to do. Any chance of a coffee and bacon roll to go?" He leant on the counter.

'No kiss then.'

"Sure." Feeling a little put out Kate went into the kitchen and turned the hotplate on for the bacon. Fiona ventured into the café.

"Morning Ryan," she said, making herself busy wrapping cutlery in napkins.

"Oh, hi. Fiona?" Ryan was flicking through the local paper.

"That's right. Don't you remember me from Leeds?"

He looked up. "No. Should I?"

"We've met a few times. At Kate's. In the house she shared with Darren?"

Ryan felt heat rush to his face. "Ah right." He turned back to the paper to hide his reaction.

"So you still in touch with him then?"

"In touch with?"

"Darren. Daz. You were best mates weren't you."

Kate came out of the kitchen bearing a bacon roll. "I've put brown sauce on, don't worry, and Gill will have your coffee in a second." She passed Ryan his sandwich.

'Thank God,' he thought, desperate to get out of there. "Thanks."

"I was just asking Ryan if he remembered me," Fiona butted in. "Apparently not." She folded her arms across her chest.

"Well, it was a long time ago Fi," answered Kate in Ryan's defense.

Gill came round with Ryan's coffee. "I haven't put sugar in," she said, thrusting the cardboard cup at him.

"Right. I'll be off then." Ryan turned away from the glare of the three women, slamming the door behind him.

They stood there after he'd left, each with their own thoughts. Kate broke the silence.

"Coffees all round then ladies? Fiona I hate to ask but I need you to help in the café today if that's alright? Mairee's phoned in sick."

"Not a bother at all, happy to help."

Once they had their cuppas they sat at a table.

"Did Mairee say if she'd be off for long?" asked Fiona.

Gill answered, "No. Think it's just a tummy thing." She stirred her coffee.

"So, do you know who might have been dipping their hand in the till then?" Kate asked Gill.

"Someone's been stealing?" Fiona was shocked.

"Looks that way. Gill?"

"Well it isn't me." Gill was affronted and huffed to show her disapproval.

"Oh God, no. I don't think it is for a second Gill. I'm sorry, I probably worded that wrong. I just wondered if you had any ideas?"

"What did Mairee say?"

"Well, it's ridiculous really, and I think she might have said it to take the heat off her, but she tried to blame Ryan."

Fiona let out an involuntary snort.

"What?" Kate turned to her. "What was that about?"

Fiona realised her mistake and immediately apologised. "Oh I was miles away, sorry. What were you saying?"

Kate wasn't convinced but she was a bit sick of everyone having such a downer on Ryan, even her own sister. She hardly knew him, and it wasn't like her to make a judgement. She explained what Mairee had said and looked at Gill again for her thoughts.

"Well, I can't say for certain but aye, I've seen him. Just thought it was petty cash for something or other and he'd forgotten the receipt."

Kate knew that her system didn't work like that. If anything was needed then the money was signed for first by herself or Jack, then it was handed over. "Hmm, maybe. You don't think it's Mairee do you?"

"Nay, known the wee lassie and her family for years. As honest as the day is long. It's no Mairee." Gill was resolute.

Fiona listened to the conversation but didn't contribute. It wasn't her place for one thing, and she had her own thoughts after speaking with Jack yesterday. She didn't want to say anything to Kate just yet though. She wanted to see if she could find out more about the whereabouts of Len. She felt sure that if she found Len then she'd know the real reason for Ryan's visit. She didn't want to see her sister hurt, but she also knew that Kate wore her heart on her sleeve and could be easily pulled into situations. You only had to look at the situation with Darren to know that.

37

R yan reversed the clapped-out Vectra along the dirt track faster than he meant to, sending gravel and debris flying everywhere. He spun the car around and drove out of the pub car park, not bothering to check the oncoming traffic. With a screech of tyres, he turned a sharp left and accelerated harder. He was pissed off and with his anger raging he took the narrow highland roads at breakneck speed. The clouds were low, a light drizzle falling on the windscreen, obscuring visibility as the worn wipers struggled to keep up. Refusing to slow down on the single-track road, he forced other cars to stop for him and more than once he had to mount the uneven verge to avoid colliding with unsuspecting walkers and cyclists.

Furious that the whole plan seemed to be going pear-shaped, he considered just abandoning it and disappearing but the lure of ten thousand pounds was too much for him to walk away. No, he'd stick it out and whether Daz liked it or not he would deliver Joe to him as soon as he was released. Ryan would find somewhere that was easy enough to do the handover discreetly, but close enough to an airport so he could get the hell away as soon as it was done and he had his hands on the money.

Finally reaching the main road out of the Gairloch, he took a right and headed for the motorway. He had an idea about meeting up in a service station, in a long-haul car park, hidden amongst the HGVs for cover and dodging any CCTV that might be installed. Once he'd done that he needed to contact Sean, Daz's cousin, who was the one doing the driving. Ryan had no idea why Daz had never learnt to drive but it wasn't his problem.

'Something else to add to the list,' he thought, 'A hire car.' He knew he would need some form of ID but giving his own name didn't bother him: he'd be long gone before anyone knew what was happening. He'd already worked out that he could catch a flight to Amsterdam from Glasgow airport, then a connecting flight to Sydney. He'd buy the tickets at the airport once he'd handed over the brat.

Pulling into a petrol station, he fuelled the car, grabbed a couple of pasties from the chiller cabinet, paid and started his journey again. It took longer than he expected, arriving at Stirling Services four hours after he'd set off. He'd have to bear that in mind when he was telling Sean the location but he reckoned it was about halfway for both of them.

Luckily there was a cheap hotel nearby so he booked a room for the night, planning on doing the return journey the following day.

Settling himself on the bed, he fished his mobile phone out of his pocket and rang Sean. It had been a while since they had last spoken and even then it was just general banter over a pint whilst he waited in the local for Daz to join them. He had no idea if Sean would remember him. He definitely would after this.

"Sean, it's Ryan."

"Alright. What's happening."

Clearly Sean did remember him, or he'd spoken to Daz recently.

"Stirling services, 7pm. A week from today." Ryan paused but there was no sound from the other end. He assumed Sean was still listening so he carried on. "There's an HGV park. I'll be on the last row at the back, near the exit."

"Got it," came the short, surly reply. The line disconnected.

"Charming," said Ryan. He couldn't care less. He wasn't out to make new friends, he just wanted the job done.

Throwing his phone on the bed, he flicked on the TV and settled back to waste some time watching mindless television.

38

Kate hadn't been able to settle all night. She finally gave up at 4am and had been sat in the living room mulling things over. It wasn't a thing she could put her finger on, more a series of incidents that didn't seem to link together, and most of it centred around Ryan. She thought back to when he'd arrived in the spring, and how things had seemed to change over the following weeks. Most of the changes had been in a good way, at least for herself and Joe. Ryan had lifted her in a way that she hadn't felt for a long time. Finally she had felt a part of something; a family, a team, but she couldn't ignore the way that Jack had been with him, and now even her own sister seemed to have formed an opinion although Fiona had barely spent any time with him. What was she missing? Could others see something that she couldn't? It was that thought playing constantly on repeat that had finally driven her out of bed and onto the sofa, nursing a cup of tea. Kate wasn't stupid. She knew Ryan was a rogue but he would never mean anyone any harm, he was just a bit rough around the edges. She'd seen Jack's response to seeing Ryan in the café the other day and, try as she might, she couldn't work out what had taken place between them, but Jack was definitely unnerved.

She heard footsteps out in the hallway, presumably Joe wanting a drink. She pulled her dressing gown tighter around her and stepped into the hallway.

"Good morning sunshine," she called as Joe tumbled blearily towards her. "Would you like a drink of orange juice?"

Joe rubbed the sleep from his eyes and nodded his head. "Is Aunty Fi awake?"

"No darling, not yet. It's still early." Kate headed into the kitchen and poured Joe his juice.

"Are we going anywhere today?" he asked.

Since Aunty Fi's arrival she had kept him busy with day trips and visits to the beach. He'd come to expect something different every day. "Not sure. I thought it might be nice for me and you to go to the park?"

Joe shrugged his shoulders and took the glass from his mum. "OK."

Kate smiled and followed him into the living room, switching on the children's channel. They snuggled up together and Kate must have dozed off as the next thing she knew Fiona was standing in front of her with a coffee.

"Hey sleepy head."

"Oh gosh, I must have been tired, sorry." Kate took the coffee from Fi.

"Bad night?" asked Fiona.

"Not great actually, a bit restless."

Fiona sat alongside her. "Why don't you have a break from the café today? It's not overly busy and I'm sure Gill can cope plus Mairee might be back today." Fiona stroked her sister's hand tenderly.

"That's not a bad idea. I feel like it's been a bit relentless what with Jack and then the whole money missing episode. Some fresh air will do me good."

Fiona looked out of the window. Although it was past 9am the sky was still an ominous dull grey with thick, low-laying clouds. "Make sure you wrap up if you do go out," she gestured to the window.

"What will you do whilst we're out?"

"Oh, I've got plenty to be getting on with. Gill has shared her recipe for coffee and walnut cake so I'm giving that a go, don't worry about me," laughed Fiona.

"Ha ha ha, fair enough. Joe?" Kate turned the TV down to get her son's attention. "I'm going to shower then what's say we hit the park for the morning?"

"Cool," came the reply, his attention immediately switching back to the telly.

After much fussing from Fiona and digging out of scarf and gloves, finally Kate and Joe set off for the park. It was only a short walk, and Joe ran ahead, making a dash for the swings. That persistent drizzle that seemed to start in September and last until the following March was in evidence again as Kate approached the bench, deciding not to sit after all. She wandered towards the swings as Joe frantically tried to get her attention and urged her to push him higher. She put all her energy behind it and gave him an almighty push. He squealed with delight as he soared through the air. Kate was so wrapped up laughing with Joe that she didn't see Janice from The Kingfisher crossing over the grass to talk to her.

"Ach, he's having a grand old time isn't he?" she said as she sidled up to Kate.

Kate laughed. "Hi Janice. Yes he is." She stepped back from the swing now that Joe had a good rhythm going by himself. She folded her arms and walked back over to the bench, Janice following her.

"How's Jack doing?" she asked.

"Oh, he's doing great, thanks for asking."

"That's good to hear. And are you busy in the café?"

"It's slowed down a bit now but it's not too bad." Kate wondered where this was going.

"Ryan seems to spend a lot of time there."

'Bingo,' thought Kate. "Yes, he's been a great help."

"Shame he doesn't spend as much time at the pub."

"Oh, I'm sure he's there more often than not." Kate refused to be drawn in.

"Aye, well he only shows himself when he has to that's for sure." Janice was clearly pissed off with Ryan. "Take yesterday for instance. Off he's gone for a few days, who knows where. I dare say Len would have a thing or two to say about it."

Kate's ears pricked up at the mention of Len: another thing that had been on her mind. "Have you heard from Len?" Kate tried to keep her tone casual.

"No, not a word. He's staying with Molly by all accounts, Ryan's sister in Inverness? I was only telling Jack the other day…"

Kate interrupted. She'd heard of Molly but had never met her and she didn't know that she lived in Inverness. A thought occurred to Kate. "I'm sorry Janice, I've just remembered we have to be somewhere." She stood up and shouted to Joe that it was time to go. She could hear Janice mumbling something under her breath but she paid no attention to her. Grabbing a hold of Joe's hand they headed for Jack's cottage.

She knocked on the door and tried the handle, it was open. "Jack?" she shouted as she and Joe entered. The living room was empty. "Jack?"

Jack and Fiona came out of the kitchen, each holding a cup of tea.

"Kate, what are you doing here? " asked Jack.

"I was just about to ask the same of Fiona," replied Kate, mildly taken aback to see her sister here. She hadn't mentioned it earlier.

"Oh, I just popped in to check on him after I'd called at the shop."

Fiona looked flustered, and had always been a terrible liar. Kate decided to ask her about it later. Right now she wanted to tell Jack what she had found out. She shook her head, clearing her thoughts. "I've just seen nosey parker Janice at the park. She mentioned that Len was staying with his older daughter Molly in Inverness. For some reason it's been stuck in my head that Len seems to have been out of the picture for a while. Do you know anything about it?"

Nobody spoke. Fiona and Jack looked sideways at each other.

Kate spotted it. "What's going on?"

Jack shifted uneasily in his seat, whilst Fiona went to sit on the sofa. "You'd better sit down."

Kate was completely confused but did as Fiona told her. "What is it? What's happened?"

Jack made a harrumphing sound in his throat, so Fiona took up the tale. "Jack and I were talking the other day, and as you know he's had some trouble remembering things."

"Go on." Kate was impatient to get to the point.

"Well, he's been making a list of the short memory bursts that he's had and he shared it with me."

Kate looked incredulous. "Shared it with you? Why?"

Sibling rivalry was never far from the surface. It always happened with Fiona and it infuriated Kate.

Jack looked decidedly uncomfortable. "Now Kate, it's nothing like that. Fiona just called in on a day when I wasn't feeling my best and I thought if I shared some of the jigsaw pieces with someone it might help me."

"So go on then, what's the big reveal?" Sarcasm dripped from Kate's lips and somehow she just knew that this would end up all being Ryan's fault.

"Don't be like that Kate. We're just trying to help Jack get his memory back," said Fiona in that patronising tone she used, noted Kate.

"So where's this list then?" she asked.

"Joe, would you mind going into the kitchen and getting the piece of paper please?" asked Fiona. She could tell that Joe had picked up on the sudden change of atmosphere and didn't want him upset by it. Joe did as he was told and passed the list to Kate. She read through it, and sure enough there was Ryan's name.

"Is someone going to explain this to me?"

Between them, Fiona and Jack ran through each of the points and waited whilst Kate digested the information. "So what does this prove then?"

"We're not trying to prove or disprove anything. Jack is just trying to make sense of the memories."

"But why is Ryan's name on there?"

Jack spoke before Fiona had the chance to jump in. "I'm not sure but when I saw him the other day I had a sense of déjà vu and thought I'd add his name." It even sounded lame to Jack. "But if, as you say, Len is staying with Molly then it makes sense for me to have gone there."

"Gone where?" asked Kate.

"Inverness," replied Jack.

The room fell silent.

"And did you see him? Len, I mean?" asked Kate.

"I can't remember, hen." Jack looked defeated.

"Well have you spoken to Molly and asked her?"

It seemed so obvious but neither Jack nor Fiona had done so. "Jack, do you have Molly's phone number?" asked Fiona.

"No. Just an address that I got from Janice."

"Well surely Janice has her number?" ventured Fiona.

"I don't know. It's all too confusing."

"Look, before we all get our wires crossed, why don't we get Molly's number and give her a ring? At least you can cross that off your list?" Fiona looked at Jack.

Kate snorted. "Or maybe Fiona, we just call Ryan and ask him? Or did that not occur to you?" She knew she was being defensive but she was so annoyed at her older sister right now it was all she could do not to rip her head off.

"Kate, don't be like that. No one is blaming Ryan for anything."

"No, not yet but you would, wouldn't you? Given the chance."

Joe looked up from the book he'd been reading at the change of tone in his mum's voice.

"Kate, I'm sorry but I've told you before, I don't trust Ryan. I have no real idea why he's even up here and don't you think it's all a bit strange that..."

"Oh shut up Fiona. You just can't help yourself, can you? Interfering in everyone's business. Why can't you see that for the first time in years I'm actually happy? I've built a new life for myself and Joe, and I'm finally happy. Why would you want to go and spoil that." As Kate spoke she took a hold of Joe's hand and headed for the door. "You're here on MY invitation, and I knew it was a mistake." Kate stepped onto the outside porch. "And as for you Jack, after all we've been through together and you go behind my back? Some friend you are." And Kate slammed the door, hard, making the little door knocker shake on its fixings.

39

Kate stormed down the harbour path, heading back to the café. She was furious with Jack and Fiona. How dare they conspire against her, she fumed. What the hell had she ever done other than try and be happy. Tears of frustration ran down her cheeks, and she wiped them away.

"What's wrong mum?" asked Joe as he struggled to keep up with his mum's rapid pace.

"Nothing Joe, it's fine. We just need to get back to the café."

"But why were you shouting at Aunty Fi and Jack?"

"It's grown-up stuff Joe, honestly and nothing for you to worry about."

"Was it about my dad?"

Kate stopped in her tracks. "No. Why would you ask that?"

Joe shrugged his shoulders. "Dunno, you just used that voice that you use when you and dad argue."

Kate was floored. They might have been gone for two-and-a-half years but clearly the memories stayed with Joe.

She knelt down so that they were eye to eye. "It wasn't anything to do with Dad, and it's not something that you need to worry about sunshine. It was just a silly argument, that's all. " She pulled him in close for a hug, guilt coursing through her body. She took his face in her hands and kissed him on the nose, much to Joe's disgust.

"Eeeew mum, that's gross." He wiped it away.

Taking a hold of his hand, she carried on walking at a slower place. "Come on, let's go see if Gill has any sausages left."

Once they were back at the café she left Joe in Gill's care and headed up to the flat. Taking off her coat and boots, she flicked the kettle on and stood staring into space waiting for it to boil. She knew she had snapped at Fiona and Jack, but her emotions were riding high and her head was all over the place. She took a few deep breaths and closed her eyes, focusing on her breathing to calm her down.

The door to the flat opened slowly, and Fiona walked in.

"Kate, I..."

"Don't apologise Fiona, it's fine." Kate took a cup from the mug tree. "Want one?"

"Erm... yes please. But look, I'd like to explain."

"There's really no need."

"I don't want you to think we were going behind your back, that's all."

"Well you were a bit."

"Yes but not in the way you think. This isn't about Ryan at all."

Kate turned from the worktop and looked at Fiona. She knew that as sisters they could be as stubborn as each other, and for Fiona to back down must mean that she felt bad about the fight. Kate had to confess that the last thing she wanted to do was fall out with anyone. She'd had enough of that in the past. "Look, we're not two stroppy teenagers anymore so let's sit down and talk it through cos I still don't really understand what's been going on if I'm honest."

The relief on Fiona's face was evident, and it was all Kate could do not to laugh. A few years ago an argument would have ended in days of not speaking. She stepped forward and held out her arms. "Let's not fall out, eh?" Fiona fell into her arms and they both laughed.

Over several cups of tea and an unknown quantity of biscuits, Fiona started at the beginning and explained to Kate what Jack had found out. She didn't hold back on her own feelings for Ryan, and was surprised when Kate didn't respond as she would have expected.

'Maybe little sis has grown up,' she thought to herself and smiled.

"So where does this leave us then? " asked Kate.

"I'm not sure. It might all be nothing. Until Ryan gets back there really isn't much more we can do. I don't want to go phoning his sister and worrying her unnecessarily."

"No," said Kate, "I agree. I've tried Ryan on his mobile again but it's still going to voicemail. He said he'd be a couple of days so if there's still no word tomorrow I'll go see Janice again and see if she had any other numbers for Ryan or Len."

"Sounds like a plan. Now, where's that nephew of mine?" Fiona placed her cup on the coffee table and stood up.

"Oh he's filling his face with sausages I imagine."

"Right, well I'll pop and see him and see if he wants to help me with that cake."

Kate took the cups into the kitchen and rinsed them off. She was glad she'd made it up with Fiona, and even though she still had lots of unanswered questions it felt good to know that she wasn't on her own.

. . .

Later that same night, Joe piled out of Fiona's car and hurtled towards the Scout hut. Fiona watched him as he was greeted by his friends.

"It's Fiona isn't it? Kate's sister?"

Fiona looked around. "Yes, that's right." She put out her hand towards the man who'd spoken to her. A rather tall, thin gentleman, he took it and they shook.

"I'm Mr Wheeler. Temporary Cub leader and Kate's friend." He beamed at her, and Fiona wondered if there was anyone in Kate's new life that didn't give off a sense of belonging.

"Oh, lovely to finally meet you. Joe talks about you all the time."

"Does he really? Well he's a lovely wee chappy and me and the wife think the world of him, and Kate of course. Is she no here tonight?" He looked around the car park which was teeming with noisy young people.

"No, she's gone to see Jack so I volunteered to drop Joe off."

"How is Jack? Wasn't he at the hospital today?"

"Yes he was, he's had the plaster taken off and just has a boot on now so he's much happier. You were there when Kate found him weren't you?"

"Aye hen I was, dreadful business."

Just as Fiona was about to reply a shrill whistle was sounded behind her, making her jump.

"Well, that's my cue," said Mr Wheeler. "Will you be picking him up?"

"Yes, I would have thought so." She looked round for Joe and spotted him lining up with his pals. "See you Joe, have fun." She waved and climbed back into the car. She was still feeling guilty for the argument with Kate, even though they had made friends again. The last thing she wanted to do was upset her sister. Arriving at the café, she let herself into the flat and saw Kate was fast asleep on the sofa. Not wanting to disturb her, she went into the spare room and opened her book to read for a while. It was pleasant laid in the warmth, listening to the relentless wind and rain batter the window outside. She felt her eyes closing and dropped the book from her hand as she fell into a deep sleep.

B oth girls were rudely awakened by someone banging loudly on the door to the flat.

'What the hell,'" thought Fiona, rousing from her impromptu nap. She sat on the edge of the bed, shaking the sleep from her head.

"Kate? Fiona?" It was Jack.

"Yes, yes I'm here, hold on."

Kate opened the door just as Fiona walked out of her room.

"What on earth is wrong?" asked Kate.

Jack burst in the minute the door opened, hobbling on his boot. "Where's Joe?" he demanded, clearly out of breath and agitated.

Kate and Fiona looked at each other. "He's at Cubs," answered Fiona.

"What time is it?" asked Kate, still disoriented from her sleep. Her head seemed to be full of fluff. She went into the kitchen and poured herself a glass of water.

"Did you send Ryan to pick Joe up?" said Jack impatiently.

Kate gulped the water down and scraped her hair back

from her face into the scrunchy that she kept around her wrist. A few shakes of her head and the fog was clearing.

"What? No!" She looked around for Fiona. "Fi?"

"I'm just in the bathroom. Hang on." They heard the chain flushing and Fiona came out, tucking her shirt into her jeans. "What is it?"

"Ryan picked Joe up from Cubs," said Jack.

"What? But he's not due to be picked up... Oh shit, what time is it?"

"It's 8:15pm."

"Oh shit, Kate. I'm so sorry I must have fallen asleep."

"But Ryan isn't here." Kate looked at Jack.

"He wasn't but he's back and Mr Wheeler saw Joe climb into a car with Ryan."

"What? How do you know?" asked Fiona.

"Mr Wheeler called in on his way home. He said that Fiona had dropped him off but Ryan turned up early and bundled Joe into the car before anyone had chance to say anything to him."

Kate was reeling. She pulled out a kitchen stool for support as she felt her legs buckling from underneath her. "But... what... I don't understand."

"I'm worried Kate. If Ryan wasn't supposed to be there and he hasn't brought him home, where the hell is he?" Jack was pacing the best he could up and down the corridor. Kate had never seen him so fretful.

Fiona stepped in. "Look, there may well be a very logical explanation. Kate, why don't you try Ryan's mobile?"

Kate fumbled in her bag for her phone and dialled Ryan's number. "Voicemail."

"Right," said Fiona. "Is there a chance he could have taken him for a pizza of something?"

"Not without checking with me first," replied Kate.

"Jack, did Mr Wheeler say anything else?"

"He mentioned that Ryan was in a different car, a new-looking one. He thought it might have been an Audi but Ryan pulled off at such a speed no one managed to get a clear view."

Fiona ran her hands through her hair. "Right... right. Well let's not panic just yet. Let's give it some time and see if he brings him home."

It was clear that Jack didn't agree with Fiona, and he didn't hesitate in saying so. "I have a nasty feeling about this."

The three of them stood and looked at each other. Fiona broke the silence. "Do you think we should phone the police?"

Kate immediately went on the defensive, "No, absolutely not."

"But Kate..."

"No Fiona. I know you and Jack have some kind of conspiracy theory going on but not the police. No."

"It's not a conspiracy theory Kate," Jack spoke so quietly they barely heard him.

"What was that?" she asked.

"I think it was Ryan that pushed me down the cellar steps."

"What!" Kate was incredulous. "What the hell do you mean?"

"I remembered last night. I didn't want to believe it at first, but it was too detailed for me to have imagined it. When he slapped me on the back in the café the other day it triggered something in my head and I couldn't let it go. I remembered that I'd been to Inverness to see Molly and Len but when I got there, Molly hadn't seen Len. I hadn't been home long when Ryan turned up at the door. Molly must have called the pub after I'd left and Ryan found out that I'd been to see her. He was threatening me and as I went into the kitchen to get something, he followed me. I opened the larder door to get the milk and that's when he pushed me."

Kate and Fiona stood and stared at Jack in complete shock. Kate's mind frantically ran through the scene that she had found when she had first discovered Jack; the second cup, the spilt milk. She started shaking and rubbed her eyes. Her left thumb and index finger pinched her forehead.

"But I..."

Fiona took a hold of Kate's shoulders. "Kate, nothing else matters now. What matters is finding Joe."

Jack had leant against the worktop for support and looked positively white. "I'm sorry Kate," he whispered. She moved across to him and took his hands in hers.

"You've nothing to apologise for Jack."

"I have Kate. I knew Ryan was trouble the minute I met him and I should have warned you. I should have tried harder to get you to see him for what he is."

"He's many things Jack but he wouldn't hurt Joe."

"I don't know lassie, I just don't know."

Kate turned and looked at her sister. "He wouldn't, would he?"

"I really think we need to call the police," was all Fiona said.

But Kate was resolute. "No!" It came out louder than she expected, pulling Jack up short.

"That wee laddie could be in all kinds of danger. Fiona's right, we have to phone the police."

"It's not that straightforward. I don't want the police involved."

"What do you mean? Joe is missing! Why can't you see that?" Fiona was trying desperately to keep calm.

"Ryan wouldn't hurt Joe," said Kate, somewhat lamely and to herself.

"I've heard the rumours Kate. I know why Ryan had to leave Leeds."

"That's all it is Jack, rumours. He was set up by... someone. Ryan may be a lot of things but he would never hurt a child, and certainly not Joe." Kate had regained some of her composure and was now pacing the floor.

"Set up... by who? I know you know more than you're letting on."

Fiona felt like a spare part. She silently left the room with her mobile in hand.

"It's best if you don't know Jack. Trust me."

"Then for God's sake, phone the police or I will."

"Just give me a minute." Kate half walked, half stumbled into her bedroom and reached to the back of the dressing table for a piece of paper that she hoped she would never need. There was a phone number and name on there that was firmly part of her past and she knew that once she rang it, it would all come crashing violently into her present. Just as she was about to dial, Fiona came into the bedroom.

"Do you still have the contact number?" she asked.

"Yeah. Never thought I'd need it though." Tears started falling. Fiona sat on the bed next to her.

"You know you have to do this, right? "Kate took several deep breaths and dialled the number.

"DC Ziggy Thornes," announced the voice on the other end.

"Ziggy, it's me. Kate Walker, or Kathryn Ward as was." Kate's hand was shaking, Fiona took her free hand in her own.

"Hell, this must be serious."

"It is. Joe's gone missing and I think he's in danger."

Ziggy stood up from his desk and raked his hands over his head.

"Shit. Right. Where are you?"

"Same place but I'm in the flat above Harbour Café."

"I'll contact the local force, then I'll kick things off here. Keep this phone with you. Kate, do you have any idea who might have taken him? "

Kate hesitated and looked at Fiona for reassurance. For the sake of protecting her son she had to give up Ryan's name.

"Kate? You still there?"

"Yes, sorry Ziggy, I'm still here." She exhaled loud and slow, feeling the breath in the pit of her stomach. "He's with Ryan Albright," she almost whispered into the mouthpiece.

"What the hell? What has he got to do with anything? Don't answer that. Right now we need to find your son. Jesus, this is a disaster." She could hear Ziggy tapping away frantically at his keyboard, probably pulling up Ryan's extensive criminal record. "Look keep this line clear and I'll be back in touch. And Kate? Stay right where you are."

The line went dead.

40

"What do you mean you're going to be frigging late Ryan?" Daz spat into the phone.

"Chill. I was late setting off. I'll be there about 11pm."

"For fuck's sake Ryan man, this had better not be a fuck up."

Ryan could hear Sean kicking off in the background. "What difference does it make, you're still getting your kid back."

"Is he there, put him on the phone."

"Nah bro, you'll have to wait until we get there. Have you got the money ready?"

"Yeah. It's all here."

"Cool, see you soon then."

Ryan chuckled to himself. He was nearly out of this unholy mess once and for all. Getting the kid had been easier than he thought. He'd spotted Fiona dropping Joe off at Cubs, and boom, there was the perfect opportunity delivered right into his hands. At least something had gone right. He knew he'd gone too far with everything else but once he set off down the road of violence he'd had no choice but to continue.

'Ah fuck it,' he thought, 'I won't be around for much longer anyway.'

He was pretty sure that Kate didn't suspect anything. She might have put a few of the pieces together but he was confident that she didn't have the whole picture. He couldn't believe how easy it had been to win her over. He figured that living in relative isolation for two years would do that to any woman. She'd been starved of affection and he'd had her eating out of the palm of his hand. He smiled to himself; Kate had lapped up every scrap of affection he had thrown her way.

Ryan checked in the rear-view mirror to see that Joe was settled in his seat. Joe had always been an easy target. He'd won the boy over the old-fashioned way; illicit sweets when mum said no and of course the shared secrets that unwittingly tied Joe into a conspiracy with him. One threat to expose the lies Joe had told had soon put him in his place.

Renting the hire car had been a doddle. He'd taken a detour via Inverness on his way back, hired an Audi S Line and driven back to Gairloch. He'd used his real name, there was no need to hide. He'd soon be on a plane out of there. He pictured himself maybe working in a beach bar, getting friendly with the tourists. The thought excited him massively. A fresh start, leaving all this shit behind him and starting again.

A little voice popped up from the back seat, "Where are we going?"

"It's a secret and we like our secrets, don't we?"

"Is it another one I'm not to tell mummy?"

"Yeah, something like that."

"Whose car is this?" asked Joe, playing with the middle armrest.

"It's my new car. Do you like it?"

"Yeah, it's cool. Does it go fast?"

"It does. I'll show you how fast when we get to the motorway."

"Have you got any sweets?"

"Course I have, here." Ryan reached onto the front passenger seat and threw a bag of sweets over his shoulder. It just missed Joe's head. The boy grabbed the bag from where it had landed on his lap and pulled it open. A rainbow of coloured wrappers spilling everywhere.

"Sorry," he murmured, glancing cautiously up at Ryan in the mirror. Joe hastily gathered together as many as he could and stuffed them back into the torn bag.

"No worries mate, just make sure you put them all back in. And put the empty wrappers in the bag too." Ryan didn't want to waste any time clearing up after the kid once he'd dropped him off.

"Are we nearly there yet?" came the predictable question.

"Not yet. Let's have some tunes on, shall we?" He was sick of speaking to the kid now. Ryan turned the radio on and some inane pop music started. He glanced in the rear-view mirror again and saw that Joe was nodding away to the music. He seemed happy enough.

Ryan's mobile rang. "What now?"

It was Daz again. "How long will you be?"

"Jesus, I've already told you. A couple of hours."

"Is he OK?"

"Yeah. He's got sweets and I've put some tunes on. He's well happy."

The call ended and Ryan checked in with his passenger. "Alright in the back?"

"Who was that? Was it mummy?"

"Nah, someone much better than that."

"Really?" Joe couldn't think of anyone else.

"Well it was going to be a surprise but we're off to see your dad."

"My dad? I thought I wasn't allowed to see him?"

"Well you can today."

"Will mummy be there too?"

"No, not today sunshine. This is a special treat just for you."

Joe didn't answer straight away. "It would be nice to see him," mused Joe. "Mummy never really said much about him."

"Remember when I told you that me and your dad used to be mates? Well, he phoned me and said that he would like to see you so that's where we're going."

"Oh, OK." said the ever-trusting Joe.

'Kids are so accepting of lies,' thought Ryan.

"Are we nearly there yet?" asked Joe, again.

"No. Why?"

"Cos I need a wee."

"I'll stop soon enough so we can get a drink and go to the loo."

Ryan turned the music back up and headed towards the motorway. His mind was already on that flight to Australia. Just the small matter of delivering Joe and he would be on his way.

41

Molly had had enough of being kept in the dark. She didn't trust a word that came out of Ryan's mouth, and now she knew that Dad hadn't been staying at Sheildaig Lodge she was confused and worried about exactly where her dad was and what the hell Ryan had done to him.

She pulled up outside The Kingfisher. It had been a couple of years since she had been back to her childhood home. Molly had left home when she reached 17 and met her husband Michael shortly afterwards. They had moved in together and married as soon as Molly found out that she was pregnant. Once mum had passed away, she really had no reason to visit. Relationships with her dad had never been great. He'd been a hard taskmaster, and although she had stuck it out longer than Ryan she jumped at the chance of a fresh start as soon as she could. That wasn't to say she didn't care about her father. He was still family after all but apart from running the pub he very rarely wanted to leave Gairloch and was content enough to live a quiet life.

Bracing herself before entering the pub, Molly took a

couple of deep breaths and opened the double doors that led into the main bar. It was fairly quiet now, just the few autumn walkers scattered around. She looked at her surroundings and noticed that the old place hadn't changed much at all since she had last visited. There was still the same wallpaper that had a yellow tinge from the smokers, and the floor was still the cheap vinyl that became gradually stickier as beer got spilt throughout the evening. She glanced behind the bar and saw Janice cleaning pint glasses. She approached and noted that the barmaid seemed to have aged since she last saw her.

"Hiya Janice, you alright?" asked Molly, leaning against the bar.

Janice looked up, "Well look what the cat dragged in! Molly hen, how lovely to see you."

Molly laughed, noticing that Janice's eyes had a sparkle in them, waiting for gossip no doubt. "Hi." Molly decided to cut to the chase, "Is Ryan around?" Molly had been trying his mobile constantly since she'd spoken to Hamish at Sheildaig but it continued to go to voicemail.

"Ryan? No lovely, he's never here. He's supposed to be looking after this place whilst your dad's away but I rarely see him. Is Len coming home then?"

Molly knew she had to be careful how she played this. She wanted to find out what Ryan had been telling people before she went into full-on panic mode.

"Do you know how I can get hold of him? His mobile's turned off."

"No, he wouldn't tell me. You can check in the flat though if you like?"

"That would be great Janice, thank you."

Janice lifted the bar access and let Molly through.

"Here, here's the key. I don't go up there, don't want him to accuse me of interfering with his stuff."

Molly took the key and thanked Janice again before heading upstairs. She unlocked the door and let herself in. The place looked as though it had been ransacked. The sparse furniture was tipped over, cushions removed from the battered old sofa, the kitchen chairs pushed onto their sides. Molly moved carefully through the debris and opened the bedroom door. If she didn't know better she would think that there had been a break-in. All the bedding was stripped off the bed, the wardrobes were open and empty and all the drawers on the dressing table were laid bare. The room was as empty as it could be.

Taking stock of everything around her, it was clear that Ryan had left, and in a hurry. She pushed the creeping anxiety down and tried to make sense of what she was looking at. She had no idea what to do next. She felt tears creeping into her eyes, but she was determined not to let them fall. She had to get to the bottom of what was going on. She jumped as she felt a hand on her shoulder.

"Oh my, what a mess." Janice appeared behind her. "Looks like he's gone then?"

"Yes," said Molly slowly. "Do you have any idea where he might have gone?"

"Nah, he wouldn't tell me. Could he have gone back to Leeds, though I doubt he'd be welcome there after all those stories I heard."

Molly turned quickly on Janice. "What stories?" she demanded.

"Oh I'm sure they're not true. I don't want to upset you. Why don't we go back into the bar?"

"What stories Janice?"

"Those about the kiddies, why Ryan had to leave."

"What?"

"I don't know the whole thing, just what I heard but he had to leave Leeds after something to do with kids. I mean I'm not saying they're true but..."

Molly interrupted. "Janice I have no idea what you're talking about or suggesting so I suggest you keep your mouth shut. I need to find Ryan urgently. Do you know who he might be with?"

Janice was taken aback with Molly's tone. "Your best bet is that café owner Kate. He's been as thick as thieves with her recently. I'm not one for..."

"Gossip, yes Janice I know. Do you have a number for her?"

'How rude,' thought Janice at being interrupted. "Yes, it's downstairs."

Janice turned to head back into the bar. Molly took a last look around and left the flat, locking the door behind her.

Once downstairs, Janice scrolled through her phone.

"I don't have Kate's number, she works at the Harbour Café. I say works, it seems Jack is handling the place..."

"Janice!" said Molly sharply, running out of patience. "Whose number do you have? What about Jack?"

"Oh did you hear about him? He had an accident recently. Fell down his cellar steps."

"It's OK, I've got Jack's number." Molly turned from the bar and fished her phone out of her bag. She rang the number that he had left her when he had visited him but it was his house number and there was no answer. Reluctantly she turned back to Janice who was looking highly pissed off at being cut off mid-sentence.

"I'm sorry Janice, I didn't mean to snap. I'm just under a bit of pressure so if you can help that would be appreciated. Do you have a number for the café, or can you get it for me please?" Molly realised that she needed Janice onside if she stood any chance of getting to the bottom of everything.

Janice's expression shifted slightly, appeased by Molly's feeble apology.

"Yes, here's the number. But listen to me first."

Molly breathed deeply and let Janice continue. Sensing that she had Molly's attention again, Janice continued with her tale.

"So, as I was saying. Jack took a tumble down his cellar steps and ended up in hospital. He was in a bad way, it was touch and go for a while I think. Anyway, just before he had his fall he was in here asking about Ryan. Now I'm not one to put two and two together but it makes you wonder doesn't it?"

Molly was confused and thought she'd missed something. "What do you mean?"

"Well, is it coincidence that not two days after Jack's in here asking questions, he goes and has a fall? Jack's lived in that house for years, why would he suddenly fall?"

Molly took on board what Janice was hinting at, but she didn't have time for that now. She had to find out where her dad was. She dialled the number Janice had given her. To her surprise, Jack answered the phone.

"Jack?"

"Aye, Harbour Café, who's that?" questioned Jack.

"Jack, it's Molly, Len's daughter."

"Oh hello hen, how did you know I was here?"

"I didn't. I'm at The Kingfisher and Janice said Kate might know where Ryan is."

Jack went silent.

"Why would Kate know?"

"I have no idea, Janice said he'd been around there a lot recently and I need to find him."

"You're not the only one Molly, we're looking for him as well."

"Why, what's happened?"

"Kate's son Joe has gone missing and he was last seen with Ryan." Jack's voice was low and he was almost whispering.

"Oh hell. Jack I'm sorry but I think Ryan is behind more than that." Molly felt an icy vein of fear wash over her. She tried to get her thoughts in order but she was overwhelmed. "I have no idea where dad is, and I think Ryan has done something to him."

Silence again.

"Jack, are you still there?"

"Yes, yes I'm still here. Look, we're waiting for the local police to turn up about Joe. Why don't you head down here and you can tell them about Ryan at the same time?"

Molly hesitated, unsure what to do. She wanted to wait at the pub in case Ryan showed up but she also wanted to find out more about Jack's fall. Could Janice's suspicions be right? Could Ryan have pushed Jack down the stairs? And if he could do that to Jack, someone he hardly knew what the hell else was he capable of? And why had he taken Kate's son.

It was all too much. She sat heavily on one of the bar stools. Jack was still waiting for an answer. She suddenly felt that she had to get away from the pub, away from gossipy Janice and escape the cloak of darkness that her childhood home seemed to be filled with.

"Yes, I'll come over," she finally answered, feeling the adrenaline that was driving her earlier action slowly seep from her bones.

42

Jack replaced the handset and stared at the phone, taking a moment to digest what Molly had just told him. He was rocked to his core. He had to stay strong for Kate, though he knew she would ask who had been on the phone; she was understandably distraught and fretful. He'd have to tell her. He had no real choice. Sure enough, Kate turned from the café table where she was sat and looked at him questioningly.

"Who was that?"

"It was Molly, Len's daughter," said Jack, sitting back down opposite Kate and Fiona. "She's on her way here."

"Here? Why? Does she know something?" Kate wasn't stupid and she knew from Jack's face there was more to it.

"She's worried about Len. She can't seem to find him."

"What do you mean, 'find him'?"

"I don't know the full story until she gets here, but I'm guessing that if Len wasn't staying with Molly as Ryan had told me and Janice then where the hell is he?"

"Oh Jack, you don't think?" Kate couldn't finish the sentence.

"I have no idea. I don't know anything anymore." Jack rubbed the back of his neck and shook his head.

Kate started crying again. "I feel such a fool. How could I have been taken in by him?" She folded her arms across the table and laid her head down. Fiona leaned over and rubbed her sister's shoulders. There was little she could say or do to comfort her. She just hoped that her worst fears weren't going to come true.

Jack felt just dreadful. Why hadn't he seen what was going on? Why hadn't he spoken to Kate about his concerns sooner? Why, why, why just kept running through his head. He couldn't sit still. He stood and walked over to the coffee machine. He had a feeling it was going to be a long night and a few shots of caffeine wouldn't go amiss. He used the time it took to make the coffee to think carefully about how to frame his next question. He didn't want Kate to retreat into herself. He knew she didn't like to talk about her past but that phone call she'd made upstairs must have something to do with it, and now was not the time for holding back information, however personal.

"Who was that you spoke to upstairs?" Jack wasn't good at doing subtle, but he did soften his tone.

Kate lifted her head, wiped her eyes on the back of her sleeve, and glanced briefly at Fiona. "It's a contact of mine from Leeds." She wasn't sure how much to tell Jack. The truth was bound to come out now. Maybe it was better if he heard it all from her. "A family liaison officer who helped me relocate."

Jack took the information in. "And Ryan? He seemed to know his name?"

"Yeah, Ryan had a bit of a reputation in Leeds."

"So I gather." Jack thought back to the rumours that

Janice had passed on and wondered if there was any truth in them after all. He set down the cups of coffee, along with milk and sugar. He pulled a hip flask from his pocket. "You might want a wee nip of this in it." He leaned over and poured some of the amber liquid into Kate's cup which she sipped willingly.

"So what's happening now then?" asked Jack.

"Ziggy is sending someone local to see us."

"Is that all? Can't they do more? I mean if Joe's in danger..."

"I don't know Jack, my head is all over the place."

There was a knock on the window of the café, and Kate shot up from her seat.

"I'll get it hen, you sit down."

Kate did as she was told and Jack unlocked the door. It was Molly. She came into the café and Jack made quick introductions before making Molly a coffee and inviting her to sit down.

"Oh Kate, I'm sorry we're meeting under these circumstances." She reached out and took Kate's hand in hers.

"I know, it's all a bit crazy. How are you?" Kate was concerned for Molly and the safety of her dad.

"I'm OK. I just have no clue where my dad is or what Ryan has done," Molly cried, big fat tears dropped onto the table and Kate passed her a tissue.

"Where did you think Len was?" asked Kate.

"At Sheildaig Lodge Convalescent Home. He told me last week that dad had been there a while, and I actually spoke to him but something just sounded off. I started to doubt him and then I thought back to Jack's visit and nothing seemed to add up." She broke off to catch her breath.

"Hey, it's OK. We'll find him. We'll find them both." Kate

tried to comfort Molly but her own heart was breaking and she found herself crying too. There was another knock on the window and Jack, who had been sat watching the two women fighting back his own tears, was grateful for the interruption. He unlocked the door and two police officers walked in. Jack recognised them both and greeted them by their first names.

Both officers walked over to the table where Molly and Kate were sat, removed their police hats but kept their high-visibility coats on.

"We're here about," the female officer consulted her notes, "Joe?"

Kate wiped her nose on a tissue. "Yes, that's my son."

"I'm PC Claire King and this is my colleague PC Steve Jones. Is it OK if we sit down?"

"Yes, yes of course. Would you like a coffee?" asked Kate, immediately switching into hospitality mode, standing up.

"I'll get it," said Fiona, indicating to Kate to sit back down.

The officers sat awkwardly on the café chairs, adjusting their coats and gear to get into a more comfortable position.

Molly butted in, "I'm Molly and my dad is missing too."

Everyone in the café turned to look at her.

"Sorry, I didn't mean to blurt it out but I'm going out of my mind."

"OK," said PC King. "Let's take this one step at a time." She turned towards Kate. "Our colleague, DI Thornes has informed us that your son is missing, and you suspect that a Ryan Albright might have taken him?" PC King consulted her notes again. "Can you tell me what has happened?"

"Well, Jack tells me that Ryan was seen getting Joe into his car outside the Scout hut on Denby Dale road. I was supposed to pick him up but Ryan got there early and took him."

Jones was making notes furiously. "OK. We know from DI Thornes that you moved here a couple of years ago from Leeds? Is that where you know Ryan Albright from?"

"Yes, that's right." 'Oh God,' thought Kate. 'This is where it all comes out'.

"And when was the last time you saw Joe?"

Kate let out a sigh of relief. "At around 7pm when Fiona dropped him off. I was going to pick him up but I fell asleep and Jack woke me up to tell me Joe had been taken." She was rambling and she knew it.

"OK, OK, slow down. Let's break this down so we can get all the relevant points," said PC Jones. He turned to Jack, "Did you see him take Joe?"

Jack snapped his attention back to room. "No, it was one of the Cub leaders, Mr Wheeler."

"OK, we'll speak to him in due course. Do you have his contact details?"

Jack scribbled the name and address down and passed it over.

King turned back to Kate. "Kate, we just need to establish a few facts. Are you OK to answer a few questions?"

"Yes, yes anything."

"So you didn't arrange for anyone else to collect Joe from Cubs?"

"No. Fiona spoke to Mr Wheeler and he knew I was planning to collect him so I don't know why he let him go with Ryan."

"And what time did it become apparent that Joe was missing?"

Kate looked at Jack, "Well I'd fallen asleep so when Jack woke me up it was 8.15pm so I was 15 minutes late. You'd have to ask Mr Wheeler when he saw Joe getting into Ryan's car."

"Why would Joe get into Ryan's car?" asked King.

"Ryan's been around here quite a bit recently and they were friends. Joe would trust Ryan if he said I'd told Ryan to pick him up."

Molly butted in, "He's emptied the flat above the pub too, all his clothes and his belongings have been cleared out."

PC King carried on taking notes whilst Jones took over the questioning.

"We'll need details of the pub etc but we can get to that in a moment. What was Joe wearing?"

Kate answered, "His Cubs uniform." Kate broke down. "Oh God what have I done," she sobbed and laid her head on the table.

"I know this is difficult for you Kate but I have to ask. Do you think Joe is in danger of harm from Mr Albright?"

"No...yes, I just don't know," said Kate through her tears.

Jack moved in his chair so that he could comfort Kate. "There's been some rumours going around about Ryan, and I'm fairly certain it was him that pushed me down the cellar steps."

Both police officers turned to look at Jack.

"OK, we can look into that but right now we have to focus on getting a clear picture to pass onto DI Thornes and his team. Can you tell me about the car that you mentioned before? Is it unusual for Ryan to be driving?"

Jack answered whilst Kate went to the bathroom to wash her face. "Mr Wheeler seemed to think it was a grey Audi. He usually drives a battered old Vectra but this seemed to be new, and it had hire car stickers on the rear windscreen."

King was scribbling furiously. "I don't suppose he got the number plate?"

"I don't think so, you'd have to ask him, but it looked like a new car."

Kate returned to the table, eyes swollen and her nose red but she'd managed to stem the tears for now.

"Kate, do you have a recent picture of Joe?"

"Yes, there's one upstairs. Jack, would you mind getting it? It's on the fridge, under the fish magnet."

Grateful for something to do, Jack scraped his chair back and headed toward the door that led upstairs to the flat. Kate took the opportunity whilst Jack was out of the room to question the officers.

"Do you have any idea where he might be? We've had a tough couple of years since moving up here." She hesitated. "You know why we moved, right?"

"No Kate, we're not privy to that kind of information, we're just interested in the facts and background at this stage. I need to run through a missing person report with you to make sure we've covered absolutely everything and then we'll take it from there. We'll see if there's any CCTV footage of the car and we'll speak to other witnesses as soon as we've left here." Constable King took a break from taking notes to pull out a MisPer report. "There's no chance that this was just a miscommunication, and Ryan has maybe taken Joe out for pizza or something?"

"No. This was deliberate I know that much," said Kate.

"What makes you say that?"

Kate was again thrown into a quandary. How much should she tell them? "It's just a feeling," she finally said.

Jack came in with the recent school photograph. "Is this the one Kate?"

She took the photo from Jack and ran her fingers gently

over her son's face. "Yes, thank you." She passed the picture over to the police officers.

Over the next twenty minutes they completed the forms, asking Kate endless amounts of questions.

"And Joe's father, where's he?" asked Jones.

"He's...he's not in the picture," said Kate

"But do you know where he is? Could he be involved?"

"I...don't know."

The two officers looked at each, sensing that Kate was holding something back.

"Kate, it's important that you tell us everything you know."

"I have told you everything," Kate replied, defensively. "Joe's dad isn't in the picture, OK?" She was starting to lose control, and deep down inside she knew that Daz was somehow behind this.

"But do you know where he is? Can you give us his name?"

Kate was stuck between a rock and a hard place. If she gave them Daz's full name it wouldn't take long for them to put two and two together. She wasn't 100% clear on police procedure, but she knew it wouldn't take long for them to find him, if Ziggy hadn't already joined the dots.

Reluctantly, knowing that her world was about to unravel she gave up Daz's name. "It's Daz, Darren Walker and he's currently in prison." She daren't look at Jack, she felt she had let him down and damaged any trust that remained between them. Her new life had been built on lies that were slowly but surely coming undone. "I'm sorry Jack." She kept her head down.

Jack didn't know what to think. He knew Kate had a past and he wasn't surprised to hear Joe's dad was inside but it made him wonder what else she was keeping from him.

"Don't worry lassie, let's just get the boy home." He rubbed Kate's arm.

43

The two police officers stood, replacing their hats.

"Hold on." Molly stood up and walked over to them. "What about my da?"

"Yes, of course," replied King. "We just need to get this information across to the team looking for Joe, then we'll take your statement."

Molly's patience was wearing thin. She'd held her nerve throughout Kate's interview. She knew Joe would take priority but it seemed to her that no one cared about Len, or where he was.

King could sense that Molly was a coiled spring, ready to unfurl at any time.

"Molly, why don't we head over to The Kingfisher to take your statement? We need to speak to anyone who may have seen Ryan in the last 24 hours, and take a look around the place for any clues so it makes sense?" She looked at her colleague and he gave a slight nod.

All three said their goodbyes to Jack, Kate and Fiona, promising Kate they would update her as soon as they had any news.

. . .

Molly left her car in the café car park and joined the police officers in their patrol car.

The weather had started to turn for the worse, with the autumn chill fogging the inside of the car windows. Molly rubbed the condensation and peered out into the mist. She was glad she had moved out of the area but looking through the gloom and out onto the landscape she did miss the open space, and the wide-ranging mountains. She couldn't help but wonder if her dad was out there somewhere. As much as she had held back on allowing the thoughts to enter her mind, she had a feeling in the pit of her stomach that something dreadful had happened to Len.

The police car pulled into the pub car park, and the occupants exited. Molly led the way and they entered through the double doors at the front. In their full uniform, the police officers looked intimidating and out of place in the sleepy local.

Janice was once again cleaning glasses behind the bar, and only a handful of locals had stopped by for a quick drink. It was getting late so most people had headed off to their homes before the rain set in.

"Oh my, what's happened?" asked Janice as the three approached the bar.

"Nothing to worry about," said PC Jones. "We just need to take a look around and ask a few questions."

Molly stepped forward. "Can you let the police officers

into the flat please Janice? I think they'd like a word with you as well so I'll watch the bar."

Janice, completely taken aback with the intrusion, did as she had been asked for once and led the way to the upstairs flat. Molly took her place behind the bar and looked around to see if anyone needed serving. Mr Wheeler approached the bar and ordered a pint of bitter.

"I think the police will want to speak to you too," said Molly, slowly pulling the bitter into a pint glass.

"Aye, no bother. Is this about Joe? I thought something didn't seem right."

"Yes, Joe and my dad Len."

"Len? Why, what's wrong?"

"I don't know where he is, and Ryan was the last person to see him."

Mr Wheeler rooted around in his pocket to pay for his pint and shook his head. "Goodness, I had no idea. I hope they're both safe."

Molly took the money offered and passed across the pint. "Yeah, me too."

Janice came back into the bar with the police trailing after her.

"Molly, can we have a word?" asked PC King.

"Yes of course. Oh, this is Mr Wheeler, the Cub leader. You'll want to speak to him too I think." Molly made her way around the bar and walked to a corner table at the back of the pub. King acknowledged Mr Wheeler and asked him to hang on until they had finished with Molly.

The cops took their seats opposite Molly.

"Janice seems to think your dad was at your house, recovering from an operation, is that right?"

Molly ran through the whole story from her perspective, including the lies that Ryan had told.

"He was obviously covering his tracks but it doesn't help me find my dad."

"So when did you last see your dad?"

"We weren't close so it was about eighteen months ago, but I did speak to him recently, and he told me he was convalescing and not to worry." Molly felt incredibly guilty for not visiting her dad sooner.

"You spoke to him? When was that?"

"Oh, erm...let me think." Molly scratched her head, trying to think when it was. "It can't have been more than three days ago."

King referred to the notes that she had written down when speaking to Janice. "So your brother, Ryan, hasn't been seen locally for the last 24-36 hours and you have no idea where he is?"

Molly suddenly felt as though she were under suspicion, as if she were somehow involved. "No, I have no idea where either of them are. Why aren't you looking for them?"

Jones stepped in, aware that the direct manner of his colleague could sometimes be questionable. "You're not under suspicion, we just need to establish a timeline so we can start to move forward. We already have officers looking for Joe and Ryan. We just need to build on the information we have about your dad."

"I know, I get it. I'm just frustrated that we're sat here when we could be doing something."

"Let's start again. Where would Ryan usually keep his car?"

"Round the back of the pub. I'll show you."

They stood and exited the pub through the rear door. The Vectra that belonged to Len, which Ryan often drove was sitting in its usual place. PC King walked round to the front of the car, and using her Maglite she shone her torch down the dirt path leading away from the pub into the woods.

"That barn there, does anyone use it?" She flashed her torch at the rickety structure. Janice had now joined them.

"Nah, hasn't been used in years," she said, arms wrapped around herself in an effort to keep out the chill.

Both officers started to walk towards the building. They studied the lock that was on the door.

"That looks new," commented Jones, pulling on a pair of gloves. King looked at it and agreed. They gave a hefty push to the bottom panels, and it didn't take long for them to give way. They squatted down and flashed their torches into the cavernous space.

"Mr Albright?" shouted PC Jones. There was no response. "Here." He passed his torch to his colleague. "I'll take a look." He dropped onto all fours and crawled under the space they had made. Having retrieved his torch, he approached carefully, taking his time to kick away the debris underfoot and look for any clues. He could see discarded medical bits and pieces; a syringe, bandages and an unknown bottle of pills.

"Think we might have something Claire, you'd better call it in," he shouted back. As he slowly edged his way to the back of the barn, fearful that at any minute the whole structure would collapse on him. He could smell something foul, and at first wondered what he was going to find when he caught a glimpse of something silver out of the corner of his eye.

"Mr Albright? It's the police. Are you in here?" Still no response. He proceeded with caution, the unmistakable odour getting stronger as he approached one of the stables. The door was hanging off its hinges, and he realised that the flash of silver he had seen belonged to the rim of a discarded wheelchair. Moving closer, he lifted his torch higher and shone it straight into the face of who he presumed was the missing pub landlord, Len Albright.

44

"Kate, it's Ziggy. How are you holding up?" The line was full of static and she struggled to hear him. Kate had stepped outside to get some fresh air. She clutched her mobile phone to her ear.

"I'm OK, wait let me go back inside." Kate pushed the cafe door open and signalled to Jack and Fiona that Ziggy was on the phone. "Is there any news?"

The line was still crackly and she could barely hear what Ziggy was saying.

"OK, I'll keep it brief. We've spotted the Audi on the A9, heading south so it seems likely that he's heading to a meet-up point. I doubt he'll risk driving all the way to Leeds."

"Meet-up point? What do you mean? Is Joe with him?"

"The CCTV isn't brilliant but it's been confirmed that there is a passenger in the back seat about Joe's height."

Kate felt her heart drop. "Oh God, what is he doing with him?" She thought back over the last few months and tried to see if there were any signs that this would happen. She had been so taken in by Ryan, how could she be so stupid.

She'd been so careful, kept her life so simple and sheltered Joe from the past, from the hurt that she'd had to go through.

"Kate? Are you still there?"

"Yes Ziggy, sorry. I'm here."

"Kate, I have to ask. Have you been in touch with your ex-husband recently?"

"No, he doesn't know where I am and anyway he's inside isn't he?"

"Not anymore. He was released on parole last week."

Kate dropped the phone. She felt the life drain out of her. Her hands started shaking and her heart bounced around her chest. Jack and Fiona, who had been sat listening to the one-sided conversation sprang up from their seats. Fiona dropped to her knees to comfort Kate whilst Jack retrieved the phone from the floor. Fiona helped a fragile, broken Kate into a chair.

"Hello?" said Jack into the receiver. "Ziggy?"

"Who's that? Is Kate still there?" Ziggy was confused at the new voice.

"It's Jack, I'm a friend of Kate's. What did you say to her? She's gone awfully pale."

"Jack, this is DI Ziggy Thornes. I'm the SIO on Joe's case. I've just updated Kate on where we are with everything. Is she OK?"

"Not really, here, I'll see if she wants to speak to you. " Jack took the phone away from his ear and approached Kate. "Do you want to speak to him hen?" Jack felt he was caught in the middle of something that he didn't understand. He had no idea what was going on. Kate took the phone from Jack.

"Sorry Ziggy, that was just a bit of a shock. Is he behind

all this?" She didn't know why she had asked, she knew in her gut that he was. She had a flashback to the last words he had shouted at her as he was taken away to start his sentence. He'd sworn he'd take his revenge on her.

"We believe so, it's a bit early to say just yet but it is a line we're following. We're covering this from every angle Kate, and it's being treated as high priority. Just stay where you are, keep this line clear and I'll update you when I know more."

"OK, thank you." She clicked the end call button and dropped the phone into her lap. Jack sat at the table, drumming his fingers and wondering what the hell was going on. He could see that Kate was still shaking and she appeared to be mumbling to herself.

"Kate, what's going on?"

"Oh Jack, it's all crashing down on me."

"What is? You can tell me."

"I don't know what to tell you, or where to even start." She looked at Jack properly for the first time since Joe was confirmed missing. His face was etched with worry, and she was overcome with a wave of guilt. "You've been so good to us Jack, you don't deserve any of this." She placed her hand over his.

"Deserve what Kate? Is it Joe? Is he hurt?" She could hear the emotion and panic building in his voice. He deserved an explanation but pride held her back from giving him the full picture, which included her lies.

"They think Joe is still in the car with Ryan and they're heading south on the A9." She held her breath before she said any more.

"But what made you drop the phone?"

Kate exhaled. "Ziggy suspects that Joe's dad is behind all this."

"Joe's dad? Why would he? Wait, is Ryan Joe's dad?" ventured Jack, something that he had suspected for a while.

"No, no he isn't. Joe's dad is called Darren, Daz. He's been serving time in prison in Leeds."

"Prison? What the hell for? Jack wasn't sure if he wanted to know the answer.

"Armed robbery," Kate admitted, tears streaming down her face. "And it's all my fault. He's been released early on parole and I had no idea."

Fiona sat and listened to Kate's words, not quite believing what she was hearing. Of course she knew about the court case and the volatile relationship between her sister and Daz but much of what she was hearing was news to her. She watched Kate closely, wondering what other secrets she was keeping.

F or Kate, all the missing pieces started to slot into place now that she had had time to digest the information. Of course Ryan had befriended her, and then some. It was so obvious to her now. She just knew that Daz had somehow convinced Ryan to abduct Joe and take his son back to him. Kate felt stupid, foolish, and naive. It had all been a big game to Ryan. He didn't care it was people's lives that he was playing with.

" I never trusted him," muttered Jack. He didn't know what to make of the info Kate had just told him, and now he knew the full story he didn't blame Kate for what she had done. She had acted to protect her son. She had needed to protect herself. Kate had done what he thought any woman would do in her situation. He was about to tell Kate this when her mobile started to ring again.

"**K**ate it's Ziggy. I have an update. It looks as though they're headed towards a service station which is where we believe the handover will happen. We have officers in place, and we'll ensure Joe's safe before we take any action. I've arranged for PC King and her colleague to bring you to us so you can be reunited with Joe once we know he's OK."

"Oh thank God. Thank you Ziggy. Please keep my boy safe or all this will have been for nothing." She hung up and relayed the message to Jack and Fiona.

"Do you want me to come with you?" Fiona was anxious to see Joe and know that he was unharmed.

"No, thank you Fiona. I know Joe means a lot to you but I think I'm better going on my own."

"Kate, I'm not sure what's going here but at least let Fiona go with you," pleaded Jack.

"Honestly, I'm fine and what could you do anyway?" Kate didn't want her sister with her when her world fell apart. She was already ashamed at how naive she had been and she couldn't bear to see that look of disappointment on her sister's face.

"Please Kate. Let me come with you, you need your family around you at a time like this. Stop pushing me away." Fiona was in tears, begging her sister to accept support just for once.

Feeling beaten, Kate relented and agreed that Fiona should go to the police station with her. She already accepted defeat and knew that Joe would need someone with him. As his aunt, it was only right that Fiona went with her.

Jack stood back and watched as the sisters clung to each other. He was no longer sure who was supporting who. His only concern was getting Joe back home, safe and sound.

45

PC King stepped precariously towards the beam of her colleague's flashlight. She was immediately hit with the foul smell that made her recoil and cover her mouth and nose.

"Is he...?"

Jones felt for a pulse in Len's neck. "Barely. We need an ambulance, and forensics."

"I've called it in, they should be here shortly."

Both officers took a quick visual scan of the area surrounding the wheelchair, noting the knocked over bottle of water and unopened energy bars.

"Looks like someone wanted to keep him alive," said Jones as his torch took a sweep of the debris lying next to the chair. His experienced eye travelled down the body, from Len's head that was slumped forward to his legs that were straight out in front of him, and the wound that Ryan had ineffectively tried to treat. It was once again weeping and oozing with yellow pus.

"That's what the smell is," he said, holding the light onto the open wound. Blowflies and maggots were having a feast on the fetid flesh.

King retched, well known for her weak stomach, she took a few steps back and inhaled deeply.

"What's happening?" came a voice from the other side of the barn door.

"Why don't you go and wait for the SOCOs and let Molly know we've found her dad?"

Relieved at being able to get away, she didn't need asking twice and made a hasty retreat into the fresh air. Crawling underneath the barn door, she got to her feet and shook her head to clear her senses, as well as gulping in the fresh air by the lungful. Molly was immediately at her side.

"Is he in there? Is he... is he alive?" She couldn't bring herself to utter her worst fears.

King pulled herself together. "Yes, yes he's in there and he's alive but only just. An ambulance is on its way."

Just as she finished her sentence blue flashing lights could be seen from the main road.

"Janice, can you direct them in please?"

Janice had been engrossed in every detail, remembering as much as she could so she could retell the story later. "Aye, aye, sure." She scurried away to wave the ambulance in.

"Molly, he's not in a good way and it seems he's been here a while. He has an open wound on his leg that needs attention and it looks as though he's dehydrated and in need of a good meal."

The two women stood to one side whilst the crew opened the doors and grabbed their response kits. Claire relayed the known information to them and watched as they made their way into the barn.

"Oh God, how could this have happened?" Molly was overwhelmed with guilt and horror.

"We'll get to the bottom of it, right now we need to get your dad to the hospital."

Janice rejoined them with mugs of sweet tea. "I thought you might need this." She passed a mug to Molly and the police officer took the chance to retrieve crime scene tape from the boot of the patrol car and cordon off the area surrounding them.

A s they stood surveying the scene, SOCO arrived. Wrightson, the Crime Scene Manager approached them.

"Evening Claire."

"Hey Wrighty, you been updated?"

Wrightson was already in full protective clothing and dropped his protective mask as he spoke. "Yeah, we had an update from Steve. Is he still inside?" He gestured towards the barn.

"Yeah, I think he's waiting with the victim. Responders are in there at the minute." Just as Claire finished speaking, Steve appeared underneath the barn door and straightened up. He acknowledged Wrightson and joined the others.

"Can you start with the barn door? We need to break it down to get Mr Albright out. If you could take a look at the padlock that's on there, might be some fingerprints."

Wrighty gave a short nod and motioned for the rest of his team to follow him. King guided Molly and Janice away from the scene so it could be secured without any further contamination. Molly was desperate for news of her dad.

"What's happening? How is he?" she asked.

"They'll be bringing him out shortly. He needs urgent treatment, they're doing as much as they can right now. Molly, the recent operation he had, was it on his legs?"

"Yes, yes that's what I've been trying to tell you. Ryan picked him up but no one has seen him since."

"OK, well..." He was interrupted with loud cracking noises as the SOCOs brutally wrenched the barn door, allowing the emergency response team to exit with Len strapped to a stretcher. Molly rushed forward.

"Dad...Oh Da, what has he done to you?" She reached forward but didn't know where or what to touch. The odour was overwhelming.

"If you could step back please, we need to get him in the ambulance." Between the two paramedics they manhandled the stretcher into the rear. They hadn't dared to undo the bindings that held much of Len in place. They'd been able to insert an IV line and cautiously tend to the infected wound but once they had him stabilised, with a more consistent and stronger pulse, the priority was getting him to the hospital.

"Can I come with you?" asked a distraught Molly.

"Yes, of course, just climb in the back here and take a seat to the side." Molly climbed in and did as she had been instructed. King's radio stuttered into life with her call sign.

"Receiving."

She listened to the message carefully and walked over to her colleague. "We need to take Kate to Stirling HQ. Looks like they've caught up with Ryan."

Happy that the scene was secure, PC Steve Jones handed the scene over to SOCOs, asking to be kept up to date with developments.

. . .

Janice looked woefully on as everyone left the scene. She had no intention of leaving while there was still a white tent and crime scene officers there!

Climbing into the patrol car, Claire looked over at Steve. "What the hell has been going on?"

"No idea. It's all a bit of a tangled web really but if this Ryan bloke is responsible for leaving his own father in that state, he needs catching."

"Sounds like Thornes is about to catch up with them, thank God. Do you know him?"

"Who? DI Thornes? Not really. I've seen him a few times but never really had anything to do with him. Seems he's well thought of though. Can't help but wonder what Kate did to get moved into witness protection though, she looks like butter wouldn't melt."

"Yeah, the whole thing's a bit strange, right?"

"Aye, it is that. So we've to take her to Stirling then?"

"Control said so, Thornes' orders."

"Great, another long night then." With that Jones started the car and pulled out of the car park, heading back towards Harbour Café.

46

The rain was lashing against the windscreen, and from her position in the back seat of the police car, Kate watched the rain sliding down the window on the outside. She traced some of the drops with her finger, wondering what lay ahead. Her main concern was that Joe was safe. She just wanted to collect him and return to their easy way of life, but in her gut she knew that wasn't going to happen. Too much had happened, and her darkest secret was nudging closer to the light.

Why hadn't she been told that Daz had been released? What would happen once the police spoke to him? And what would Ryan tell them? All of these thoughts whirled around her head and she felt physically sick.

After what felt like eternity, they pulled up outside Stirling police headquarters, and Kate was shown into the family room. She had just sat down when the door opened.

"Kate, hi." Ziggy stepped into the room and shook Kate's hand. "Didn't expect to see you again."

"No, me either. Where's Joe?" She had forgotten just how tall and imposing Ziggy was.

"He's fine, don't worry. He's sleeping in the next room."
Ziggy sat down opposite Kate. The family room was set up
to look like someone's living room, with sofas and soft
furnishings. There was a box of toys in the corner and a
bookcase sat on the wall behind Ziggy.

"When can I see him?" asked Kate.

"You can see him in a short while, I just need to ask you
a few questions first."

Kate felt the colour drain from her face. "Questions?
What about?"

"I'll get to that. Would you like a drink or anything to
eat?"

"No, no, I'm fine thank you. Can we just get this over
with?"

Ziggy moved around in his chair so that he was leaning
forward and placed a brown folder on the coffee table that
stood between them.

"So as you know, we've arrested Ryan, Darren and
Darren's cousin Sean. It has come to light that Darren was
paying Ryan to abduct Joe and take him back to Darren."
Ziggy was chancing his arm with that last statement. He'd
yet to interview any of the suspects.

Kate gulped. Although she felt that Daz was behind it,
hearing the words made it real and she couldn't believe he
had been so desperate to see his son, and hurt her.

"During the interviews with Darren, some new evidence
has come to light and I'm hoping you're able to help me
make sense of it all." Ziggy glanced up from his notes and
looked at Kate, who could barely sit still. She caught him
staring at her and she flushed bright red.

"OK," she ventured tentatively. She shrank back into the
lumpy sofa, trying to make herself as small as she could.

Ziggy sat back and crossed his legs. "I'd like to take you

back to the day you handed in the gun at the police station. Remind me again, how did you come across it?"

Kate paled and ran her hands through her hair but didn't reply. "My son Joe and his friend found it in the back garden of the house I shared with Darren in Leeds." She paused. "Wait, am I under arrest?"

Ziggy looked up from the notes he had been taking. "No, you're just helping with our enquiries at the minute, but it would help if you could answer my questions as honestly as possible."

Kate took a deep, shuddering breath and weighed up her options. Tell the truth and face the consequences or continue with her lie? Different scenarios ran through her head, none of them appealing. Eventually the emotions became too much to bear. "You don't understand. Daz was a bully, he made my life hell. I couldn't see any other way out." She was sobbing now, tears streaming down her face that she made no effort to stem. She had known this day would eventually come but she couldn't have imagined how wretched she would feel.

"Kate. Tell me what you know." Ziggy passed her a tissue.

"Can I see Joe?" She blew her nose.

"You need to tell me what you know Kate."

"Well this is a holy clusterfuck of a mess," exclaimed Ziggy Thornes, running his hands over his shaved head. He hadn't expected to hear from Kate again. When he had last seen her, he was handing her over to the CPS and the allocated safe house. He had passed her his number out of courtesy more than anything. He had felt sorry for her. She had escaped an abusive marriage in an effort to protect her son, and possibly save her own life. Ziggy had been the Senior Investigating Officer throughout the trial and sentencing. They had built up a bond over that time and even though he always advocated his officers against it, he'd found himself pulled in. Ziggy's son was the same age as Joe, and at the time Ziggy had been going through the break-up of his own marriage. He reasoned with himself that he had been vulnerable and his own emotions were high. He'd allowed himself that one slip in an otherwise exemplary career, and it hadn't happened since. When he heard Kate's voice that first time it had taken him right back to a time in his life that was full of drama.

P ushing the past to one side, he walked into an office that had been allocated to him; Stirling HQ being the nearest station to the motorway services where they had apprehended Ryan Albright, Darren Ward and his cousin Sean. Joe had been safely taken by a child protection officer and was currently sleeping on the sofa in the soft interview room. He sat behind the desk, and accessed his emails, looking for any updates whilst he waited for the interview room to be free. It was set to be a long night.

O ne of the duty officers knocked lightly on the door.
        "Yep?" called Ziggy.
    "Guv, all prisoners have been processed and are waiting to be questioned."
    "Thanks, I'll be down shortly."
    Ziggy had mobilised two of his senior officers to accom-

pany him to Stirling to help with the interviewing. He called for DC Harrison who was writing up notes at a nearby cubicle.

"Which do you want to do first?" Harrison asked as he entered the temporary office.

"Albright I reckon. Just had an update from Steve Jones. Albright's father was being kept hostage in a barn behind the pub that he was working at. Could be looking at a murder charge yet."

"Really? What the hell has gone on?"

"No idea. Albright has a record for petty crimes as long as my arm, but this isn't his usual style. He's been suspected previously of more serious stuff, but we've never been able to get enough evidence."

"Could be our chance now?"

"Oh yeah, though his dad is in a bad way he's already blamed his son for it. No such thing as family loyalty there."

"So how do you want to play it?"

"Let's see what he has to say for himself shall we?" Ziggy pushed his chair backwards, grabbed his notes and together they headed downstairs to the interview rooms.

"Interview room 2 is ready for you guv," said the Custody Sergeant.

Two uniformed PCs escorted Ryan from his cell into the interview room. Ziggy hit record after making the usual introductions and advising Ryan of his rights, and then started the interview.

"Are you comfortable there Ryan? Would you like a drink?" Ziggy started soft, aiming to build rapport.

"Nah, I'm good thanks." Ryan had his arms folded across his chest but other than that he looked completely unperturbed.

"OK, what can you tell me about the events that have taken place this evening Ryan?"

No response, much as Ziggy expected: it really was going to be a long night.

"Ryan, this is your chance to tell me your version of events. Whose idea was it to abduct Joe?"

No response. Ryan slumped further down in his plastic chair.

"Did Darren Ward put pressure on you?"

No reply.

"Do you owe him money?"

A snort escaped from Ryan. Ziggy jumped on the small involuntary tell. "Is that what this is about? You owe Darren money?"

"No, he fucking owes me money but that's not happening now is it?" Ryan crossed his legs under the table.

"So you did do this for money? He was going to pay for abducting his son?"

Ryan realised he'd dug a hole for himself. "No comment."

Ziggy inwardly sighed, dreading the no comment interview. It was the bane of his life and a reason he hated interviews.

"Yeah, this isn't TV Ryan. No comment will only get you so far."

Ryan looked up at Ziggy and smiled, "Whatever."

Ziggy decided to change tack. "Tell me about your dad."

Ryan's head snapped up and he readjusted his position. "What about him?"

"When was the last time you saw him?"

"Dunno."

Ryan looked distinctly uncomfortable.

"Isn't that why you've been up in the Highlands? To look after his pub?"

Ryan knew he had to be careful how he answered now. If he admitted he was there to take over the pub then he would have to admit to seeing his dad recently. "No comment." It was the easiest route he figured.

"Ryan, this is your chance to tell me what you know."

"I don't know anything."

"I think you do. I think you've set out on a path that seemed relatively easy money and you've ended up digging a massive hole for yourself. I don't think you meant for circumstances to go so far and you've lost control. Am I close?"

'Are you close? Fucking spot on mate,' thought Ryan but he chose not to answer.

Ziggy decided to let him stew and ended the interview. Hopefully when they next spoke they would have more forensics and Ryan wouldn't have any excuses.

47

Z iggy walked out of the interview room and kicked the wall, immediately regretting it as he stubbed his big toe. He swore out loud just as a young PC was passing. He apologised and headed for his makeshift office. How could he have been so stupid? But he had no time to dwell on his own failings as he prepared to interview Darren Ward. He watched closely as Darren was led from his holding cell to the interview room. He was running out of time and patience, and he certainly wasn't in the mood to build rapport. It was late, he was knackered and just wanted to wrap this up as soon as.

Darren was brought in and seated in the chair that Ryan had just vacated. Once again Ziggy went through the set-up procedure and read Darren his rights.

"How much money did you offer Ryan to abduct Joe?"

"What? Is that what he said?"

"You've just been released Darren, what were you thinking?"

"I should never have been sent down in the first place and you know it."

"Oh really? Why's that then?"

"Oh come on. Don't pretend you don't know. That gun wasn't mine. I had nothing to do with that robbery. It was all bullshit made up by *her* to take my son from me."

Before leaving the station at Leeds, Ziggy had asked for the case file on Darren's conviction. Despite Darren's not guilty plea, it was Kate's testimony along with the t-shirt that had convicted Daz. Ziggy had asked for forensics to test the gun again for fingerprints and was waiting on the results.

"That bitch took my son and I wanted him back. Ryan fucked up. He had one job and he fucked it up." Daz kicked the underneath of the formica table, sending pens, cups and notes flying.

Ziggy was taken aback with the vitriol in Darren's tone, and his sudden lashing out. It was easy to see why Kate needed to get away. He collected his notes and calmly addressed Darren. "So you don't deny paying Ryan to plot and abduct your son?"

"Not much point is there?"

"Not really to be honest. Tell me," said Ziggy, changing tack. "What do you know about Len Albright?"

"Who?"

"Len Albright, father of Ryan Albright?"

"Not a clue mate, never met him."

"So you weren't involved in the kidnap then?"

Daz laughed. "Useless piece of shit, he's really done it this time."

Ziggy sighed inwardly. He was certain that Darren had nothing to do with the disappearance of Len but he had to ask the question. Getting back to the main point, Ziggy started his questioning again. "So who came up with the idea to take Joe?"

Darren looked at Ziggy. What was the point in holding

back now? He knew they had Ryan and Sean in custody and it wouldn't be long until one of them gave up the information, if they hadn't already. "Ryan."

"Really? How did he contact you?"

"He was on my allowed calls list."

Ziggy rolled his eyes. Every number was supposed to be closely vetted before being added. He wondered how it had slipped through the net. "And what? He just contacted you out of the blue one day and came up with the grand plan?"

Darren reached for his cup of tepid tea. "Yeah, something like that."

Ziggy didn't believe him. "I'm not sure Ryan's clever enough to be honest. So you had no input into the plan?"

"Oh yeah." Darren pushed his tea away in disgust and stretched his legs out, pushing himself back in his chair. "But he was the one who started it all."

"How so?" asked Ziggy.

"Told me one day that he'd happened across Kate in Scotland, where his dad lives. Pure coincidence by all accounts. Apparently he'd gone back to his dad's pub for some reason."

"Bit of a huge coincidence don't you think?"

"That's what I thought but you could see it as fate as well." Darren placed his hands behind his head, grinning.

Ziggy looked on, taking in Darren's very casual approach to what would likely result in another five years inside at least. "I must say, you seem to be taking this all very well considering you're looking at another spell inside," he observed.

"Is what it is, isn't it?" came the reply.

Ziggy couldn't help but think that Darren was holding something back. What more did he know? What was Ziggy missing? "So Ryan contacted you, and you came up with the plan between you?"

"Yep, that's pretty much it."

"I can't help but think I'm missing something Darren. You seem to be too willing to confess. What am I missing?"

"Ha, that's rich. You're the detective, you tell me."

The heavy atmosphere was broken with a knock on the door. "Message for you guv," relayed the PC who poked his head around the door.

Ziggy pushed himself up from his seat, suspended the interview and left the room. "What is it?"

Harrison was waiting for him in the corridor. "Forensics are in for the gun."

The two detectives made their way into Ziggy's office where he opened the email and reviewed the contents. "Shit."

"What now?" asked Harrison.

"Take Darren Ward back to his cell. I need another chat with Kate. Under caution this time."

Z iggy had left Kate in the family room, where she was joined by Fiona. The two sisters had barely spoken a word, despite Fiona having so many questions. All she had been able to get out of Kate was that everything had been her fault. Fiona had spent most of time holding her sister and passing tissues. She felt like an outsider and didn't have a clue what was going on. She had been allowed to see Joe but he was, thankfully, fast asleep unaware of the chaos unfolding around him. Ziggy entered the room and acknowledged Fiona with a nod of the head before addressing Kate. "Kate, can you come with me please?"

Kate stood and rubbed her hands on the front of her jeans. She turned to look at Fiona. "I'm sorry," she said. She reached out for Fiona's hand. "Will you look after Joe for me please?"

"Of course, but what's going on?"

Ziggy led Kate away, leaving Fiona confused and frightened for her sister.

Once settled in the interview room, Ziggy realised that he could no longer pussyfoot around Kate. It didn't matter what kind of bond or rapport they'd developed in the past. Kate was in serious trouble and he had to get to the truth.

"Kate, as you're aware Darren Ward and Ryan Albright have been arrested and charged with abduction, namely of your son Joe."

Kate looked at Ziggy and fidgeted in her chair. His tone was completely different and it terrified her. Was he waiting for an answer? She was just about to speak when he spoke again.

"Kate. I want to take you back to the time when you handed the handgun into the police station. Do you remember that night?"

"Yes. We've already talked about it and I told you what happened." Kate ran her hands through her hair, she was shaking.

"That's right, and I'd just like to go through in a lot more detail exactly what happened that day."

"Why? I've already told you everything and Daz was charged so what's the point?"

"Well, that's what I want to discuss. Your now ex-husband,

Darren Ward, was arrested and charged with armed robbery on the strength of your testimony and the evidence presented at the time." Ziggy paused and rearranged his paperwork. He allowed the silence to fill the room. "Do you have anything you would like to say to that?" He met Kate's eye, and instead of the usual glint of stubborn determination he saw a scared young woman whose life was about to change irrevocably. He sat back and waited for her to answer. When she didn't he continued, "Kate, I have here the statement you gave earlier today regarding the handgun and how you found it." He consulted the piece of paper in front of him. "Earlier you said that Joe and his friend found the gun in the back garden of the house you shared with Darren Ward, and as it was wrapped in Darren's t-shirt you assumed it was his?"

Kate gulped. "Yes, that's right." She could barely get the words out.

"And that you remembered seeing Darren with the gun in the past and that you were convinced it belonged to him?"

Kate nodded. Her throat seemed to have closed over.

"So you handed it in to the police?"

Where was this going? She thought.

"Kate. I don't believe you."

There, he'd said it but she was in too deep now to claw her way out. "Why not?" she mumbled.

"We've had the gun re-tested for fingerprints. Forensics have come a long way in the last few years Kate."

Kate felt cornered but she let him carry on.

"Further examination has found another set of finger-prints on the gun. Those of Ryan Albright."

Kate felt herself crumbling from the inside, out. She hung her head and let the tears fall.

"Did you know Kate? Did you know that the gun belonged to Ryan?"

No answer. Just the sound of a sobbing woman filled the room.

"I believe you did. Here's what I think happened. We know from Ryan that you and he were having some kind of relationship. We also know that on the day you brought the gun to the police station Ryan Albright moved out of the area after visiting you and your then husband."

Kate looked up, sniffed, and asked for a tissue. Ziggy's colleague left the room momentarily to grab a box from the office. In the silence Kate continued to sob but appeared to be more in control. Ziggy waited for his colleague to return and for Kate to blow her nose and wipe her face.

"Kate, it's time to tell your side of the story." Ziggy leaned across the table, his voice softening as he spoke. "Come on Kate, if not for your sake then for Joe. Tell me the truth."

At the mention of Joe, Kate closed her eyes and took a deep breath. Her head was buzzing. It was late. She was tired and had a headache. She had to admit defeat.

"Yeah, I knew. I didn't know he'd used it in a robbery but I did know it belonged to Ryan."

'At last,' thought Ziggy. "Now we're getting somewhere. Carry on."

Resigned, Kate continued. "He called by the house one day and asked me to hide it for him. I refused but as he forced the gun on me, Daz came home and I bundled it into one of his t-shirts. I was outside hanging the washing out. When I went back into the kitchen Ryan had gone. I found out later that he'd left Leeds."

"Why did you hide the gun? Why didn't you just tell Darren what he'd done?"

Kate snorted. "Are you kidding? You've seen Daz's temper, what do you think he would have done?"

Ziggy recalled how Darren had reacted violently in his interview. He knew Kate and Darren had a troubled relationship, it was the whole reason for putting her into witness protection.

Kate continued, "I was scared that if Darren had a gun, with his temper it wouldn't be long before he took it out on me or even worse, on Joe. I used it to get us away from him."

"So you lied?"

"It wasn't like that I swear."

"So what was it like?"

"I wasn't thinking straight. Daz had already kicked off when Ryan turned up at the house." She paused and took a sip of water to combat the dryness of her mouth. "I wasn't thinking straight. I tried to tell you I'd made a mistake, but it was too late."

"Kate, you went through the whole court case and never said a word."

Kate didn't have an answer as the tears, fear, and anxiety engulfed her body.

Ziggy had had enough. He stood up. "Take her to a cell."

48

K ate sat on the hard bench that passed for a bed with her arms wrapped around her legs, head resting on her knees. She felt utterly bereft. All she had ever tried to do was keep Joe safe and she had failed him spectacularly. She sobbed quietly and didn't dare to think about her future.

The lock on the outside of the cell door rattled and she lifted her head. Ziggy stood there, and she felt a tremendous amount of guilt for having lied to someone who had taken herself and Joe under his wing in the early days. She'd let everyone down.

"How are you holding up?" he asked as he entered the small, claustrophobic room. He sat on the bench beside her. She wiped her nose on her shirt sleeve.

"How do you think?" she asked, sniffing. "I'm sorry..."

Ziggy cut in, "Save it Kate, I don't want to hear it." His words sliced right through her. "I'm here to tell you that you'll be taken to Leeds tomorrow and formally charged."

She nodded, resigned to her fate. "Can I see Joe?"

"Yes, I'll arrange for you to see him for a few minutes.

Your sister's still here, and she has said she'll take care of him. I'm guessing that's OK with you?"

"Yes, yes of course. What's happening with Darren and Ryan?"

"They're already on their way to Leeds to appear in court tomorrow, charged with kidnapping."

Kate looked up at Ziggy. "I really am sorry Ziggy, you were so good to us."

"Yeah well. You know you're facing a custodial sentence Kate don't you?"

"I figured as much."

He left Kate to her thoughts and headed to the canteen. He felt so let down. It was rare that his gut instinct was wrong and it would take some reconciliation with himself to come to terms with that. He took his coffee and a muffin over to a table and sat quietly, lost in his own thoughts. He felt a tap on his shoulder and turned round. The two PCs from Gairloch were hovering in the background.

"How's everything?" asked Claire.

"Yeah, bit of a mess really. Sorry, I didn't realise you were still here."

"We thought we'd hang around to see if anyone needed taking back."

"Ah OK. Let me check with Kate's sister, I'm not sure what her plans are."

The two PCs left and Ziggy looked regretfully at his muffin, he wasn't much in the mood for eating anyway.

· · ·

Back downstairs in the family room, Fiona sat alone not knowing what she should do or where she should be. She'd tried to phone their parents but it went to voicemail which wasn't surprising considering the time. She'd checked on Joe a couple of times but he remained fast asleep. She was just about to go looking for someone when Ziggy stepped into the room.

"Sorry I haven't been able to update you Fiona. Can I get you a drink?"

Fiona sat back down and asked the accompanying PC for a coffee. Once settled, Ziggy sat opposite and brought Fiona up to date with what was happening.

"So Kate could be looking at time in prison?" exclaimed Fiona. She never expected that would be the outcome.

"Unfortunately she lied under oath, that's perjury and it's taken extremely seriously by the justice system. If you want to help her then you need to find her a damn good lawyer."

Fiona's head was spinning. "Oh my God, I can't believe this is actually happening."

Ziggy gave Fiona a few minutes to gather her thoughts. "You need to consider Joe as well."

Fiona's head snapped up. "What do you mean?"

"He'll need someone to look after him, and with both parents likely to be in prison the courts will allocate a legal guardian or place him in foster care."

"Of course he'll come with me, there's no question."

"Then when you speak to a solicitor you need to advise him of that too."

It was all too much for Fiona to take in. She was determined not to cry; Kate had done enough crying for both of them. She had to get practical and organised. "Can I see Kate?"

"Just for a few minutes. Do you want to wake Joe so she can see him too?"

Ziggy instructed the custody officer not to handcuff Kate as she was led from her cell to the family room. He figured it be would hard enough for Kate and Joe as it was. He opened the door and Fiona rushed forward and threw her arms around her sister. The two stood there sobbing on each other's shoulders until they felt a tap on their legs. Joe stood with his tired eyes wide, staring at his aunt and mum.

Kate crouched down. "Hey sunshine, are you ok?" She stroked his ruffled hair and wiped sleep from the corner of his eyes. He looked confused and on the verge of tears.

"What's happening mum? Where's dad gone?"

"Oh baby, it's all a bit much to explain right now, and I don't have much time."

Fiona took a hold of his hand. "You're to stay with me for a little while. Is that OK?"

Joe looked up at his aunty. "I guess so. Are you coming too mum?"

Kate felt her heart shatter into a million pieces. "Not just yet sweetheart but I will, soon –- I promise."

Ziggy left the room, leaving the custody sergeant with them. It was heartbreaking to watch and it was at times like that he had to remind himself he was a police officer with a job to do, no matter how difficult. He gave them more time than he should have, mostly for Joe's benefit before he went back into the room.

"Time to go Kate."

The three of them were seated on the sofa, Joe sat on Kate's knee even though he was far too big. She held him tight and gave him a last kiss.

"Erm, does anyone need taking back to Gairloch? The local PCs are waiting," asked Ziggy.

Fiona looked up. This was actually happening then. She had to leave her sister whilst she took her nephew to his home. She felt as though she had entered some kind of parallel universe. She looked over at Kate but couldn't find the words to say goodbye.

As if sensing her sister's difficulty in speaking, Kate spoke first. "Right you two," she said with fake positivity. "You need to get yourselves off and let Jack know what's going on." She stood and straightened her back, trying to summon a strength she didn't feel. "Come on Joe, put your coat on." She helped him into his coat and fastened his shoelaces for him, even though he protested that he could do it himself. A few more minutes passed, with Fiona and Kate hugging each other and promises from Fiona that she would sort everything out until they could no longer delay the goodbyes.

ate watched as her sister and son walked away from her and towards the exit. Her life was over.

49

G airloch Spring 2001

K ate looked out of the coach window at the unfolding scenery. She'd missed the rolling hills and vast open lochs. After spending six months in custody she feared she would never see wide open spaces again. When the train had reached Inverness and she disembarked she had inhaled deeply, swearing that the air was fresher the further north she travelled. She was nervous, and the butterflies in her tummy could easily have been mistaken for fear and not the excitement that they actually meant. It had been hard, harder than anything she had ever done in her life but on her release she realised that she felt a weight lifted. She no longer had to look over her shoulder or hide her past. She felt a sense of freedom and finally whole but with just one vital piece missing: Joe. As the coach entered Gairloch, passing the golf course and heading round the bay, she held her breath. She knew that around the next corner she would see the harbour, an image that she had maintained in her head during her time away. It had helped her escape the confines of her cell and lulled her to sleep on most restless nights. Then there it was, Gairloch Harbour. She grabbed the backpack that was on the seat next to her and stood up, walking to the front of the bus, waiting for the driver to stop. Lifting her bag onto her shoulder, she climbed down the steps and stepped onto the pavement. There was no party to greet her, she hadn't let anyone know she was on her way. She was ashamed of her previous actions, and though Jack had been to visit her in prison it had been awkward and uncomfortable for them both. She knew Fiona was visiting for the Easter holidays, she'd offered to pick Kate up on her release date but Kate had put her off. She needed to do something for herself after months of being told when to sleep, when to eat, when to exercise.

A s she walked past the post office she spotted a familiar face walking towards her, and her anxiety levels shot up.

"Kate!" exclaimed Mr Wheeler. "Why isn't that a lovely surprise. I had no idea."

Kate laughed nervously as Mr Wheeler gave her a hug. "Thank you. How are you?"

"Never mind me lassie. How are you?"

"Not bad, thanks. You're the first person I've seen." Her hands were shaking, and her voice wobbled.

"You mean no one knows you're here?"

"No, I've literally just arrived."

"Well then, isn't this a cause for celebration. Come on." Mr Wheeler turned and walked alongside her as she headed towards Harbour Café. He held the door open as Kate stepped inside. Everyone looked up and a hush descended. Jack poked his head from the rear of the kitchen to see why it had suddenly gone quiet. A few seconds later there were cheers and Kate was surrounded with friends who were shaking her hand and welcoming her with open arms. Jack stepped forward and wrapped Kate in a bear hug until she had to beg him to let go.

"Why didn't you tell us you were coming?" chided Jack, pulling up a chair so that Kate could sit down.

She felt a little overwhelmed but took it all in her stride. "I wanted it to be a surprise." She unfastened her coat and pulled off her hat.

"Well it's that alright," commented Gill, pushing a cup of tea and a slice of cake in front of Kate. Gill was grinning from ear to ear.

The little bell above the café door tinkled and Kate turned to see who it was. Fiona came into the cafe, with Joe at her side.

"MUM!" shouted Joe, who pushed everyone to one side and threw himself at his mum. He'd only visited Kate twice while she was inside and she could see that he was uneasy on each visit so she asked Fiona not to bring him anymore. They had written to each other and had regular phone calls which had helped to sustain them both.

"Why didn't you tell me?" He refused to let go of her, as if she might slip away again.

"I wanted it to be a surprise." Tears were streaming down Kate's face and her heart felt so full of love and gratitude she thought she might burst with happiness.

Fiona stood back and watched as Joe and the regulars of

Harbour Café welcomed Kate and hurled questions at her. She could see that Kate was getting overwhelmed so she decided to step in.

She clapped her hands together and raised her voice. "Come on now, give Kate a chance to catch her breath." Everyone laughed and slowly went back to their tables.

"Come on you," said Fiona. "Let's go upstairs." Kate followed Fiona to the flat upstairs. As soon as the door opened, Kate felt completely at home. Fiona had been a frequent visitor, determined for Joe to keep contact with Jack and his own friends in Gairloch. They entered the kitchen and gathered around the worktop, all talking over each other.

"So Len's back behind the bar then?" asked Kate.

"Yep, he's doing well. Not back full time but Janice is pulling her weight and Molly does some of the weekends so he's on the mend, but it will take a while."

Jack wanted to broach the subject of Ryan, but Fiona jumped in before he had chance.

"Ryan had another year added to his sentence last week."

"Why?" asked Jack.

"He attacked a prison guard."

"What an evil..." He stopped just short of swearing in front of Joe.

Fiona had explained everything to Joe, and though he was young he had shown a level of understanding and seemed to take it all in his stride. He had readjusted to life in Leeds, knowing it was temporary and their frequent trips back to Gairloch had helped. Now Kate was home it was decision time for Fiona. She was torn between staying in Leeds or relocating to Scotland. That was a decision for another day, she thought.

Kate leant back against the worktop and looked at the people she had around her. There was a new lightness to her heart that she couldn't remember feeling before, and she fleetingly wondered what it was before the answer came to her from nowhere – she was finally home.

ENJOYED THE LIE SHE TOLD?

Please consider leaving a review on Goodreads, Amazon
or contact the author directly.
cat@catherineyaffe.co.uk

READ ON FOR EXCLUSIVE EXTRACTS FROM
THE WEB THEY WOVE
(Book 2 in the Tangled Web series)

ACKNOWLEDGMENTS

Thank you goes first of all to you, the reader. Thank you for selecting this book, and if you enjoyed Kate's story please do consider leaving a review as these are hugely important to any author. If you've enjoyed The Lie She Told then please tell all your friends!

Thank you to my wonderful, supportive husband Mark for putting up with me as I went through several versions until I felt it was just right.

Thank you to my amazing son Daniel who has always been my biggest cheerleader.

Love you sunshine.

Of course, this book would not be possible without a whole host of experts; former Met DCI Steve Gaskin (The Crime Lab), Shaun Wrightson, Adam Lloyd and the fantastic team over at UK True Crime Podcast. Bridget Braund for being an amazing proof reader (any mistakes are all my own!) and Dr Stephanie Carty (@tiredpsych) for helping me with character development.

Finally, to my parents for their limitless love and support.

September 2021

A whole year has passed since The Lie She Told was released and I am still blown away by the reviews and feedback I get for my 'first born'. Thank you so much for helping me to celebrate this one year anniversary, and keep an eye for more books in the Tangled Web Series!

Cat x

THE WEB THEY WOVE

FOLLOW ON FROM THE THRILLING FIRST BOOK IN THE TANGLED WEB SERIES

NOT ALL KILLERS

ARE WHO THEY FIRST SEEM...

The mutilated body of a young female is found in a popular recreation ground in Leeds City Centre. D I Andrew 'Ziggy' Thornes and his team are at once assigned to close the case as soon as possible.

With little to no forensic evidence left at the scene, Ziggy struggles to pull the strands of the case together. When a second boy turns up in the same place, under the pressure from higher up and increased scrutiny from the media, Ziggy must drive the case to a rapid conclusion as fear spreads through the city.

Realising that the victims have been held captive prior to their gruesome deaths, Ziggy delves deeper and relentlessly chases down every lead.

When the investigation leads him dangerously close to home, will time run out before the tangled web of evil destroys everything he holds dear?

Available on Amazon mybook.to/thewebtheywove

PRAISE FOR THE WEB THEY WOVE

"As always, Catherine Yaffe has crafted a thriller/police procedural that grabs you and won't let go! These characters get under your skin and you can't help but keep reading even though you should be doing other things. The pacing is tight, the twists keep you off-balance and the ending is near stopping. Pick up this book and be prepared to immerse yourself in the story! Brava Cat!"

"Loved it! The main characters are believable and the plot kept me guessing, but the clues are there if you spot them. This is the second book I've read by this author and am really looking forward to reading more. I'd love a Ziggy series! Highly recommend, it's a page turner that's so easy to read - great for holidays."

"This is a brilliant read.
Wonderful well written plot and story line that had me engaged from the start. Love the well fleshed out characters and found them believable. Great suspense and action with

wonderful world building. Can't wait to read what the author brings out next. Recommend reading."

READ ON FOR A PREVIEW OF THE FIRST 2 CHAPTERS OF THE SECOND BOOK IN THE 'TANGLED WEB SERIES'.

Not All Killers
Are Who They First Seem . . .

CATHERINE
YAFFE

THE
WEB
THEY
WOVE

PROLOGUE

June 2002

The heel of her shoe snapped as he dragged her along the stony path. She struggled, trying desperately to free herself from his grasp, reaching up and hitting the hands that yanked her along by her ponytail. Her shoes finally lost their grip and slipped from her feet. She could feel the small, sharp flints from the path slashing at her heels. Her feet tried to gain purchase, but there was little hope. The little black dress she was wearing had risen up around her thighs, exposing her bare legs to the cold night air.

She had resorted to holding onto her scalp with her hands to try to alleviate the pressure as she begged him to let go of her hair, every tug screaming at the roots. She shouted and yelled, trying to make as much noise as possible, hoping to attract attention, but the wind blew the screams back into her mouth, trapping them in her throat.

With a jolt, he released her and forcibly pushed her flat onto her back, the damp, uneven ground soaking into her dress. The stones pushed sharply against the fabric, breaking through and embedding into her flesh as his weight bore down on her.

He shifted, straddled her chest, and slipped a silk scarf around her neck.

'Please, no... Don't...' She gasped as she fought for her life.

He laughed, a cruel, hollow sound, and looked down at her prone body beneath him. Crossing the scarf, he pulled tight on either end. She looked directly into his eyes, silently pleading for him to release her whilst twisting her head from side to side, but this only made breathing harder.

She stopped thrashing and lay still, tears running down the side of her face, diluting the mascara she had so carefully applied earlier in the evening. Multicoloured dots and stars appeared in her peripheral vision, then blackness enveloped her.

Smiling, he watched the rise and fall of her chest as it rose, fell and stopped. He pulled himself upwards and gently wrapped the scarf around his gloved hand. He lifted it to his nose and inhaled, pleased that the faint smell of her perfume still lingered: Estée Lauder Youth Dew. For a moment, he was transported to a different time and place; a place he'd fought hard against, but one that had ultimately consumed him.

He liked it when they fought back. The feisty ones were always the most satisfying. When their bodies were still, screams silenced, and the life leached out of them, he felt at his most powerful.

It had been many years since his last one; she had fought hard too.

Despite the lapsed time, he was pleased to find that he

still felt satisfied. Yes, he thought as he sat back on his haunches. It had been a good experience, a good way to start.

He'd raise the ante next time. Because there would definitely be a next time, of that he was certain.

SATURDAY 1 JUNE 2002

DI Andrew 'Ziggy' Thornes took a deep breath as he stood behind the armed officers as they prepared to break down the door. Following a countdown, the door crashed open and Ziggy stood to one side while the premises were searched by Armed Response. Pretty soon, five of the gang members were led out in cuffs to the waiting police vans.

The search teams followed them in, and after donning a Tyvek crime scene suit, Ziggy, along with his deputy DS Sadie Bates, took a look around. A violent gang had been plaguing the city of Leeds for weeks now, committing raids on jewellery shops, and Ziggy and his team had been on the case, trying to catch those responsible. The covert team had had the ringleaders under surveillance, and it was finally time to see what their hiding place had to offer.

'Regular treasure trove isn't it?' commented Sadie as they moved from room to room.

'Isn't it just? And we haven't even been upstairs yet.'

The hiding place was a mid-terrace house in Harehills, Leeds. From the outside, you wouldn't know that a violent gang operated from there; washing was hanging on the line, garden bins were lined up neatly against the wall in the tidy back yard and net curtains framed each window. Hidden in every possible space was over one million pounds' worth of jewels that would take forensics days to seize and store.

Once they'd ensured the crime scene had been secured, Ziggy handed over to the crime scene manager and headed back to West Yorkshire Police's Leeds HQ to brief his team.

DS Nick Wilkinson, DC Angela Dove and DS Sadie Bates had worked together for the last five years. During that time, they had developed an almost intuitive way of working that saw them with the highest arrest and conviction rates of the region, and as their senior officer, Ziggy was proud of every one of them. They each had their strengths, and they were utilised to the full.

Sadie was massively ambitious, and Ziggy knew that she wasn't destined to stay in his team forever. She was due to take the next step in her career within the next twelve months and he had done everything he could to support and promote her, even though he'd be sad to see her go. She acted as his deputy on all major cases, and her unfailing enthusiasm spurred everyone along when the going got tough.

Nick was the warhorse of the team; diligent, laid-back and very rarely phased by anything. He'd reached the rank of detective sergeant with ease but was happy to stay there until he retired. Somewhat older than the rest of the team, Nick – or 'Wilko' as he was affectionately referred to – remembered a time when policing had been done using good old fashioned shoe leather rather than fingers on keyboards.

In complete contrast, Angela, the youngest and most recent member of the team, was a whizz with anything technical and was also the most organised of them all. She thrived in her role as office manager and organised anything from the incident room where she played a vital role in co ordinating all the information that an enquiry generated to team birthdays; Angela could turn her quick, analytical brain to any task. She worked speedily and efficiently, though Ziggy often suspected she had a tendency to like things a little too perfect.

His team complemented each other well, and Ziggy was there to bridge all their abilities, having spent time working for Missing Persons, Child Sexual Exploitation and the drugs squad over his twenty-five years in the force. He liked variety, but he had found his feet with the Major Investigations team as detective inspector.

Pulling into the car park, Ziggy reversed into a parking space and he and Sadie exited the car. The building was new by policing standards. It had been purpose built and was equipped with all the latest technology. The Major Investigation Department was located on the top floor of the building in a large, open plan office. It was filled with workstations, separated off by low partitions, and when they were in the throes of an investigation, the noise levels were tremendous.

Ziggy's team were located in the far corner, near the windows that looked out on the city of Leeds. His own, rarely used office was situated at the back. He preferred to be out, in amongst everyone else. He enjoyed the buzz and thrived off the energy that an investigation invariably generated.

He did have his foibles, though. As a very visual person, Ziggy needed to see the progress of an investigation. Whiteboards were fine, but Ziggy also had flip charts around the room where he could work things out on paper. His mind maps were legendary and had proved useful on more than one occasion; tiny details that at the time made no sense were meticulously noted down and left visible for everyone to see, for the dots to be later joined and the resolution of cases achieved.

Making his way to their corner of the floor, Ziggy watched as Angela took down the various images and sheets of paper that had been Blu-Tacked to the walls for the jewellery robbery case. Everything would be filed away as they built the case for presentation to the CPS and, further down the line, in court.

As they walked across the office, Ziggy headed to check his emails and DS Sadie Bates headed for her own desk. 'After that success, lunch on you, right?'

Ziggy laughed. 'Sure, fish and chips all round. Sound good?'

'Hell yeah. Wait until I tell Wilko – he'll be beside himself.'

Ziggy grinned and shook his head as Sadie walked away. He felt his phone vibrate in his trouser pocket and pulled it out to look at the screen; it was the control room.

'DI Thornes,' he answered.

'Sir, a body has been found on Woodhouse Moor, near the university. Scene of crime officers are on their way, and I've been asked to assign you as deputy senior investigating officer by DCS Whitmore.'

Ziggy immediately felt his adrenaline pumping. 'OK, send me the details and we'll head over there now. Who's on the scene already?'

'Uniform, they were alerted by a bunch of kids. They've set up the cordon and started the log. As I said, SOCOs have also been informed.'

Ziggy ended the call and walked into the incident room.

Everyone had packed up their desks and were waiting for Ziggy to join them for lunch.

'Lunch is cancelled, I'm sorry to say. Just in, body found on Woodhouse Moor.'

The whole team stopped chatting and started removing their coats and replacing their bags on the floor.

'What do we know?' asked Sadie, walking forward, raring to go as always.

'Not much, call was from Control.' Ziggy stood, shaking the creases out of his carefully pressed trousers.

Sadie pulled her jacket from the back of her chair. 'Let's head over there. Nick, we'll give you a call once we know more.'

'Sure thing,' said Nick, logging back into his computer.

Angela stood up and walked to the whiteboard, setting it up for the information that would be coming their way.

Sadie drove the unmarked pool car through the back streets of Leeds. Ziggy had lived in the city for twenty years and still didn't know all the shortcuts. Sadie was a risky driver at the best of times, and even with the blue light flashing on the dashboard, she honked every car out of her way.

'Calm down, the body isn't going anywhere,' said Ziggy as he gripped the overhead handle.

'Sorry,' she said, clearly not meaning it.

Ten minutes later, Sadie dumped the car at the side of the road, and they made their way over to the edge of the green expanse.

Woodhouse Moor was a large recreation ground right in the heart of the university district, surrounded by a plethora of take away shops. Popular with locals and students, it was notorious for large social gatherings in the summer months, but more nefarious activities when the nights drew in. The weather recently had been typical of the British summer; scorching hot one day, then November-like winds and unusually low temperatures the next. That day, the weather had settled on 'quite pleasant'. Well, it wasn't raining, at least.

Ziggy and Sadie made their way onto the grass and ducked under the outer cordon. They signed the log and followed the designated approach path. The white forensic tent had already been erected, protecting the body from prying eyes. Once they were fully clothed in protective suits, they entered the tent and edged closer until a hand was frantically waved towards them, stopping them in their tracks.

'Careful! And move – you're blocking my light,' cried a woman dressed in a forensics suit without looking at them. Dr Leila Turner, or Lolly as she was more widely known, was somewhat unconventional but the best pathologist that West Yorkshire Police had at their disposal, and it didn't hurt that she'd been best friends with Ziggy since childhood. Not that it improved her manners at all, either way.

'Oops, sorry.' Ziggy stepped over to the right. 'Good to see you, Lolly. Drew the short straw, did you?'

Lolly looked up from her kneeling position. 'I was in the area when the shout came in. Couldn't resist.' She grinned. A quirk of the job; not many people in Ziggy's life would be thrilled to receive a call about a body being discovered.

As Lolly continued with her careful examination process, Ziggy and Sadie took in the scene in front of them. The body of a young female was laid flat on her back, and for all the world, it looked as though she was sleeping – if you discounted the blueish tinge to her lips. No matter how many times they were confronted with a dead body, the sight never got easier to digest.

'What can you tell us?' asked Ziggy, pulling his face mask away from his lips as he spoke.

'Looks like asphyxiation. See the marks here' – Lolly pointed a nitrile gloved hand towards the throat of the victim where there was considerable bruising around the neck – 'which also fits with the petechial haemorrhaging around the eyes.' Lolly shone her pen torch so they could get a better look.

'How long do you think she's been here?' asked Sadie, itching her head. The nylon suit created a scratching noise that made Ziggy's toes curl.

'Overnight, definitely. Full rigor mortis and distinct lividity to the underside of the body. Plus, there's mottling on her legs, which would fit with the temperature change overnight.' Lolly stood up. 'Take a look at her feet.'

Ziggy and Sadie moved down the body as directed and bent to look at the soles of the feet. They were shredded with tiny stones embedded. Lolly joined them and lifted the left foot in her gloved hand.

'Looking at the heels, it would seem she has been dragged along the path.'

So where are her shoes? Ziggy wondered as he leaned in closer and saw the dried blood on the bottom of the foot and around the Achilles heel. 'Ouch, whilst she was still alive by the looks of it.'

'Yep. And it's the same on the backs of her legs, and I suspect on her back as well.'

Ziggy stood up. 'When will you get to the post-mortem?'

'Later today, just need to finish up here.'

'OK, we'll see you there later.' The officers said their goodbyes and left the tent. Ziggy and Sadie headed to the crime scene manager, who was busy outlining the scene to his team and adjusting the outer cordon. The SOCOs had already started work, on their hands and knees at the far edge of clearing where the body had been found, carefully searching the tarmacked area. A yellow marker had been placed at the side of a black, high-heeled shoe, minus the heel.

'Any ID found?' asked Ziggy. 'Any sign of the heel to that shoe?' He pointed towards it as he spoke.

'No ID, and that's all we've found of her shoes so far. No bag or coat or anything on the victim either. We've just extended the search perimeter based on information from Dr Turner, so we might find a student ID card or bus pass or something.'

'Right, OK.' Ziggy looked around for Sadie, but she had wandered off to speak to the first attending officer. He walked over to join her.

'Have you spoken to the witnesses?' Ziggy asked the young police constable who'd been first on the scene.

'Yes, I've moved them over to the bench just there. A group of skateboarders trying tricks on the handrails came across her. They called it in from their mobiles. I think their average age is around twelve.'

Ziggy took the information on board and glanced at the youths who were chatting on the bench. 'Great, thanks. I'll head over and have a word.'

'I've taken preliminary statements, sir,' the constable said, 'but I don't think they're involved.'

Ziggy raised his hand in acknowledgement as he turned and walked away.

Sadie started the conversation with the skateboarders. 'Now then, lads, we hear you found the body?'

A tall, gangly youth stood up and flipped the skateboard he was holding. 'Yeah, man, I mean, scared the life out of us. Thought it was a dummy at first.'

Another one of the boys jumped in. 'It wasn't us,' he said defensively.

'No one said it was, sunshine. Have you given the police officer your names and addresses?' asked Ziggy.

They all nodded.

'Was she murdered then? Will we have to go to court and that?'

Sadie smiled. 'No, it doesn't quite work like that.'

The lad seemed disappointed; clearly, he had found the whole thing exciting. 'Shame, never been to court.'

His mates pulled his arm and made him sit back down. 'Shut up, Ned, you dickhead.'

Ziggy's instinct told him that they were unlikely to be involved, so he told them to go home and that if any further information was needed, someone would be in touch.

Once he'd made sure the boys had left the park, he turned to Sadie. 'We need to get uniform down here, start a house-to-house. Also, let's see if the CCTV over that parade of shops reveals anything.'

'On it, boss. I'll give Wilko a ring and update him.'

Ziggy took a few steps away from the scene, as he was known to do, and looked around him. He'd attended a couple of incidents on Woodhouse Moor over the years. For a while it had been the much-disputed territory of two rival gangs, and fights had broken out, often involving stabbings. There was the odd scuffle with drug dealers and the occasional sex worker was arrested, but nothing like they were facing now.

It would be highly unlikely or extremely unlucky to turn up no clues in an area that was as popular and as busy as Woodhouse Moor. Of course, it also ran the risk of being too popular, potentially diluting any real traces of the killer. He watched as SOCOs continued their painstaking search through the grass and undergrowth. But why had the body been dumped so publicly? Was it a pick-up gone wrong? But it didn't appear accidental; it was too precise for that, based on his experience. Had the killer been interrupted?

Looking back from the edge of the green where he now stood, he saw that the deposition site was just off the main road. The location meant it was just off the usual well-worn path and carefully placed. The killer must have needed a car or some mode of transport to bring her here. Somebody must have seen something, surely?

The killer was either extremely brave or innately stupid to leave a body so exposed. Ziggy hoped it was the latter.

Buy the book online now
mybook.to/thewebtheywove
Also available at all retail outlets
(just ask at the counter)

I love to connect with my readers on social media so feel
free to join me on all the usual platforms;
Twitter @catherineyaffe
Instagram @cat_yaffe_author
Facebook /catherineyaffeauthor

You can also join my mailing list &
FREE SHORT STORY
'FEEL THE FEAR'
by visiting my website
https://www.catherineyaffe.co.uk

 facebook.com/CatherineYaffeAuthor
twitter.com/CatherineYaffe
instagram.com/cat_yaffe_author

Printed in Great Britain
by Amazon

83813668R00171